CURSE ME

CURSE ME

(Book 1)

Elle Chipp

Copyright © 2023 Elle Chippendale

All rights reserved.

For more information contact ellechipp@gmail.com

ISBN: 9798396837232

Imprint: Independently published

DEDICATION

For those who gave it all for love.

And *especially* for those who got nothing back.

Playlist

"Fingernails" - Don Broco

"I Did Something Bad" - Taylor Swift

"Breakfast" - Dove Cameron

"DARKSIDE" - Neoni

"Wreak Havoc" - Skylar Grey

"Vigilante Shit" - Taylor Sw

Prologue

The pipework hanging above his head leaks a drop of water for every step he takes while travelling deeper into the alleyway. Almost all of the sunlight is hidden by the layers of industry connecting the two buildings together, leaving only a few streams of light that are able to fall to the ground.

The two walls on either side of the man are covered in a layer of thick moss that is damp and dirty to the touch, yet he clings to them anyway. Any method to find his footing and to continue moving forwards is well worth the soiled garments. After all, he'll be worse off coming back and he can't help but grin to himself as he pictures his motivation.

Her silky dark hair is flashing through his mind as the darkness claims him over and over again. Her pale skin that was exposed to the sunlight still haunts him as he moves, but not nearly as much as those eyes that held contact with his just long enough to make him follow.

He'd only seen her briefly before making the hasty decision to follow her inside.

The seclusion is just what he needed and the pulsing below his belt still entices him onwards with cruel intentions haunting his consciousness. This is not his first time in pursuit of a victim, and as far as he is concerned, she is his to find.

'It's her fault for having such a pretty face.' He thinks to himself as he stalks further on with more speed. He can see her skin glowing in the distance and his saliva escapes out and down his lips as he locks in on his target.

She fixes her cold gaze upon his face as he approaches. She is able to see him perfectly in the dark and is not surprised to find that the pathetic creature is following her.

He is no man, this monster crawling towards her. He insults the species from which he came as far as she is concerned and she knows the desires that are inside of him, his previous misdeeds but there is no fear clouding her.

He's about to find out that there is more than one kind of villain, a lesson she's always enjoyed teaching.

'This might be a willing target.' He thinks to himself as he mistakes a glimpse of her hungry glare for desire.

A mistake indeed.

Her full lips are pursed together in a straight line, and he traces the shape eagerly with his straining eyes. Ideas are running through his mind, ideas that would stir the hardest of hearts, and she watches as each and every one of them stains his soul further.

"Why don't you come closer?" His voice breaks from his dry throat, signalling how his patience is failing. He will not be able to wait much longer before taking action.

"Why don't you?" Her voice sounds like velvet, and it's with this that he cannot hear the hidden malice laced inside each of her words.

To comply, he edges forward eagerly only to find that she is faster, and once in front of him, she leans in as if to bestow a kiss, only for the man to fall to the ground cold and dead.

Well, almost dead.

That would be too easy. She smiles as she thinks of the people who will not have to endure his presence again, and of what is waiting for him below. His soul is hers now and there is no question as to where it's going once she is through.

CURSE ME

Chapter 1

"Do it again, that felt good." I purr in the face of the idiot standing in front of me.

His face looks as gormless as ever as we watch my red fingernail fall to the floor next to my bare feet. They're lucky that I didn't want those shoes anyway, blood is impossible to get out of suede and I'm not the type to spend my time scrubbing at stains.

As I look around, I can sense that there is a faint smell of piss in the air and the chair under me has long since rusted. The room is lit by a single bulb that the red-haired woman keeps pushing around on its wire, as if it's meant to trigger any emotion other than disgust at how tacky this all is. It's taken straight out of an eighties movie, and a bad one at that.

The man in front of me almost looks ill from the sight of my finger as the bleeding starts and I laugh at him openly. He's got to be new at this, bless his soul.

He takes a deep breath before picking the pliers up once more, moving to my middle finger now and I wonder how long it takes them to realise that this is pointless and to just start talking already.

My fingernail is pulled again, and I sigh. "Well, you fucked that one up, didn't you?"

His eyes widen and I roll mine in reply. "You want to keep it rough and ragged. Pull it straight out like that and it doesn't sting enough to get them to talk." I lecture, though I doubt he knows what sort of an expert sits before him.

I look over to the blond man in the corner, the person who is clearly in charge. "Did you train these goons at all or is this their induction?"

He only smiles in response and both the idiot, and the woman exchange a look. Unfortunately for them, they're starting to lose my interest already.

"Well, as fun as this is and as much as I needed an excuse to get my nails done again, what's this all about?" I ask while zoning in on my fingers for inspection.

I can see clearly inside of the bloodied mess that the regrowth is peeking through already and I know that my nails will be back fully within the hour. It was a nice colour though, and it took me ages to find the right shade.

"You know why." Red snaps and I look up at her now, taking the time to actually examine her face.

She's pale and freckled like most redheads, but she has a piercing on her lip that I notice too. I imagine that would be rather painful for her if I decide to rip it out, I suppose that it depends on just how boring this really gets.

"I can assure you that I do not." I sigh dramatically. I mean, why else would I let them bring me here?

"Mark Burnley." She says as if the name is meant to shock me into submission.

"And he would be?" I wish they would get to the point.

"The man you killed." The fool with the pliers says.

He's gathering a bit of personality now, and giving me what appears to be his best attempt at a scowl. His dark curly hair looks greasy in the orange light and his stubble is at least a few days old.

"You're going to need to be a little more specific than that." Fuck, if I took the names of everyone I killed I'd have no memory left.

"So you're an assassin?" The boss deigns to speak up for the first time since I arrived.

His voice is low and rough, I'd be turned on if I wasn't insulted by his question.

"Oh, I have no need for money." I wink at him.

"Why'd you do it then?" The brunette in front of me asks and it's starting to annoy me to have different questions coming from around the room. They've clearly never done this before which surprises me given the setting we find ourselves in.

"Do what?"

"Kill him." Red hisses at me and my grin widens.

"Why, was he your boyfriend?" I mock, earning a growl in response and I realise quite quickly how easy she is to play with, to the point where it's almost unfair to continue. I can even see the boss smirking.

"Again, I can't confirm. I need a few more details... please." My voice is flirty as I use the word 'please' and the brunette pales considerably.

"We found his body behind a dumpster." The boss speaks again, and my face remains blank, half of the shit I leave behind ends up behind a dumpster.

"On fifth street." The brunette says, and I pull a face intimating that nothing rings a bell, then a vague recollection springs to mind.

"When was this?"

"Tuesday."

"Did he have disgustingly bushy eyebrows by any chance?" I say with a smile, both the brunette and the redhead inhale sharply which lets me know that I have the right guy.

"Ahh, I know who you mean now. East-Asian, tall, and a tattoo on his neck wasn't there?"

I've been wondering who that guy was. He didn't strike me as anyone that important to be honest but then again, I didn't care to ask about his day job.

"So you did kill him?" Red clarifies through her teeth.

"Yeah… that was definitely me," I bob my eyebrows smugly and I see the boss tilt his head at me in curiosity, so I mimic the gesture back.

"Why'd you do it? How'd you find him?" The brunette spits out and I raise my hand to wipe my face, snapping the rope around my arm as if it was made out of tissue paper.

"I wouldn't do that again if I were you." My voice changes and they both take a step back. "I did it because I wanted to, and I found him because he was already there, annoying the fuck out of me."

I laugh coldly, enjoying the fear growing in their eyes. "Are you telling me he was meant to be hidden?"

"What was he doing?" The boss asks, stepping forward an inch.

"I'd tell you, but it might upset Red here." I tilt my head in her direction and give a face of mock concern.

"He was hitting on you?" Brunette asks, not looking nearly as shocked as Red.

"If you can call it that, he got what was coming to him." I turn to Red. "Exemplary taste of yours by the way, he was a complete gentleman." I wink with sarcasm running thick through my voice.

Red steps forward and the boss clears his throat in warning.

"Aww leave her be, I think it's only fair that she gets a few hits in. I did kill her boyfriend after all." I tilt my head to the side, daring her to step forward.

I know that I can rip her spine from her skin in under five seconds, I've timed it.

"Dan, take Abbey." The boss mutters while stepping forward into the light. Dan does as he is told and moves to escort Abbey from the room.

"Bye Abbey." I blow her a kiss and watch her stiffen at the gesture.

"Who are you?"

I'm alone with their leader now and my smile broadens. I pull my tied hand free as easily as the other and do the same with my legs, crossing them and leaning forward on my elbow to look at him closely.

"As much as I know a walking cliche like you would want me to... I can't find it in myself to answer with *your worst nightmare*." I mock the phrase as I say it, rolling my eyes.

"You think I'm cliche?" He stands up straighter, and I have to respect the fact he's not terrified at how I just freed myself. I love to see a reaction to that.

"What film did you steal this place from?" I gesture around me in disgust.

"It was my father's." He concedes as if he knows it's a bit much.

"Where's daddy tonight then? I'm a bit offended that I've only got the second in command." I lean back again, trying to analyse the best way to make him squirm. "That is… if you even rank that high?"

"I'm in charge here." His voice is thick, and I raise my eyebrows.

"Could have fooled me," I say while checking my nails and seeing how they're already halfway back to normal.

"Wh-" His voice cuts off as he notices too, his eyes widen and his jaw drops. "What are you?"

Always the same question.

"Does it matter?" I shrug, rising to my feet and looking around. This place is a shit hole and not worth my time.

So, I turn to him, giving him the full force of the ice in my eyes before demanding, "Tell me in as few words as possible, why am I here and what sort of operation is this?"

His eyes glaze over, as they all do. "You're here because you killed my lead distributor, we work with the Lord of Ashes."

The compulsion wears off and he shakes his head as he comes back to himself.

"Wait, how did you do that?" He looks horrified at what he's just confessed, and *this* is the reaction I wanted before.

"I'll do it again if you like." My voice is smooth and seductive as I summon back the ice. "Why is your father *really* not here?"

"He's dead." The trance wears off faster this time and his eyes go round again as he comes back to himself.

"Good to know." I pause. "Well, I'm going to shoot. Tell little Abbey to avoid fifth for a while as I do love to take them out in pairs."

His face is a picture of disgust and I smirk before adding, "After all, it's only fair to give them someone to travel down with on the way to hell."

Personally, I hope it's filled with fire and pain, much like the suffering they caused while still here on earth but at that point it's out of my hands.

"How d'you know they're going to hell?" He can't help but ask and I love the fact that he has, even if it means sticking around another second to answer.

"Because I only kill the darker souls." I bite my lip to emphasise my point, "They taste better."

Chapter 2

I walk into the light again and can't help but wonder how the hell his soul was so pure.

Every single person that's come out of that organisation has been as dark as midnight and while he had no clue, I couldn't have laid a hand on him even if I wanted to.

I wonder if they know about me, about my curse. Maybe they're starting to take measures and hiring innocents to stop me from killing them all. It makes me question, should I be killing them all?

I didn't go after that arsehole because he worked for the Lord of Ashes, I killed him because he was a rapist and had it coming to him. I haven't really got a strategy; I had no clue where to start from the very beginning.

CURSE ME

All I know is one of these dark souls will set me free and for that, I'll keep killing as many as possible. At this point, who cares? If I'm ridding the world of those that tarnish it then really, I'm doing it a favour. At least this is what I tell myself to feel better about how much I enjoy it sometimes.

There's nothing quite like the cry of someone in pain, knowing they'll never be able to do that to another person again and knowing that I'm the one that gets to serve the vengeance.

It's still early outside as I pad barefoot along the footpath, ignoring the broken glass and bits of rubble that get caught under my feet. Pain doesn't bother me anymore, if anything it's a nice reminder that somewhere deep down inside there's a human there, or at least I hope there is.

Having my nails pulled before was like a cat scratch and I think the most uncomfortable I've been since it started was getting shot in the head, and it was like nothing more than a weak slap. I still remember the look of the man who did it, how the blood drained from his face, and how he screamed when I threw the bullet back at him with so much force that it was like I was a gun myself.

It doesn't take long before I'm riding the elevator up to my apartment. I say my apartment but really, it's my victim's. She was a real piece of work, and her latest offence was blackmailing her staff. She was threatening to deport them if they didn't sleep with her, so I impaled her on a spike in the living room and watched her bleed out onto the now-replaced flooring.

She'd been on my radar for a while, luring young men into the drug scene, sending death threats over the internet (with the receipts to follow through if needed), and abusing every pet she's ever owned.

Sometimes I think I went too easy on her, I like dogs.

That being said, while her soul was rotten her taste in fashion was pristine. All it took was a bit of compulsion, a fake ID, and I am now Elisabeth Robertson.

She has a pretty little bank account too that's still being filled by her father each month. A text here and there and he's none the wiser that she's at the bottom of the local river. As far as I can see I don't even pay the rent for this place, the only bill is for her phone and if that's the price to pay for a decent place to crash, then so be it.

I walk into my living room and am greeted by the comforting scent of French vanilla. While I might have no soul, I sure as hell know how to live in comfort. The entire east wall is a window showing the city far below, the sun is glaring down this morning and the trees in the park are a vibrant shade of green.

Elisabeth must have paid extra for soundproofing because while I can see the traffic, I can't hear a peep and after a few experiments when bringing work home with me, I have concluded that it probably goes both ways.

CURSE ME

There's a soft leather sofa in the centre of my living room. The rich chocolate brown compliments the pink tones that she had incorporated around the room and I can't help thinking that if she'd given up being a degenerate, she could have had a successful career in interior design. I guess her loss is my gain.

I walk across the hardwood floors and into my bathroom, the tub is sunken into the floor and has enough room to house a family which was a pleasant surprise when first looking over the facilities. I can still smell the disgusting room I was just held in, so I run a bath with an extra dose of lavender to soak it away while I plan my next attack.

On most Saturdays, I allow myself the time to relax. Trouble tends to find me in the evening and all I have to do is put on a pretty dress and smile for my targets to come to me. One of the weapons given to me by the curse was that it enhanced my looks, making me the perfect magnet for the wrong sort of attention. Unfortunately, that can make it quite hard when trying to stay under the radar but it's not like anything can hurt me anymore.

I lather rinse and repeat several times before rising from the tub. Of course my nails are back now, but I frown when noticing the difference in colour between the rest. I'll have to get them redone again before tonight, as my higher calibre victims would notice something like this from a mile off.

With a heavy sigh, I pull on a dark purple day dress that blends well with my black hair and will complement the chill in my eyes should I need to use any compulsion. I slide into a black pair of Louboutin's and as usual, feel rather smug that Elisabeth and I shared the same shoe size on top of everything else.

Now that I look more human (no pun intended) I grab an iced coffee out of the mini fridge by the door and head out into the city once again. My heels click against the pavement whilst I make my way to the nail salon, and I can feel the heat of the day clinging to my dark hair as it swishes past my shoulders.

The salon I frequent is just around the corner from the main stretch of designer shops, and I make a mental note to pick up some more suede shoes on the way back to complete my collection again. I still can't believe that I let that prick spill blood on them. I'll have to keep them hidden away for special occasions from now on if kidnappings are going to be a regular thing.

Margaret, the owner greets me as I walk in by bringing over another iced coffee, something that she knows I love and it's all due to the fact that I tend to tip well when it's not my own money.

I love the bitter taste of it against my tongue and while caffeine doesn't affect me anymore, it's almost as if there's a placebo effect in place and it makes me feel more alive sometimes.

The walls here are covered in mirrors and flowers and it's the perfect spot for socialites to visit and paste pictures up on their Instagram walls. I personally avoid the mirrors, I like to look and feel good, but seeing what I've become doesn't always appeal to me. There's only one mirror in my apartment and I use that to check over myself before leaving for the night, to make sure the curse is in full effect and that I can make the most of it.

It's hard to look in a mirror and not remember the freckles I used to have, how my black hair was once brown or how my eyes were a darker blue while now they're just ice. But at least I don't have to see that brand on my chest, the tattoo-like mark of a heart meant to symbolise the deal I made.

The deal I regret.

A part of me wishes they'd left that all alone as with the other perks I'm more than capable of killing anyone I need to. This just feels excessive and more of a punishment by taking more of myself away and leaving behind the reminder I can never seem to scrape off.

After the initial greeting from Margaret, I'm escorted over to a seat that resembles more of a throne than a chair and Sacha, the nail tech is sat there waiting for me. I smile at her but it's not a warm smile. Nothing about me is warm anymore and I can tell that they're afraid of me behind the poker faces plastered on top. Margret trains them well but there's no fooling me about this sort of thing.

Between here and my hairdresser, this is the best it gets. I tip well, and I answer questions but nothing about me is nice. Kindness has no place in my life anymore and they all know that. In fact, I find the fear useful because while they haven't seen my abilities, it's like they can sense it and they pander to my needs more desperately.

They don't know that because their souls are clear, I can't harm them and even if they started greying, I'd be tempted not to. Like I've said, that nail colour took ages to find and I'm rather attached to it now.

My hands are massaged while I listen in on the gossip between the other patrons sitting along the row, receiving less thorough attention than I am. I mean, at this point, Sacha doesn't even need to ask what colour I want, and I nod my head in approval when she pulls it from the shelf.

"Just for you." She adds as if trying to increase the already substantial tip coming her way and I smirk at the fact that they reserve it for me now and no one else.

The red is the perfect shade to match blood. Not just any blood but the blood of darker souls. I've noticed that the innocent bleed more vibrantly, not from my own hand of course but from what I've witnessed before reaping vengeance. The darker souls bleed almost purple, and I want to be reminded of that as much as possible.

To remind me what I need to spill to be free.

After Sacha is done, I shop around a bit and by the time I return home, eat and dress it's almost 8pm. It's gotten to the point lately where I swear that the curse has found a way to make these infinite days go faster, but I don't mind.

It's not like I can live a normal life anyway when I'm trapped like this.

Before leaving I glare at the thing in the mirror and take in the loose, silver dress that's draped over my body tonight. There's barely enough boob tape in the world to keep this thing from falling from my breasts but I can't find it in myself to care as long as the brand is covered. They're not mine anyway, mine were smaller before all of this.

The apartment is dark, but I can see just fine. The twinkling lights from the city below are shining through the window and if I didn't have things to do, I'd happily just stare at them all night. There's something peaceful about it.

The first bar I find is more glamorous than the ones I intend to end up in, but the night is young and Elisabeth's credit card is burning a hole in my purse, begging to make up for a disgusting morning. So, I order a glass of champagne and sit at the bar, looking at the orange lights illuminating the liquor bottles and the shining marble acting as my table.

I listen in to the conversations around me and can't help but wonder what percentage of people in here are wicked. How many of them can I kill and are there *any* that are off-limits?

You see, the rich hide it better but there's no changing the colour your soul turns once you're tainted, and I like to challenge myself sometimes by guessing the verdict before taking a look to confirm.

After four years I'm almost always right and the only time I've been wrong in the last few months was this morning and that was with that pure soul working for the Lord of Ashes. It's still bothering me, and I keep asking myself how that was even possible as I don't like to lose, even when betting against myself.

But there's no use dwelling on it tonight so I shake the thought from my mind and survey the room again. There's so much wealth and fashion on display tonight but like every time I come here, the fact that a few blocks over people are begging for food makes my teeth grind.

I wouldn't class myself as the epitome of charity or anything, but if the small percentage of Elisabeth's money isn't going towards bits and pieces to please me, it's going anonymously to the places that need it more.

Yes, knowing that Elisabeth would hate for her money to be given to the poor causes me no end of ironic amusement, but a big part of it is that I like to think I'm not a *complete* monster if I do this.

Or at least not yet anyway.

But the people dining here wouldn't know what charity was if it hit them in the face, and they don't have a soul-stealing curse to blame it on. There's a waiting list a mile long just to get a reservation here and the cheapest meal is closer to three figures than two if they deign to eat.

I know it's a bold assumption, but when I overhear businessmen pathetically gloating to their dates *every time* about how they managed to work their way in with bribes and flaunting wealth they don't deserve, it makes me want to burn the place to the ground.

So I drain my glass and move to leave as while the location is stunning, the people disgust me and I don't know why that fact still surprises me after all this time.

Chapter 3

There's a tear in my dress and if the man wasn't already dead, I'd have killed him all over again for it.

It's partly my fault. I no longer care enough to look out for weapons and when he slashed at me with a knife, I just laughed rather than trying to protect the garments covering me. It could have been worse I suppose, if anything the tear along my thigh makes this more provocative and it'll save me putting in more effort to speed up the headcount for the night.

I spit at the body below my feet as this man was particularly disgusting and I'm glad that he fell into my trap so easily. Usually, with a murderer it takes more attention to reel them in and just for that, he deserves his fate.

CURSE ME

It took him 20 minutes of monologuing before he actually got to the trying to kill me part, and it was useful to hear his past history. It got the rage flowing and I was rather creative when using his own methods against him, if I do say so myself.

While pouring the liquor bottle that I swiped from the bar over him, I run a match down my leg to trigger a flame and throw it down on my homemade BBQ. I watch for a couple of seconds before I leave, it's satisfying to see the smug look on his face melt away and I swagger out of the alley onto my next location.

There are two places that I know are bound to bring me something tonight and I toss a coin from the dead man's wallet to decide. The Grasshopper it is and it's a good thing too as I could use the walk to calm down.

Before making my way over, I stop at an ATM with the ice behind my eyes to obscure the camera. I empty his bank account of the $4000 he had left which means I now have a new budget to enjoy myself with. If I go light on the iced coffees this will last me until the end of the month and I can justify the new Persian rug I've been eyeing up. I was distraught when the owner was pure-souled or I'd have taken it there and then. Unfortunately I'll have to pay for this one.

The Grasshopper is as busy as usual and I nod to the bartender, John in recognition. We're not friendly but we've seen each other often enough that I leave him be. He's only greying slightly in the soul department, and I confirmed the other month that it's from extorting money from the seedy owners.

I'd have done the same so I can't really fault him to be honest.

As always, I order a glass of champagne and sit on a barstool under the display lights, recalling the shittiest catch of the curse so far, the fact that I can't get drunk. The closest I get is after a dozen bottles, then I can feel the faintest buzz in my ears, but that's all and it's gone in minutes.

Now I just like to drink because it compliments my ego when I watch the reactions of the men around me. Sometimes I like to act drunk to lure them in but mostly I like to strut around the room with grace to show them how much stronger I am in comparison after drinking the whole damn bottle.

As I said, I have to make my own fun now.

My dress throws its shimmering reflection around the room and it's not long before John nods at me to indicate that I have a credit waiting, courtesy of a fellow patron eyeing the trap.

I down my drink and order another, using my finger to stir the strawberry thrown in there and wonder what sort of fool will dare to approach me next. After my latest kill, I have high expectations and if it's something as petty as a thief I'll be seriously disappointed.

CURSE ME

If the soul is dark enough, I sometimes don't even bother to ask what they've done, either they'll break the curse, or they won't and those sorts of people are worth terminating anyway.

Across the bar I see a dark-haired man with a perfectly groomed beard raise his glass in a greeting and I find the muscles I need in my face to smile back. His soul is bad, but I've seen worse, and I suppose I can always go for number three when I'm finished if I'm still eager.

"I thought that was you." A low voice says as a blond man slides into place beside me.

I grind my teeth as I recognise the waved hair that's swept back to fall just beneath his ears. I don't even need the face to turn to me to know that it's the man from this morning. As tempted as I am to change my target, he's off limits and thinning my patience as a result.

"You're brave," I say while levelling a glare at him. To his credit, he doesn't react until I turn back towards my drink.

"I have some questions." He replies but nods his head as if to say that my comment is duly noted.

"And a death wish apparently." I add sweetly, hoping that the words will carry him away from me.

I don't want the full extent of my venom to get out when I'm trying to lure the man in the corner at the same time. I can see him looking over now as I'm approached by another prospect, so I smile in his direction to reassure him, you know, because I'm nice like that.

"Yeah... I'll be honest, it took a few drinks before I dared to come over." He shrugs like it's a compliment and I can't help but raise my eyebrows.

"I'd have stuck to my gut if I were you."

I look away again but keep my expression pleasant, there's something sinister about a threat coming from a charming face and it's worked quite well for me in the past.

"I'm afraid I don't have that luxury." He smiles and he's caught my attention with that answer.

"And why is that?" I ask, sipping at my glass and clocking another nod from John.

"Answer my questions and I'll tell you." He swallows subtly and I smirk at the courage he's obviously trying to maintain right now.

"You do remember my party trick from before, right?" I ask, licking my lips seductively when angling my head towards my target again, killing two birds with one stone. "I can find out one way or another."

He takes a deep breath. "That's one of my questions."

Oh, that's what this is about. He's going through the whole *what are you?* routine and I'm disappointed that I even asked. I try to avoid that line of questioning where possible, especially if I can't kill them at the end of it like with Blondie here.

"Did your mother never teach you that it's rude to ask personal questions?" I summon a glimmer of ice behind my eyes, and I swear his hands shake when he finishes his glass in one drink. Good.

I chuckle to myself quietly and summon another helping for him with my credit as I admire the effort. If I had the time, I'd probably play with him a bit more.

"My mother's dead." He says after drinking from his new glass.

"An orphan, interesting." I muse. "Now run along before you stop being so." I wave my hand and turn away.

The crowd is picking up now and my mark is staring over so I bite my lip slightly and take a bite from the strawberry that's in my drink. He's hooked and I wonder how long it'll be before he approaches.

"I'm good right here." Blondie smiles, it's a weak smile but he manages it anyway, though it makes me narrow my eyes now.

"This is becoming tedious."

I don't even try to hide the displeasure on my face. If my mark gets frightened I'll just track him down or maybe he'll take it as a compliment that I'm not interested in any other men. It's just a shame that my attention isn't the sort of thing he's going to want in the end.

"Three questions and I'll go." He bargains.

"Be careful who you make deals with boy." My voice is thick with promise, and someone should have said the same to me, but they didn't.

"Boy? You're younger than I am." He laughs.

"Am I?" I raise my eyebrows and he gulps.

I would say we're the same age, but he doesn't need to know that, the expression is enough to entertain me and I purse my lips, waiting.

"What's your purpose?" He shifts in his seat and I can tell that he's uncomfortable but at least he skipped ahead a few questions compared to the usual ones.

"Who's to say I have a purpose?" I tease him.

"You can't just go around killing for fun." He frowns and I hold back a laugh.

"I can't?"

He only replies with a look. I can't remember the last time someone dared to do that after knowing what I am. I wonder if he knows that I can't hurt him.

"My purpose is to remove wicked souls from the streets." My voice is like honey, as if I'm telling him that I'm a schoolteacher or a veterinarian.

He nods, letting it sink in. "Are there any catches?"

This time I do laugh. "You can't imagine I'd tell you if there was?"

He cringes, nodding again as if he should have seen that coming and to be honest, he should have.

"Last question," I say while leaning in, testing the strength of the courage behind the mask he's trying so desperately to keep on. It's stronger than most and for that, I'll give credit where it's due.

"Would you consider a partnership?" He breathes heavily through his nose in anticipation, and I tilt my head when hearing it.

I didn't expect that one from him. Not because I haven't been offered it before, but because his soul is supposedly pure. How is that the case if he's approaching a monster like me with a proposition?

"Because you've had the balls to even approach me. I'll give you a gift." I wave my hand to John to get another drink and sure enough, there's a credit waiting.

"I'll let you explain your motives yourself before I extort the truth in...other ways." I grin, downing the beverage in one swallow.

He doesn't reply but instead looks around the room and I can see the sweat on his forehead starting to build up.

"We can go somewhere more private if that's what you'd prefer." I dip my chin and look up at him through my lashes.

"Can you guarantee I'll walk away?" He asks, ignoring my suggestive tone.

So he doesn't know about the curse, that's even more interesting. He's lucky that I even waited to confirm that as, catch or not, I'd have found a way to kill him if he did.

"I might be able to extend a promise… in exchange for satisfying my curiosity." I shrug.

"Follow me then." He gestures over his shoulder and I swallow, a scowl making its way to my face after being told what to do. Nothing annoys me more.

"While you might walk away, I'd be careful with your words if I were you," I say softly in his ear after catching up to him with ease.

He jumps at the closeness. "Sorry… Please follow me?" He tries again and I merely nod.

He takes us into an alleyway and if he wasn't untouchable, I'd say it would be a lovely coincidence that he lured me here and not the other way around.

"Speak," I say, indicating that my limited patience is reaching its end.

"My brother is the Lord of Ashes; he killed my Father four years ago and I've been looking to take him out ever since." He takes a deep breath, clearly unable to believe that he's letting this slip.

"I was approached by a…. vigilante group before I was due to join the family business and have been working as a double agent. It's mostly tax and accounts but it's enough to help. I want him gone but I need your help to stop him."

I have to admit that what comes out of his mouth wasn't what I expected. To the point where I've just had to compel him to confirm if he was lying but he wasn't and now I'm almost impressed.

"Approach me in three days and I'll give you an answer." I say after noticing the panic behind his eyes from what he's just risked in passing along this information.

"Where will you b-" He starts before I cut him off. "If you want to work with me you have to be able to find me."

"Okay." He claps his hands together.

"Okay," I smirk. "Now leave."

"Can I give you a tip?" He's a bit more confident now before clocking my raised eyebrows. "Call it an incentive." He adds quickly.

"I'm all ears." I cross my arms.

"The man buying you drinks doesn't work for him... but his friend does."

"Our targets aren't the same." I remind him.

"Maybe they should be." Is all he replies before turning to walk away.

I want to reprimand him for turning his back on a predator as he could be dead by now. If what he says is true, he needs to be a lot more careful.

After that odd little encounter, I end the night by killing both the man from the bar and his friend. I have to concede that the friend's soul was darker but I'm happy with the result nonetheless. Unfortunately, the curse remains and it's just another night of taking out the trash.

    I leave the bodies to be found out of curiosity as I wonder if the fallout will be the same as it was with Mark Burnley. I don't fancy another trip down a tacky cellar but if there's information to be had it may be worth it.

    I pocket his phone after turning it off, as if I decide to take up Blondie's offer it would be useful to come bearing something and it crosses my mind for a second that I don't even know his name.

    I bet it's a rich boy's name, something like Tristan or Chad.

    It might not even matter yet though as I can't decide whether to shake him off next time or not. The first test will be if he can find me again.

    I won't be making it easy.

Chapter 4

I don't see him in the next three days, though I do manage to get a Persian rug. It's not as nice as the one I had my eyes on, but it's close and when I saw it in the woman's home, I couldn't help but take it.

Like Elisabeth, this bitch was a blackmailer, but she was old enough to have numerous crimes under her belt by the time I found her.

Her fatal mistake was threatening Sacha online or I'd probably not have noticed. Sacha's phone had been buzzing quite a bit when I got my nails done a few days ago and when I ran into her yesterday, I remembered she was a bit more nervous than usual, so I compelled her to fess up.

Apparently, the woman wasn't too old for the classic death threat routine, but what I found more interesting was the reason behind it. The idiot was having an affair and made the mistake of using her boyfriend's credit card over her husband's one day at the salon. Sacha wouldn't tell a soul; she knows better than to do that, but the woman was paranoid and now she's paid the price.

I must say though, the rug looks fabulous under my sofa now. It was just what I needed to be able to bring in the plants that I wanted to add around the place.

It's Tuesday and I don't have that much to do. It's not a busy sort of night and I can't be bothered to walk around aimlessly.

Blondie was meant to find me by now, but I think it'll be more interesting if I can find him first. After all, who doesn't love a game of cat and mouse?

The first place I go to is The Grasshopper and I enter through the backdoor this time. I know my way to the office and the lock is so pathetic that I don't even think I need to use my increased strength to snap it open.

The fluorescent bulb that shines down on the room is so depressing and there's a collection of shitty posters that have been hung around it, as if that would make a difference. I decide instantly that whatever John gets paid isn't enough to work here. I'd hate every second.

I log onto the computer, with the ID foolishly written on a sticky note, and search through the security tapes to find the time that Blondie placed his order. 11:52pm is displayed on the screen when I see him and from there, I look through the credit card receipts and find his name.

Jeremiah Smith.

I'm willing to bet a lot of money that it's not his real name but there are no other orders placed at that time, so I take the address from the card and go from there. I end up leaving via the window just to shake things up a bit and to avoid detection in case he's better at tracking me than I thought.

I walk a couple of blocks in the right direction, I can tell that it's going to be a nice area as the dirty streets become cleaner the farther I go. I should have known sooner from the fact that his father owned his own torcher chamber, but I know not to go straight there from the information he imparted earlier.

As I walk, I can't help but think of the words he said to me and I smile to myself at how interesting it all is, it's sort of like a gossip column but useful. Who'd have thought such an attractive, innocent-looking man would be related to a family like that?

The building complex is new and empty and I curse him for a second before looking through the window for the business names. The floor I need is four and the business listed is 'Ambrose Industries'

I do a quick internet search to find the company and the owners but the fact I don't know his name doesn't help so I save all three addresses and start with the one closest to me.

As luck would have it, the last one gives me what I need and it's not his home but an office that is actually occupied. It's about 8pm at night so there's a very slim chance that he'll be there but I can walk in anyway.

I enter through the doors, using the ice in my eyes to obscure the cameras, a lovely little trick I learned by accident, and I compel the night guard to unlock his computer and take a ten-minute break.

After looking over the security tapes from this morning I find him, bright and early at 7:34am walking through the front door. The suit is a nice look on him, but I can't help but wonder what he looks like in normal clothes. I'm sick of suits at this point as it's all anyone wears in this damn city.

Now that I've confirmed that he works here, I go back a few days to see if there's a particular time he likes to show up and leave. 7:30am - 5:00pm seems to be his normal business hours and not the most ideal period if you were to ask me, but it's just what I need to know to tail him tomorrow.

CURSE ME

I log out, clear the history and spill coffee down the hard drive for good measure as I'd rather they not see the glowing eyes obscuring the cameras as I entered.

Now that the hard work is all done, I go home and run myself a bath. I deserve a break after all I've just done.

By Wednesday at 4:30pm I'm camped out on the street opposite Blondie's building with a coffee in hand and a phone in front of my face.

My long dark hair is pulled into a bun on top of my head, and I have fake glasses covering my eyes. Sunglasses are always suspicious when someone is standing still, facing one place, so I've opted for real ones, and I quite like the look to be honest.

My first thought was to climb to the roof and follow him that way but after glancing up a few times I can see that they've got bodies up there and I'm not in the mood to kill someone just for doing their job.

At 5:15pm he walks out of the building, and I swear he's late just because I'm waiting. Rather than follow, I go the opposite direction as I can make the most of my speed by cutting through the alleys and this is the best way I've found to avoid suspicion.

He stops at a deli nearby and if that's his dinner I'm disappointed. I was expecting steak or lobster, you know, high end stuff and for someone making as much money as I imagine he is, I'd expect he'd be eating nothing but the best every day. That's what I'd do.

After he grabs his sandwich, we make our way towards a seedier part of town and I keep following, stepping into shops every so often and then catching up again when I feel like it's been long enough.

I make sure not to look at him directly, as even humans have that sort of sixth sense where they can tell when someone is staring at them, so instead I look at the pavement in front of him and I'll know if he spots me.

He makes a sharp left and nobody seems to notice but me. I've seen this sort of move before so rather than follow, I cross the street to the right and walk over the path so that I can see where he's turned. He's looking over his shoulder when I do but not in the way you would if there was real suspicion, so I wait five minutes before following behind him.

My feet already know how to make no sound and I listen to his footsteps echoing in the distance. I stop when I catch an exchange of voices and I almost laugh when I hear what must be a password leave his lips. His father may be the cliché, but he's not far off. Verbal passwords, really?

He disappears behind a door and a guard is left in his place. I can see no red light indicating any cameras and they lose another point in my book for that, even if they'd do nothing to catch *me*, they still need to do better.

As I approach the guard with the ice in my eyes, I compel him to forget he sees me while seeing me and I love this trick. I circle around him just to make sure that he's under my spell before proceeding. I think better of walking straight through the door, instead I scale the wall to a window as I want to listen in before I do anything more.

I balance on the window ledge with the precision of a cat, and I can hear the conversations through the glass with ease. Below me, there is a small warehouse of sorts and thankfully there's no equipment or anything lying loose so I think it's just a meeting point.

I'd like to think that they have the sense to switch it up each time and that this is a one-off thing as for that, I could forgive the lack of cameras and personal awareness.

"The last place we saw it was at The Grasshopper." One reports and I grin when realising it's me that they're talking about.

There is somewhat of a compliment hidden in there for me, that I'm too terrifying to be a woman and must be something else entirely. I rather like it.

"Did you see who she left with?" Blondie asks and I smile wider, he thinks that I'm still off killing things and not tracking him.

"No, we saw it enter through the back door but not when it left."

It pleases me to know that it was a good decision to leave through the window after all. My instincts are better than I give them credit for, and I could have a lot more fun with this in future.

"Before then?" Blondie is getting flustered. I love to hear that I'm the cause as he rubbed me the wrong way a few times last night, and this is the closest I can get to that for now.

"It seems to have taken out Cheryll Connors this week as well, they found her hanging in her wardrobe on Monday."

That's where I got my rug, it felt like a fitting punishment for the public to think she did it herself when she'd have sacrificed the world for a chance of survival.

I know that because I asked.

"Are we sure that was her?"

"Yes-" His companion cut in with "Cheryll wasn't the type."

I lean in to get a better look at the numbers. It's just Blondie and three others and while I did feel the need to do this incognito, I can't deny the urge to jump in and scare the hell out of them as I could use a good laugh.

"Any others?"

"None of consequence."

I snort at this and feel the need to explain that the others were far worse than old Cheryll.

But what stops me from doing just that is the fact that I haven't decided my answer yet. While it would be good to get some info and targets handed to me on a platter; their shoddy practices and the pure cliche of it all have me second-guessing.

If they can be bothered to discuss anything but me, I can pick up something decent from this meeting and be on my merry way. Maybe even do them a favour and take out a few bottlenecks in the process.

But something tells me that I'm not going to be able to avoid Blondie forever. It would be annoying to have to re-plan all of my usual haunts and I hate the idea of leaving a loose end alive and out of my control.

It wasn't long ago that I suspected that they were aware of my curse, and they could find it out now, all because of this human. At the very least I need to wipe his memory as I can't just leave it like this.

Chapter 5

"Any news on Craig Lessing?" The taller of the four asks, blissfully unaware of my presence.

"None since they found him. With his friend being there, they're not too sure about the message," Blondie responds, clearly thinking that this is a good thing despite putting the target in my head in the first place.

"Do you think it'll accept?" Another asks, almost tentatively and I allow myself to be seen now while walking slowly into the light.

"Well, there's only one way to find out, why don't you ask it?" I call over to him and all three of them pale instantly.

Blondie only smiles. I narrow my eyes as that's not the reaction that I was after, but he never seems to do what I want him to. I wonder if he's wired differently to the rest of them or something.

"I thought you'd make an appearance." He muses and seems a lot braver now that we're no longer one-on-one which makes me tilt my head in scrutiny.

I don't know if that's cowardice or because he wants to be seen as a leader. Usually, I'd lean toward the former but with him, I'm not too sure. He actually looks happy to see me which I find rather unnerving.

"And I thought they paid you more than that. If you can only afford a sandwich for dinner, then I'm not sure it's an organisation that deserves my time." My tone is mocking and I can see three pairs of eyes darting between us.

He blinks, processing the information that I've just given him. I smile while patiently waiting for a reply.

"I take it you've found my office?" His voice is steady, but I can hear his pulse rise slightly.

"Yes, lovely office. Your staff need to be more careful with their coffee though." I bob my eyebrows in emphasis to make sure he doesn't miss that it was me.

"Three days isn't great, but it could have been worse." He turns to his colleagues as if it's a judgement on them all that I found him so fast. It annoys me that this is the second time that he's turned his back on me.

Besides, with a statement like that, well, it would be rude not to correct him now, wouldn't it?

"Please." I purr, "I found you in hours not days."

He exhales sharply. "For how much of that did you use your... gifts?"

"Wouldn't you like to know?" I retort.

I'm slightly pissed off that he's questioning my talents. Gifts or no gifts, I found him way too easily and he should be more bothered about it, they all should if they want to play with the big boys.

"Were you followed?" One of the men pipes up and I zone in on his face.

"No, but he was." I nod to Blondie.

I feel like they are missing the point, and this is going to suck if I have to keep spelling it out for them each time. They're more entry-level to all of this than I thought.

"Yeah, I gathered that," Blondie says under his breath. I tilt my head.

"And here's me thinking you wanted my help with something... My mistake or you'd have gone about that a very different way." The reply comes through my teeth and three of them take a step back, wisely so.

"I'm only saying that you've made your point." He raises his arms, and I can't stand the fact that I'm unable to wipe that look from his face.

If I hit him without my added strength would that work? I'm sorely tempted but I don't know what the consequences would be and I'm too not keen on finding out to be honest. It's not worth it... yet.

"No, making my point would be detailing how easy it was to find you. How obvious your fake name is, how stupid it is to use an address that can be traced back to you online. How you allowed yourself to fall into a pattern, how you actually use verbal passwords. And not in the least the fact that you turned your back on someone like me when a character half as dangerous could have put a bullet in your back." I list the points out on my fingers and I swear each time I do, the men take their turns swallowing.

"Anything else?" His face is cold and if he wasn't getting under my skin, I'd respect it.

"Yeah, if this is your regular meet up I'm not working with you." I snap.

"At least you're considering it." He winks and the ice rises to my eyes as my patience is well and truly met now. "Okay, sorry! Just trying to lighten the mood." He chuckles nervously.

"Try again and I'll lighten your head off your shoulders." I almost yell and nobody responds.

So I take this opportunity to calm down and pull the phone from my pocket before throwing it at him, I don't use my strength but don't make it go lightly either and he catches it before holding it up in question.

"Craig, I assume?" I nod toward it, though I didn't know his name until I got here.

Blondie's face lights up and he tosses it at the guy to the right. I take this time to notice each of them now, trying to differentiate between them better.

The tallest is a darker blond than my guy and his hair is a lot shorter. The one in the middle is a bit pudgier and has dark skin, brown hair, and glasses, real ones. While the last guy to the right has very long hair, is East Asian, and has terribly thick eyebrows that have me narrowing my eyes in recognition.

"Haven't I killed you before?" I call over to him and his eyes widen, like a deer caught in headlights.

"That was his brother," Blondie answers for me hastily and I nod.

"Thanks for that." The long-haired man nods and I tilt my head.

"If that's sarcasm you need to pick your targets with more caution."

The rage inside of me is flaring up far too easily around this crowd and if they're not careful I'll be making an anonymous tip, just so that I can actually do something to punish them.

"Easy tiger, he means it. They weren't on good terms." Blondie cuts in, standing between us and the man shoots him a grateful look.

"So, is this your regular meeting place?" I ask, picking at my nails casually to change the subject and keep my cool.

"No, it isn't." He grins and my face slackens. "But we do have one, I hope that's not going to put us deeper into the bad books?"

I let that comment slide because sooner or later I need to follow through. "Do you have cameras and please tell me there's no word of mouth?"

"Of course we have cameras but the word-of-mouth thing is real. I didn't like the idea of things being traceable online and this was the next best thing." He shrugs as I process his words and sort of see where he's coming from.

"Okay, give me a target and I'll make sure they end up dead," I say, as why else would they want my *gifts*?

It'll make finding my prey easier and if they work with the Lord of Ashes there's a higher chance that they may be the one I need. It's the dirtiest organisation in the city, countless murders get ordered each day and Blondie here is the only one I've seen come out of it with a clean soul.

All four of the men release a breath and I smile. It's nice to see that the fear is still strong in them all. I clock how three-quarters of them are off-limits but the darker blond is tainted enough that I could probably get away with killing him.

If I need to make a point he's the one I'll kill.

"That wasn't quite the arrangement I had in mind," Blondie starts to say. I sigh.

"Look, I'm not here to join your club. I have things to do, give me a target, or let us be done with it and I'll wipe you all now." I snap and swear that the one with the glasses whimpers a little bit, making me laugh.

"I mean your memory, Sherlock."

"You can do that?" Blondie asks, more curious than scared and I wonder what on earth is wrong with this man.

"I wouldn't have mentioned it if I couldn't now, would I?" I bite back.

The dark blond smiles slightly at this and I give him a look as I'd love to understand the hierarchy better. I thought Blondie would be the highest-ranking but after that, I don't know. I'd never let someone under me smirk at an insult headed my way.

"Who's in charge here?"

"In charge of what?" The dark blond asks and I narrow my eyes.

"The rest of you." I wave my hand as if it's obvious.

"Well..." Blondie hesitates. "No one. We all have different areas."

Nothing is straightforward with this lot is it? Surely one of them has to rank higher than the rest?

"No one is in charge?" The disbelief is thick in my voice.

"The way we see it is that the Lord of Ashes is one person that rules all, that's where things went wrong. Our approach is that we all have our own thing but for the big decisions, we vote." The one with the glasses says, his voice getting quieter the more he notices my gaze on him.

"Huh, interesting." I nod as it's not the worst idea I've ever heard but I can imagine there are limits to what four people can vote on without coming to an impasse.

"You say that a lot." Blondie comments and I bite my lip to hold back a glare.

"Bro, shut up." The long-haired one hisses at him, and I nod my head in agreement.

"Yeah Bro, listen to your friend and shut up." I mock him from between my teeth.

Blondie looks between us with a smile rising in the corners of his mouth and he claps the back of the long-haired man before turning to me.

"You need to lighten up, you both do." He says.

"And you need to take your life more seriously." I'm too tired to say this with any particular tone now.

"I'll try if you do?" He quips, raising his hands and grinning at the same time.

"Target, let's hear it?" I say, grabbing the bridge of my nose in exasperation.

If they don't give me a direct reply I'm walking out of here right after I wipe their brains to mush. That much I know I can do.

"Scott Hughes." The dark blond cuts in before Blondie can even try to speak to me.

"Thank you," I say calmly before turning on my heel to go.

If I ever have to see them again it'll be too soon. The last time someone sassed me like that they didn't live to see the morning and I like it better that way.

"No, wait! Before you go." Blondie starts and I don't even turn around to answer with "No."

The others whisper to him to stop but he doesn't listen and walks out the door to follow me. The guard doesn't see me, and Blondie must notice too because he looks between us with an open mouth for a second before rushing back over.

"Can you stop for a second?" He sighs and I swear I've never wanted to rip a head off more in my life.

"Do you realise how lucky you are-" I cut myself off realising that I'm saying it out loud and bite my tongue aggressively as punishment. It doesn't so much as sting, and I swallow back the blood.

"Lucky how?" He's like a kid at Christmas.

"Nothing."

"No, seriously what do you mean? You were going to say something there." He pushes.

"It was nothing pure ears like yours should be plagued to hear." I might as well give him something if not the whole truth, now that I've let that slip.

"Pure? Did you just call me pure?" He almost laughs until he sees my serious face. "Wait, does that mean you've seen my... soul?" He hesitates when saying it and it's my turn to grin now.

"Yes, and it's clean." I stop and try not to scowl at the fact.

"Is that why you haven't snapped my neck yet?" He asks, half joking but I stop breathing for a second as I had thought he didn't know.

"What do you mean?" My voice is sharper than I intended.

"You said the other day that darker souls... taste better. I guess that means I'm not your type?" He sounds disgusted when he says it and I calm myself with the idea of his ignorance.

"Something like that." That's as much as he's getting from me on that score.

He ponders this for a second. "What's your name then?" He asks, tilting his head to the side expectantly.

"Elisabeth," I reply automatically while continuing on my walk.

But he laughs at this. "What's your real name?"

"Elisabeth," I repeat through my teeth, handing him the ID from my pocket.

"That's funny, last time I checked Elisabeth Robertson had blonde hair. I've not seen you around lately, you used to be on the docks far more often." He shrugs, keeping up with my pace.

"What's your name then?" I snap, knowing that he's got me there.

"Adryan Ambrose." He nods, waiting for my reply.

Smug arsehole.

"Camilla." I finally say and I don't know why I didn't just use another fake name, that would have been a better idea.

"Camilla?" He looks taken aback and I glare at him which makes him raise his hands in defence. "I just... that's a very, you know, normal name. I was expecting something...Different."

"I was human once," I say while turning a corner sharply, hoping he doesn't bother to follow me around it. I'm growing tired of this conversation and I need to prepare for tonight.

"How'd you change into this?" He asks, barely a step behind and leaning forward in genuine curiosity.

"Keep asking questions like that and I won't care how you taste." I smile sweetly.

He takes a step back again. "Okay never mind, Cami."

My breathing hitches and I feel the pain and anger rise to the surface.

"I wouldn't repeat that word if I were you." My voice is deadly, and my pulse is rising.

His eyes go wide. "What's wrong with Cam-" A snarl from my chest cuts him off before he can finish.

"What about Cam?"

This man has a death wish, honestly.

"If you can't pronounce Camilla, it's a wonder you left school." I glare at him, but the fire is dying away already.

"So, you're okay with Cam? Got it." He grins and I just sigh. I'm regretting working with him already and it's been ten minutes.

"Let's get something to eat? I have a few more questions." He asks, bobbing his eyebrows in a cocky expression.

"I'd rather eat glass." I retort, not missing a breath.

"*Can* you eat glass?"

"Is it always like this or do I need to speak to the Lord of Ashes?" I sigh irritably, coming to a stop in the middle of the walkway. I swear if I could get headaches I'd have a migraine right now.

"That's not even remotely funny." He frowns.

"Neither is annoying me to death." I snap.

This is why I don't spend time around people, they never shut up and the questions are constant. All I wanted was an easy way to have targets picked out for me without having to make the effort of finding them myself... was that too much to hope for? Or is this the price I need to expect?

"If we're going to work together, you'll have to get used to talking to me." He shrugs.

"Consider this my resignation."

"Then how else are we going to stand a chance?" He snaps and he looks almost pissed off for the first time since we've met.

It seems it's not just *my* patience that is wearing thin here, but it's not like I instigated this round of conversation.

"Watch your tone, I could literally fry your brain into mush." I threaten with venom in my voice.

"Go ahead, at least I won't have to watch this city go to shit after my brother is done with it." He shouts back and he's serious, I can tell this just from his tone.

It makes me think for a second, remembering his motives and that he's not just another criminal trying to get me to do his dirty work.

Knowing all I do about him and seeing that pure soul staring up at me is still something I find tough to compute but it's hard not to jump the gun when he keeps pestering me like this. I'm not used to... people, especially ones with such little self-preservation.

But for some reason I decide to drop it after that. I mean, at least he cares about something more than himself and it's more than most of the people I've been around lately.

"You can buy me a drink, nothing more."

Chapter 6

"You don't eat?" He almost shouts and I kick him under the table, not with my full strength but it is hard enough to shut him up.

"I do eat, I just don't have to." I shrug while taking a sip from my glass of champagne.

I ordered the most expensive brand in here to punish him for annoying me and I plan to order the bottle if he keeps going, which is more than likely.

"Why would you bother?" He asks, scrunching his brows in thought and I almost laugh.

"Have you ever had a steak?" I tilt my head, sipping the drink again.

This brand really is delicious, I should order it more often. Life's too long to drag it out with shitty alcohol and if I'm stuck here, I definitely might as well have a good time, right?

"Yeah...?" He looks at me like I'm an idiot.

"That's why. I like nice food." I stare like it's obvious, surely a rich man like him should get that.

"Then why wouldn't you eat with me?" He frowns, revisiting my refusal and it's almost too easy.

"Because I don't like you." I don't hesitate to respond.

How arrogant can he get? Assuming I'll eat with him just because he asked me to. Someone needs to take him down a peg or two and I have a feeling it'll need to be me.

"Harsh, but I appreciate the honesty." He shrugs with a light smile and the expression suits him.

"So why'd your brother kill your dad?" I ask, not breaking eye contact.

Maybe if I turn it around on him, he'll quit bothering me so much with the questions. Plus, I'm rather curious about the answer to be honest.

"Wow, you really don't beat around the bush huh?" He jokes but sees that I'm not going to reply until I get an answer, so he does. "Power, why else?"

"Well I could see by his playroom that he wasn't a good man, why are you so bothered?"

That's the part that I really don't get, if anything it seems like his brother did us all a favour. He saved me a job at least. If my father was like that, I'd have beaten my brother to it and if my brother was worth half a damn he'd have thanked me for it.

"It wasn't just my dad." He adds. I understand now, I should have read between the lines but he's not always that easy to judge, it's rare.

"He killed your mother too?" I raise my eyebrows.

"He's my half-brother, she was my dad's second wife." He looks at the table and it must be bad for him to go all shy, I've been begging for silence all day but now that I have it, I almost wish I could take it back. Almost.

"Is he blond as well?" I change the subject and I don't know why but it feels like the merciful thing to do.

I've never been able to picture the Lord of Ashes and it would be good to get an idea of his appearance for when I have an opportunity. If they have the same hair, I imagine he'll be easier to spot.

I swear Adryan's is like a beacon sometimes.

"No, we don't look alike. He's got dark hair and eyes; we took after our mothers." He shrugs.

"You've just described 80% of the male population..." I say to highlight how unhelpful that was.

"If I was an artist I'd draw you a picture." He rolls his eyes, sarcasm running strong in his voice.

This is the most normal conversation that I've had in four years. I don't know if I needed it or if I hate it, but it's starting to flow quite easily. I'd almost forgotten what it's like.

"So, what else do you have?" He asks, downing his drink.

"What do you mean?"

"You know the compulsion and the soul thing, what else?" He acts like I'm telling him fun facts.

But I'm not some circus attraction that he can come and ogle at, I'm a predator that stands at the very top of the food chain.

"Some would think that'd be plenty." I batter my lashes at him to look innocent and he just raises his eyebrows, waiting. His lack of fear is rather interesting to me and I wonder if his half-brother is the same?

"I can't be killed, and I don't feel pain. The closest thing you humans could think of is vampires, only I come with more perks." I admit, for the first time since it all happened.

He pauses, processing that. "And pure souls aren't your type?"

"No." I shake my head, drinking again.

"Thank fuck for that." He grins and it's the smartest thing I've heard him say yet.

"Neither are blondes." I muse, eyeing his hair in a way that makes him check it for being out of place.

"Is there anything about me that you don't find repulsive?" He laughs and I like that he takes it on the chin, it shows him to be a better sport than I thought.

"If I find anything I'll tell you." I smile before finishing my drink.

"Another?" He asks and I nod.

As he walks away, I realise how glad I am that I opted for office attire when following him as the dress I have on is a simple black number and it can fit in anywhere. I feel confident as I cast a look around the room, searching for potential business out of habit.

There are plenty of people around and a few try to catch my eye, making me wonder how long Adryan is looking to drag this out for. Surely there's a point to all this?

Most of the tables are filled with couples but a few are housing bachelors. I could have sworn one of them was about to walk my way before Adryan's started to trail back over. Perfect timing, he's pure anyway and I'm not in the mood to play nice.

"I have a confession to make." He says when setting two more flutes of champagne down on the table.

"Is that what this is for, Dutch courage?" I laugh and take my glass from him in a swift movement.

"Something like that..." He pauses. "I didn't just bring you here for a few questions."

His heart thumps in suspense and I wonder if he knows how much of a giveaway that is when around me? Then again, I didn't mention the increased senses as sometimes I forget about them.

"Are you trying to tell me that you didn't want my riveting company?" The mockery in my voice resonates and he purses his lips to contain the disappointment.

"You suspected?"

"I assumed you weren't dumb enough to lure me here without reason." I lean back as I say this, watching the expression on his face.

"Well, I have a gift for you. Something to say thank you for offering your... services." He hesitates on the last word, and I ignore the fact that it makes me sound like a hooker.

"Do tell." I raise my glass in thanks and take a sip.

"Scott Hughes has a few habits. One of them is that he likes to drink on a Wednesday night." He says, tilting his head towards a table in the corner and I see three men in a booth.

"Ahh, and which of these unfortunate souls goes by Scott?" A wicked grin grows on my face. I love how easy he's just made it for me.

Half of the challenge is having to pick which one to go with and I hate when it's revealed to be the wrong choice. At least this way I have someone else to blame it on.

"That's the thing, they all work for my brother and my rationale was, why stop at one?" He smirks and I raise my glass in cheers.

"Maybe you're not so terrible to work with." I muse. "Just control that mouth of yours and you could prove to be quite useful." I can't help but add.

He rolls his eyes at this. "Would you care to know where they're heading after here?"

"If you'd be so kind…"

"Laurie's, it's a dive bar down the street. There's an alley to the left of it-" I cut him off, "I know where I'm going."

"Well then, happy hunting." He nods his head before looking around, probably to find someone he knows.

"I'm dismissed then am I?" I laugh, finishing my drink.

"I just assumed you'd want to be in position." He fumbles a bit, like he didn't expect me to say that.

"You did hear the part about vampire perks, right?" A smirk grows on my face.

"Oh, right… Another drink then?" I hand my glass to him in answer before turning back to the booth to survey my targets.

I want to stay here until they leave, memorising their faces and how they interact with each other. Partly because it'll be useful but mostly because I'm curious.

One of them looks my way and I fake a simpering blush in reply, his chest puffs out and I can hear the arrogance in his voice from here.

I can't wait to burst his bubble.

Adryan comes back with a bottle, and I can't help but grin in reply.

"You're growing on me Blondie." I sigh when pouring the lovely liquid into my glass, I may not get drunk off it, but I can enjoy the taste.

"Blondie? Are you serious?" He laughs, taking it from me and gives himself a portion.

"I didn't know your name and you know, you're blond." I shrug.

"Glad to know you remembered that much." He mutters and I finish my drink.

After a few more glasses I decide that I don't want him dead, he's annoying as hell but he's decent company and a thought crosses my mind that worries me.

I'd hate for any rash actions to spoil the future information I can get from his friends, and I can't trust him not to piss me off in future. He's got a big mouth.

"Tell me not to kill them," I say, instantly gaining his attention and wishing my voice didn't sound so concerned.

He looks like I'm speaking another language, "What?"

"Are you deaf?" I snap and he squints at me as if he's trying to figure it out.

"No I heard you, but I just don't understand."

"Have you ever organised a kill before today?" I ask, pouring more into my glass while keeping my expression neutral, as I can feel a gaze on my face from the men in the corner.

He thinks about it for a moment before answering, "No, not unless you count telling you who Craig works for?"

"There's a chance this could darken your soul a bit if I kill them on your order, tell me not to and it may or may not help." I shrug.

The temptation would be too much, I know it.

"Why'd you care?"

Why can't he just take the information I give him? This could save his life and he's sat here asking me why I should bother.

"I could use the information and I can't promise I won't react next time you open your mouth," I say sweetly. "Now say it."

"You're a delight, do you know that?" He rolls his eyes. "Don't kill them."

"Try and be a bit more convincing."

I give him a look to tell him to take this more seriously before I stop caring myself. If he doesn't get his arse in gear, then it's really not my fault if he gets on my dark side and I'm shocked I've gone as far as to speak on it.

"I don't know how... you know I want you to." He laughs nervously and his hand grazes the back of his neck.

My voice drops, "Does it not bother you that three lives will end tonight, directly because of you?" I see a reaction behind those eyes the second my tone goes serious.

So, I emphasise this as I continue, "I'd have gotten to them eventually but now it's sooner. Their families will suffer, they will suffer...All. Because. Of. You." I take my time with the last few words.

It's hard trying to call to mind my human morals while saying it. Right now, I don't know why this is working but stating the obvious seems to be doing the trick.

"Don't." He murmurs, biting his lip.

"That's better! Try and home in on that guilt, that's what's protecting you." I sound cheerful and he glares at me. "From now on I'll need to compel targets from you, if you don't give them voluntarily it might help."

I study his face, half looking at him and half scoping out the three men as a huntress never loses sight of her targets and mine are right behind him.

"Surely you can kill me anyway if I piss you off so much?" He grumbles and I grind my teeth in automatic response.

How does he keep getting so close? Maybe I should compel him to tell me all he knows, but then if he knows nothing, he will become suspicious.

"True, but it's far less tempting this way." My poker face hides my irritation, or at least I hope it does.

"I suppose we're even then." He replies.

"Not for long I'm about to give you some gifts later, have you ever watched The Godfather?" I grin and his face falls, clearly remembering the horse in the bed scene.

"Relax, I'm only joking, I'd hate to ruin my shoes," I say lifting my heels up so he can see the sparkle and I love that I can wear them all the time without the pain or incoordination.

"You'd think you'd lose your sense of humour, given you know...What you are." He says.

He's beating around the bush a bit but then again, I can't exactly correct him because I don't know what I am.

"How else do you think I lure in my victims?" I ask, giving him a sultry look, consisting of biting my lip and looking up through my lashes. I can't count how many times this has worked for me and I've long since stopped caring about how I carry out my business.

He swallows and I snap out of it instantly and laugh. "Honestly, it's too easy sometimes."

CURSE ME

"D-Did you always look like that?" He stutters, fumbling for his drink like a blind man, unable to look away from my bait.

"No," I reply sharply, no longer laughing and not wanting to talk to him about before. Why does he always have to ask questions?

Luckily for me, the three men have risen from their seats at the same moment, and I take this as my cue to leave.

I walk to the door slowly, making eye contact with no one but with a look on my face that I know they won't miss. The lighting in here sucks but my skin is pale enough to reflect what little it gives out and I wonder if it would help to have blonde hair sometimes, then again it might be harder to blend in when I want to.

I don't even bother saying goodbye to Adryan, knowing him he'll end up asking something else if I do, and I'm still pissed that he asked me about what I was like before.

In what world would I reply to that positively? I'm not going to roll over and swap personal stories with him just because he gave me a few names and an easy kill.

Making my way into the street, I walk a good few paces before waiting for the door to open and as soon as it does, I wobble on my heel and pretend to go over on my ankle. It's one of my favourite routines, the damsel in distress act, and one of them rushes over to help me to my feet. I force tears to come to my eyes and I give him a sad smile when saying I'll be fine.

For a second, I wonder if I'm being too dramatic when I whimper as I put some weight onto my foot, but it doesn't take long for his arm to go around my waist. I swallow my automatic hiss at the contact but it's a necessary evil I remind myself.

"Surely you can't leave your friends?" I ask with my voice high-pitched and pathetic.

"Don't worry about them. Scott, Doug, come here and help me you arseholes!" He shouts and I couldn't have planned it better myself, even if I was compelling them.

"I'm fine really, if you just prop me against that wall, I can call my friend. I'll be out of sight and safe there." I sniffle and indicate over to the alleyway.

Scott and Doug exchange a look and as I thought, they are more than eager to help. One takes my other side and the other just walks behind, staring at my arse and I make a mental note to make him pay for that.

I may lay the trap well with the clothes I wear, but it's set for a certain type of person. Wearing a black dress doesn't give them permission to take advantage and for a second, I'm glad I'm no longer human as I don't have to put up with this crap anymore if I don't want to.

CURSE ME

When out of sight of the main street I turn on them faster than they can blink and drag forward the dumpsters to block their exit.

Each of them stares at me with open mouths and I don't know what has shocked them the most, the fact I'm not hurt, the fact I'm fast as hell or the fact I've just pushed something heavier than all three of them put together like it was no more than a shopping trolly.

"Which of you knows Nolan Emrys?" I say, my voice deadly and the ice is shining through my eyes.

I have to get through my usual line of questioning while I can be bothered this time. Maybe one of them has a lead.

I thrive on the colour leaving their faces and it even takes repeating the question for it to register as requiring a response from them.

But unfortunately, they shake their heads and I stomach the disappointment of knowing that they'll just be another kill on the list.

Chapter 7

"Did you *have* to burn them?" Adryan asks, taking a seat across from me in my favourite brunch spot. I like the view of the park from the window and the bitterness of the blend of coffee that they serve here.

"Did you *have* to interrupt my lunch?" I reply in the same tone.

"You looked like you could use the company." He shrugs, taking a bite from my pastry and I count to three, willing the anger to fade while wishing that I hadn't saved his soul after all.

"Going forwards, let's just assume I don't want it." I grind out through my teeth.

"Come on, you enjoyed the drinks the other night."

He picks up a menu and I fight the urge to tell him to leave. He can't be here just to socialise, and I want another target. I like not having to think about it or choose which one comes next as it helps with the disappointment.

"I tolerated them, there's a difference," I say while pulling my plate back to my side of the table.

He orders himself a coffee and I notice the look the waitress pulls when she asks him what he wants. The double meaning in her voice is oh-so-obvious and it irritates me slightly. Maybe it's because he's clearly loving the attention and my solitude is ruined even further as a result.

I've never given much thought to the people who work here, and I take in her light hair and freckles which only pisses me off more when realising they resemble mine. I glare at her, and she scampers away, not giving Adryan a second look. This makes me smile before he turns back to address me.

If he wants to spoil my fun, well, I can do the same right back.

"Anyway, I've been wanting to ask, did it...Did it make a difference in the end?" He looks around gesturing to his chest for some reason and it takes me a second to understand what he means.

"I'm not a psychic and you better not come to me for a reading each time." I roll my eyes, checking his soul and shaking my head to confirm it's the same.

He nods his head, processing the information and I hear him discreetly breathe out more heavily which makes me raise my eyebrows.

"I did some thinking on what you said, it turns out I do care." He gives me a small smile and I wonder why I even asked. It doesn't matter to me why he does what he does.

"I'm not a therapist either." I laugh, taking a bite of my snack and decide that it wasn't worth the effort of eating as it's too dry.

I don't push him to cut to the chase right away as I didn't mind the banter with him before, but I didn't realise it would have to be a regular thing. It's the most I've talked to someone in a while, and I doubt I have the patience for it in the long term.

"Hey, you cared before, it's only fair to tell you that you were right" He raises his hands and I smirk, as I do like being told that I'm right and he can probably sense that I'd have that trait.

"Got any more?" I ask after looking around the room.

It isn't just the coffee and views that I came here for, I also like this place for its variety. There are so many different types of people that walk through the doors and it's as close as I come to socialising when studying them all, though I draw the line when it comes to regulars like his little waitress as I'm not looking to make friends.

"I couldn't possibly say." He replies with a voice thick with sarcasm and I roll my eyes before summoning the ice.

"Give me a target," I order.

"Roland Gardner." His eyes unglaze and I tilt my head to smile.

"Thank you, I'll find you when it's done." I say as if I'm filing paperwork for him, and really, it is just that simple for me. It's basically my day job and it can get boring sometimes.

"Are you not interested in knowing more?" He asks, thanking a different waitress for the black coffee and I smile, knowing that I've scared the first one off and spoiled his fun in the process.

"More of what?"

"What we're doing, the big picture." He seems genuinely curious for my answer.

"Is It going to affect me at all?" I give away nothing from the expression I make.

"As much as you love to disclose details, it's hard to see what would benefit you." He raises one eyebrow and I smile. He's got me there but it's not a bad thing.

"All I need is access to the baddest people you've got," I say before sipping my drink, most of the ice has melted in the summer heat and it could use another shot of espresso to strengthen it up again.

"And I want the worst." He firmly replies and I know that he means his brother.

I think on this for a second and there's no denying that the Lord of Ashes would be a nice notch on my belt of conquests.

"So you're really going to kill him?" I ask.

"It'd probably be easier if you did, but yes." His voice is strong, and I look at him properly this time.

"What would that solve? I mean, doesn't all of his power just go to you instead? Big difference."

I've paid a bit more attention to human affairs recently compared to what I used to, but I can't even guess when his father was killed and when the power was last transferred. It can't have made that much of a difference in the grand scheme of things.

"You wound me." He's more serious when speaking now and his voice is rough. "I don't want power; I want it gone. No more drugs, no more murders and no more deaths. I want peace." He finishes simply and I try not to snort.

"Peace? Does such a thing exist?"

"To me it will, and that's what I'm fighting for." The passion is thick in his voice, and I'm reminded of the sound of it back in the cellar, a leader's voice.

"Okay, set me at him," I say, it can't be that hard to kill a human and that's the second time that voice has won me around.

"He's completely off the grid. The last time he was cornered was in my father's time and he got away." The irritation clear in his face and I try not to laugh at that little revelation.

"Yes, well *I'm* not incompetent, so we can assume that that won't happen again once you give me a location." I tilt my head and I can see him clench his jaw.

"If you're so great, why don't *you* find him?" He challenges me and I narrow my eyes.

"I'm merely offering to help you out while you make my life easier for a while. Half the effort is finding someone to go for and if I have to do it all myself, the alliance holds no value for me." I lean forward, daring him to challenge me.

"I'll get you a location." He concedes and I smile.

"Happy hunting" I repeat his own words in mockery as he tries and fails to frown.

Roland Gardner is someone I actually know of, he owns a bar downtown, and I've heard of him from a few people. I didn't think he was *that* bad but at least I know where to find him.

I dress in a shimmering blue top paired with white trousers. It's not the most feminine thing in the world but it compliments my curves and it couldn't hurt to use them to my advantage tonight.

It's been a week since I was first in that cellar, and it's gone from clear nights to absolute cloud. If it rains, I will not be amused and I make sure to avoid anything too absorbent just in case.

    I pull on a leather jacket as I leave my apartment, it's still dark from when I got home hours ago and I wonder if I should leave the lights on, just so that the electricity bill isn't suspicious. I remember to shoot a text to my fake dad as I'm walking, just to remind him that Elisabeth is still meant to be alive and then I leave the phone at home as I'd rather it wasn't traced.

    I'm wearing platform boots and I love the feeling of power I get from stomping my toes on the floor. I'm not the tallest of women and this really makes up for that fact.

    The bar comes into view. I can't recall how many times I've been here before, often enough for it to leave an impression and I hope that it stays open after I'm done. The bathrooms here are half decent and the crowd is a good mix.

    The low cut, sequin top I'm wearing gets me admitted right away and I strut my way over to the bar. I feel at least three pairs of eyes on my back and I flip my hair over my shoulders for good measure. It always feels weird for me even now, luring people in with looks that aren't really my own.

    I order my usual glass of champagne and the bartender smiles at me, but I don't know him as well as John.

After my first credit, he awkwardly walks over to let me know and I fake a blush to act flattered. I wouldn't be surprised if it was coming from him by the way he keeps eying my chest and I hope Roland gets here soon as I'm not in the mood tonight.

I perch right in the centre of the room, both to maximise the free drinks and keep an eye on the entrances. The dancing will be starting soon, and I have a nasty feeling I'll have to try it if he doesn't hurry. I hate dancing, it's so joyful and lively that it feels out of place for a thing like me.

Just when I'm about to give up and change my target to a man in the corner, the tell-tale red hair walks in, and I know right away from the handshakes and turned heads that this is my guy.

I wait five minutes before approaching the bar, I don't even look at Roland because I know the type and by the time I'm back at my table with another glass, I know I've hooked him. His eyes are practically glued to my arse and I can feel him staring at it as he walks over to my solitary table.

"And what's a pretty-little-thing like you doing sitting all alone?" He purrs and I want to vomit in his face.

"Waiting for some company." I tilt my head and smile playfully, trying to push the violent thoughts aside... for now.

"Let me oblige you?" He asks as he sits opposite, not waiting for an answer and I make sure to lean forward as if I'm interested in my newfound companion.

"What's your name, darling?" He says out the corner of his mouth and I bite my lip to stop scowling as an automatic response. I know that's not his real accent, I heard him speaking at the bar and this is just cringey more than anything else.

"Lizzie." I reply, knowing Elisabeth might give me away and I keep biting my lip as it appears to be working to my advantage. "What's yours?"

I pretend to stare at his lips as if I'm entranced and I can hear his pulse raise in response to the point where he's so predictable that it's not even fun anymore.

"Roland." He practically growls and I make myself blush as much as possible. "So where do you come from, little one?"

He winks at me, and it takes all that I have not to roll my eyes at this, I mean, come on! Little one? Is this dick for real?

"Oh you know... around." I make sure to reply with a low voice and keep his eyes locked on mine. "What about you? What brings you here?"

"I own the place." His face is a picture of pride and I pretend to be shocked and impressed. Little does he know my questions are carefully chosen to help us cut to the chase, as I don't give a fuck about his star sign or where he's from. I just want to kill him already and get on with my life.

"Wow, you own the whole place?" I bite my lip again and just like that, my work here is done.

"Say, Lizzie." He pretends to take a look around the bar. "It's pretty loud out here, what would you say to a private tour?"

I shift in my seat as if that excites me and dip my head in acceptance. He takes my hand in his and my cheeks plaster on a smile as he escorts me across the room.

As we walk up the stairs, I note the different exits and need to remember to wipe the camera's before leaving as I frequent this scene too much to risk becoming a suspect.

Roland unlocks the office door and escorts me inside, the biggest mistake he'll ever make.

"I didn't realise who you were!" I try and place something like awe on my face when he tells his colleagues to leave. I pretend not to notice the door being locked behind them.

So that's how it is. Well, I'll enjoy it much more than I thought in that case.

"Yes well... I own many things, but nothing as fine as you." He licks his lips and I'm glad I can finally drop the act.

The room is large but quite snug as the furniture is all dark leather and the wallpaper is a deep red. It's got a gothic study vibe to it and I actually quite like it to be honest. To the point where I wonder if the next owner will be more worthy of such a place.

"Before I even start, I have to ask. Has that ever worked?" My voice is my own now and his face is a picture of confusion.

"What are you on-" He's cut off by the ice in my eyes and I repeat the question.

"Yes, I use it most nights." The voice is zombie-like, and I sigh at the people that have been here before me. It's got to be either the money or the hair because there's nothing else vouching for him.

I ask the usual string of questions while pouring myself a drink from his personal supply and spit the cheap bourbon on the floor the second it assaults my tongue.

"Really?" I snap at him, and he shrugs, still glazed over as I've already told him to remain calm.

"It's for guests." He replies and I shake my head in disgust.

Surely a bar owner could afford a half-decent drink to offer his visitors? It's not like he needs to scrimp for pennies and my respect for him is falling faster by the second.

I look through the drawers of the desk before finding what I want, knowing his kind all too well and pour it *all* into the liquor that I hand to him.

"Drink up." I grin and naturally, he does.

Chapter 8

When I wake up in the morning I feel the urge to go back out there and do more. There was no real violence or satisfaction in what I did last night. It may as well not have happened.

I feel useless and lazy; and it'll look like his own mistake anyway. I could have done more, I know I should have. I mean it's been four years and the curse still is going strong.

Part of me is getting tired of the disappointment and I think that's what is getting to me the most. The only thing for it is to find myself another target and when working with Adryan, at least I know that they stand a real chance of breaking it. You know, compared to risking it on the sleazy idiots that I find in bars.

One thing I know for sure though, is that there's not a chance in hell I'm waiting until tomorrow to lurk outside his office, I need to find another one today.

It takes me an hour to find his address, all while lying in my bed with a coffee in hand. If it wasn't for the fact that only *one* of my tech-savvy connections could find him, I'd scold him on this too, but he was well hidden, and my source is compelled to always keep his findings to himself.

I can't decide what would be more fun now that I have his home address, to courier something to his place with my compliments and a meeting place... or to turn up myself.

When realising that I'd not get to see the reaction to the former, I decide to make my way across town. Scaring the life out of him on a Sunday morning seems like the best way to repay his annoying personality and I'm curious to see where he lives.

I don't usually visit homes with the intention of leaving the inhabitants alive and with that in mind I've kept my outfit smart when dressing. I want to blend in well in case he has guests over and I'm not sure what I want to do afterwards. At least this way it won't close any doors.

It's early enough when I set out and there are not many people in the streets which is always a nice surprise. The smell of coffee is strong in the air and a few dogs are being walked for their morning toilet breaks.

I can't help but think that I wouldn't mind having a dog, especially when I see a particularly stunning German Shepherd bark at a stranger. The only downside is that I'm not around enough to justify it and it would probably smell the monster inside me and get scared.

As I keep going, I instantly hate the fact that his apartment complex is nicer than mine, something I notice as I turn around the corner. If he didn't live here, I know that I'd be looking up the neighbours and considering a move. Even the views are nicer, and I scowl when entering the red and gold elevator.

Of course, the rich bastard has a penthouse so I go all the way to the top and wonder if it would be too petty to throw him off the roof to claim it for myself.

His door is to my right when I step off the lift and it takes barely a push of my strength to open it silently and walk through as if I own the place.

Like mine, it is filled with all hardwood flooring, but the details are a surprising scheme of grey, black and gold. It's a completely different vibe to what I'm used to, and I have to say I didn't pin him for the type.

His kitchen/living room is first up. It's an open-plan layout of the two together which I always enjoy seeing. I check the fridge out of habit for coffee when noting that he's obviously not in here but unfortunately, there's nothing cold.

I spy that there's a warm pot freshly brewed on the counter, so I pour myself a mug before continuing and I have to admit that it feels weird to have it hot at this point.

Following the sounds ahead of me to what I assume is his bedroom, I make my way inside quietly before taking in the walls around me. Just like the main room, it's empty with the ensuite door closed and the sounds I heard were him in the shower. I decide to be patient and plonk myself onto the bed rather than explore any further. I was human once after all and there are some boundaries I still respect.

While wondering what sort of face he will pull when he sees me sitting out here, I sip at the coffee and pause when I think I can taste cinnamon. It's an odd combination for July and I don't know how I feel about it. I have enjoyed the odd pumpkin spice latte in the past, so I'm not disturbed enough to spit it out at least.

The sheets are soft, and I can see a massive wardrobe hidden behind the panelling as if it's meant to be a secret room. It's a nice touch but I feel like everyone in this city has a walk-in these days, so at least something here is what I expected.

The water shuts off and I can hear him pottering around before he walks through the door. A towel is wrapped firmly around his waist and I'm the first thing he sees when looking up.

CURSE ME

"Why's the only coffee in here warm?" I complain as a way of greeting and the horror-struck expression is almost worth the effort of trekking up here.

"Wh-How?" He stutters and I laugh.

"What's with the cinnamon too?" I stick out my tongue in exaggeration and his eyes are still as wide as saucers.

It's a rare thing to see Adryan lost for words and I rather like seeing him dishevelled like this, not just because of the view.

"My mother liked cinnamon." Is his only answer and I shrug, not wanting to pick *that* apart any further, knowing his family history.

"Roland is dead," I comment when he walks into his wardrobe and out of sight.

I lean back on my elbows and hear him release a breath deeply as he tries to control his nerves, he's not doing a great job because his heart is still racing, and I swear I hear him mutter 'Same here.' which makes me laugh quietly to myself.

"That was fast." He calls out, wanting to be heard now and I nod even though he can't see me.

"I've come for another." I state the obvious.

"I don't have another." He replies tentatively and I stand up in impatience.

My eyes roll automatically as I speak, "I've come to compel another then if you want to be pedantic."

"I don't have another." He chuckles at having to correct me as he walks back out, buttoning his shirt.

I look over at him to see that he's trying to dress in another suit. I frown at the sight. Does he own any *normal* clothes? I'd like to go a day without seeing one for a change and it's a Sunday for crying out loud.

"What?" He asks, looking down.

"I'm sick of this look," I say, pointing to his general appearance.

"And what would you have me wear?" He sighs, accepting that this is happening and that I've infiltrated his apartment. I mean, I expected him to cave but not so soon, he must have only just woken up.

"I don't know, Jeans? Chinos? Anything but that, you've overused it now." I sigh back at him, knowing that I'm getting under his skin, and I like it.

It's been a while since I've had a regular person to annoy and even in my human form, I loved to tease my friends now and again for a bit of banter. But in this life, there's no room for friends and this is the next best thing I suppose.

"I didn't realise fashion was one of your special skills." He mutters before walking back in.

"Well, we know it's not one of yours." I don't miss a beat in throwing back at him, it's too easy.

I've just realised that the bedroom is smaller than mine but to my dismay, the view is to die for. There's a balcony attached, and I walk out onto the patio to look down on the streets below. Part of me wonders if I could fly if I jump off right now and the other part wonders if I could kill someone by throwing down the chair next to me.

Rather than test one of my theories, I study the place inside again and his sheets, walls and rugs are all some shade of dark grey. The only colour in here is coming from outside and I'd hate to sleep here, it's suffocating. It's so gloomy compared to my bright open room that I wonder if he decorated it himself.

"Happy?" He asks when stepping out in black jeans and a skin-tight jumper, unsurprisingly, grey.

"Are you depressed?" I ask, turning around to examine him in general.

"Not that I'm aware of, why?" He asks sceptically and I raise my eyebrows.

"Everything in here is bland and dark. It's killing me." I gesture around.

He laughs. "It'll take more than a quick change to fix that I'm afraid."

He's right so I only purse my lips and walk back in.

While making my way to the living room I listen to his bare feet padding along the floor as he follows. It's an interesting look, Adryan dressed like a regular person. I can appreciate an attractive man when I want to and he's not bad at all.

"You should get some plants, a bit of life in here might help," I comment before nodding to myself at my own conclusion.

"Anything else?" His sarcasm is strong, but I ignore it.

"Have I mentioned no iced coffee? That's the worst part."

He smiles. "Give me notice next time and I'll make sure to stock it."

He walks to the kitchen to pour his own cup and I park myself into the soft grey sofa that basically swallows me whole. It's smoother than mine and I like the feeling on my skin better than the leather I'm used to.

"You're not as shocked as I thought you'd be," I confess when looking over to him.

"I basically shat myself?" He questions while pulling a face.

I shrug. "Meh, I've seen worse." I really have and I smile at the memory.

"I suppose it helps to know we're on the same team." He sits on the opposite end of the couch, and I look around again.

I decide that it's not worth being jealous of the place, it would take more effort to redecorate than it would to just stay where I am. Plus the rent is paid for and I doubt I'll get that lucky elsewhere.

"Why don't you have a target for me?" I break the silence after a few minutes.

It didn't feel awkward to me, but it probably did for him, I have that effect when staring silently and I don't really care to change that fact.

"I'm fine thanks, and how are you Cam?" He narrows his eyes. I wasn't expecting the sass again so soon.

"Do you really care for the small talk?" I ask, draining my mug and standing to get more.

"Believe it or not, murder isn't my favourite topic of conversation." He snaps and when realising what he's done, his gaze follows me nervously as I walk across the room to fill my mug again in silence.

The stress alone is enough to punish him for that slip-up and I listen to the thrumming of his heart for a second while appreciating how intimidating I must be to be able to do that to him without breathing a word in reply.

"I'm peachy. Any other pleasantries you'd like to put out there?" I sit back down and wait for him to reply.

I haven't really done small talk in a while, unless you count luring people in as real small talk? I suppose I could try and see if that gets it out of his system, I mean I've got time and it wouldn't hurt to practise for when I'm faking it.

"I'm surprised you're humouring me." He frowns slightly and I shrug.

"It's hard to hate something without trying it first for reference."

"Do you not have like... friends?" He leans forward and we're back to the annoying personal questions again. He really needs to pick his audience.

"My purpose is to kill, what would be the point?" I snap.

"Is that all you do?" He scrunches his brows like he finds it hard to believe and I return the gesture.

"What about you, where are your friends? What do you do?"

I might as well ask because he was about to leave here dressed in a suit. It's not exactly a hobby/friendship attire and it's the weekend. He can't judge me if he's just as bad.

"At least I know how to converse." He counters back and I purse my lips at what he's just given me.

"So you admit it then? You have no life and no friends?" Hopefully, this teaches him not to ask so many intrusive questions.

"I'm a busy man." He shrugs and that's that.

"Can I ask now?"

"You can't compel me because I haven't been to a meeting yet. You killed four targets in three days, we didn't prepare that many." He laughs and I take the compliment where it's due. "If you're eager, you're more than welcome to come and join me. Especially if it avoids you going into my head." He shivers at the recollection for some reason, it can't be that bad.

"I don't go into your head, I just…" I sigh. "Where's the meeting? I'll come if only to critique the security," I remember it pissed him off last time and I rather enjoyed the experience.

"Describe it to me… and then I'll tell you the meeting place." He leans back in his seat and while we both know that I can get the information either way, I appreciate the attempt he's making to even the power dynamic.

I'd be doing the same if I were him.

"I summon it and it's like there's this tunnel vision from me to you. I know then that anything I say you have to follow." I wait for his reaction but he sits on it for a second.

"What's the worst thing you've made someone do?"

At this, I laugh and tilt my head back. "Don't ask questions you don't want the answers to."

How would I even begin to decide how to reply to that? I can't count how many times I've done it and I've not exactly gone out into the world with the intent to be kind lately, my only goal has been to free myself.

"Okay… What's the best thing you've made someone do?"

This stops me and I have to think for a second. What was the best thing I've made someone do? It's the easier of the two to answer, that's for sure.

"I made a woman get sober." I simply say in the end.

"Why?"

How did I know he was going to ask that? It's never enough for him to just take a bloody answer.

"I killed her husband and she had a child." I surprise even myself by adding. "He wasn't there to abuse them anymore, so she had no need for that amount of escapism."

Chapter 9

I killed three men and two women yesterday. A record for this year, but it feels like nothing.

After leaving Adryan's apartment I couldn't stop thinking about the young boy with purpled arms and I couldn't stop picturing it happening still elsewhere. It doesn't take much to find the area where it's most common and by the time it was dark outside and the fifth was done, I still didn't feel any better.

When I was human, I used to volunteer at shelters, I was new to the city and wanted to get to know it, to put towards it. I felt so helpless when seeing cases like those and now that I can actually get revenge for these people, the feeling still doesn't fade. Like it doesn't matter because it still had to happen.

I can understand the rage, hell, I can even understand the blood lust, but I can't understand how someone can look at a defenceless child or partner and take it out on them. Someone that has done no harm, someone they claim to love. It confuses me and worse still it disgusts me. Me!

Tomorrow there is a meeting Adryan has invited me to and I have already found and scouted the location. The urge to wreak destruction and vengeance is finally gone for now and the question he asked me yesterday is still ringing in my ears.

Is that all you do?

I treat myself, I shop, I drink coffee, but I don't really do anything. I mean, what's the point?

I'm a monster, doing anything but that is just pretending to be something I was, something I'm not. Sometimes I wish they just took it away, the small part of me that still remains. They took my soul but there's still a sliver remaining, a taste of what I once had and a reminder of what is gone. Because of that, I know that I will never be able to forget what I am, and I think that was the intention.

Part of me wonders if maybe I died the day that I turned. If maybe this is hell, and I did something truly horrible that I can't remember.

I can't help but feel that even some of the darker souls I find wouldn't deserve this. But then again, I suppose they wouldn't mind it as much. They wouldn't really change.

I rise from the bath in which I was sulking and physically shake my head. There's no point feeling sorry for myself. I asked for this...technically.

Some people would kill for my power, to be able to force minds and to withstand pain. I don't know what's gotten into me, but I refuse to linger on it.

While dressing slowly, I pay attention to the small details of my gold belt and jewellery against my black dress to ground myself. I don't plan to go out tonight for a change, I haven't got the mindset for it so I'm going to try something else, something I've not dared to do in four years. I'm going to visit the library.

I don't know if it's pride or pain that has stopped me from frequenting the same places that I did in my mortal life, but so far I have avoided them. I probably still will but I want something to help pass the time and reading can range across a thousand subjects. If I pick the right book I can call it strategy or something.

The library close to my apartment has a lot of historical novels, and it wouldn't hurt to look up great tacticians from the past for some forgotten tips. If Adryan takes too long I might as well say to hell with it all and find the

Lord of Ashes myself, if only to piss him off. It can't be that hard, but it doesn't hurt to over-prepare when I'm bored.

The sun is out as I stroll downtown with my hair pulled into a long, dark ponytail and I love the feeling of it swishing against my back as I walk.

The heels I'm wearing are terrifying and I remember that the second I saw them, I knew I had to have them. They are black with gold studs all the way around them and it's almost like they are a metaphor for myself.

The click click click of the shoes echoes off the walls of the buildings as I walk down an alleyway not far from my destination out of habit. I do it just to see if there's anyone up to no good, but instead of turning around afterwards, I find myself staring at an apartment window.

My apartment window, or at least it was.

The day I changed was the day I'd closed the deal on it, and I can still remember every detail inside of those walls. My throat feels dry, I don't even know how that is possible, so I force myself to turn around and continue on. I should have recognised the area sooner to avoid it, a mistake I will not be making twice.

The security guard on the door outside of the library makes me laugh inwardly. As if he could stop me from entering if that's what I wanted. The thought cheers me from my deflated mood.

CURSE ME

The place is just how I remember it and I look up at the high ceilings with the gold details. I have to admit it's always been a stunning location and I love how quiet it is here. Shelf after shelf of books are stockpiled, and I inhale the musky scent of the paper that fills each room.

It's great how it's socially acceptable to be mad at someone for speaking to you while here and I'll probably come back again just for that.

The historic section is near the back, and I pick up a volume on Napoleon before finding a nearby chair to sit myself at. The only vice here is how uncomfortable they all are, I'd kill for a sofa cushion. The best position I can seat myself in is with my back against one armrest and my legs dangling over the other. I get a few nasty looks, but I dare them to come closer and try it again.

It's lovely just to be able to lose myself in something and stop thinking for a while. Well, not stop thinking but stop directing my own thoughts. Right now, the author is talking and some of the notes are actually quite interesting.

Essentially Napoleon succeeded by playing with three key areas, speed, control and exploiting his enemy's weaknesses. Just reading some of the things he managed to get through successfully, never mind alive with his army is insane and while his values aren't my own, it's hard not to be impressed with some of the feats.

I've got speed and control nailed thanks to my curse, but I do love the idea of exploiting weaknesses to my advantage. It's not like I'm invading a country or anything, I just need to pick off a few bad apples until the right one falls so I might as well have fun with it.

By the time the librarian walks to my table with crossed arms, I am on the final page of the book, I finish it before bothering to raise my head. It's 6pm and my eyes are tired, or I'd have told her to piss off and give me more time to find another.

Instead, I just rise silently (but not meekly) and walk past her and out the door. She was nice enough but there's something about standing in front of me with crossed arms that annoys me.

The summer sky is still quite bright and while I'm not hungry, I could use a good meal. It would be nice to take advantage of my day off (of sorts), so I saunter in the direction of a Michelin-star restaurant a few blocks from here. Even with compulsion, I always feel smug when gaining admittance to a place like this out of the blue.

I find myself in a comfortable chair in the middle of the room with a tall glass of bubbles. There's a wine menu that can be paired with it and while I usually partake, I don't tonight because I am celebrating taking time for myself today, and for getting myself out of a mood without violence.

CURSE ME

A lot of the couples dotted around the room are older and clearly in a position of considerable wealth. The best way to tell is from the way their noses point in the air whenever a server brings a dish to their table. I know for a fact that I wouldn't have the patience to come here all the time for that reason.

It probably makes me a hypocrite to hate seeing them think that they are better than the rest, I mean I have days where my ego is unstoppable, but at least I know when to come back down to earth where it really matters, and I don't quite believe that they share that skill. Plus, I'm not exactly wrong, I am better than mortals in a lot of areas, they just so happen to be in physical strength and agility.

If I really run out of ways to amuse myself I should enter a street fighting ring, the results would be beautiful but somehow it doesn't seem quite fair so it'll stay towards the bottom of my list, for now.

My first dish is brought out with speed and it's tiny.

I expect to see 12 of these little babies brought out to me tonight because normal portions just won't do in a place like this, I pop the smoked sea urchin into my mouth in one swift motion. It's creamy in texture and has a strong mineral flavour to it that I cleanse with my champagne.

I never used to eat fish but I've warmed to it recently.

By the fifth dish I start to see the main food come out and there is a tiny raw steak, a pigeon's leg and some sort of salmon mousse for my next three. Before I turned, I never cared for things like that, not only could I not afford it, I didn't understand it. But when you remove the need to eat for survival it becomes more of a treat than a chore and that's when I truly discovered food, ironically.

By my seventh glass of champagne the server gives me a look as if to *ask are you sure about that?* And I reply with one that says I'll drink your blood if you don't bring me another.

He might not know the exact words behind it, but he gets the gist and the bottle is left on my table. If only he knew the hefty tip waiting for him, he would have offered to lift it to my lips for me.

The last dish is a tiny golden chocolate in the shape of a skull, and I look at it between my fingers before placing it lightly on my tongue. It starts to melt instantly, and I love that it's dark. The flavours are rich, and the cacao bean is bitter which makes me comment to myself how dark chocolate and coffee must be my love language.

I let the food rest for a bit before I pay the bill and walk out of the room with grace. The look on the face of my server can either be from the cheque I have left for him or the fact that I'm able to walk in these heels without falling on my face after what I've just drank.

To solidify the smirk on my face at his reaction, I wink before disappearing completely and he seems like a decent person. I just hope that Elisabeth is watching from beyond in utter fury at the amount I left behind me, as even in death she can't escape my scorn.

Chapter 10

Today I'm meeting Adryan at my coffee shop before 5pm to walk to the meeting together. At first, I was tempted to tell him to piss off for even implying I couldn't find it myself, but then he said it would help him cover better if he wasn't walking in the middle of nowhere alone.

He has a point, and while no one can follow quite as well as I can, it would be good for me to be there to scope the place out and make sure there are no unwelcome visitors.

We arrive at the coffee shop at the same time but there's not a chance in hell that I'm walking past without grabbing a drink first. So, I order a Frappuccino for myself and I even get Adryan a black coffee with cinnamon sprinkled on top.

CURSE ME

It's been a while since I've met someone this regularly and I wonder if this is a small fragment of the real Camilla coming through and being nice...I don't know if I like it or not but it's only coffee.

When I walk back outside to meet him, I hand him his cup with an innocent expression and the shock registers on his face, but he takes it from me anyway.

"What have you done to it?" He asks suspiciously before taking a sip.

I roll my eyes. "If you thought I tampered with it, then why the hell would you drink it?"

He doesn't reply for a second while we walk, I clock the exact second he tastes the cinnamon. He gives me a look that I can't quite diagnose. I only face forwards again and keep going, letting him take on the brunt of the conversation should he require it again.

"I figured if you wanted me dead I wouldn't have woken up this morning." He says in an oddly cheerful way.

"Fair deduction." I acknowledge, sucking at the straw that's stabbed into the middle of my drink. The cream is thick and cold against the hot day, which is just what the doctor ordered.

"You know Cam, I'd have taken you for a black coffee type." He comments, eyeing the plastic cup in my hand.

I'll take that as a compliment. While I am dark and bitter, I do like to have sweet drinks where I can, and I don't care about my image enough to give those up.

"I don't need a coffee type to prove how big and bad I am," I smirk, and he smiles playfully.

This makes me raise my eyebrows as we walk, and I take a break from scanning every face in the crowd around us on the off chance they look familiar and sketchy.

"I didn't realise you thought of me that way... seeing as I *am* a big bad black coffee drinker." He replies, his expression smug.

Real Camillia should learn not to waste her breath in future, and with this in mind, I swiftly snatch the coffee cup from his hands before depositing it into the nearest bin.

"Well, that was uncalled for." He sighs.

"What did you expect?" I say sweetly and we round a corner onto a street with fewer people around.

The sky is cloudless, and I wonder if sunglasses would have been a better idea to go with this look as it would have helped with the incognito aspect.

"You know, for a person that talks shit as much as you do, you need to learn to take it as well." He looks at me and I glare back.

"And why would I need to learn that?" I ask, knowing fine well that I don't have to learn anything if I don't want to.

"Well you don't... but I bet it's a pain in the arse getting butthurt every time someone opens their mouth." He grins and I resist the urge to take the bait right away. It's too easy to bite back and I think that's what he's after.

"You know, if you weren't such a dick, I'd be worried about you." I muse.

"Why?" He scrunches his eyebrows and I tilt my head as if in concern.

"Because you clearly have memory loss, forgetting just who the hell you're talking to." I let a bit of the ice rise into my eyes and he just grins at me, the bastard.

"Old news-" I cut him off by flipping him onto his back in the middle of the dirty street, before he can say anything else.

"You may look like a dumb blonde, but do you have to act like one?" I sigh in exasperation and it's a good thing that I saved his soul when I did.

"How long have you been wanting to say that one?" He asks, gingerly rising to his feet and brushing the dirt from his grey suit.

Of course, he's wearing another damn suit.

"A while." I concede and we walk the rest of the way in silence.

The building we enter is a bakery of all places and we go through a side door that's only accessible via the alley. I see the red lights shining on us from the cameras and a bulky man dressed in a baker's outfit casually smoking next to it.

I mean, I saw all of this yesterday but it's still better than I thought.

As we walk through, Adryan opens a fridge door and lets me walk in first which is strange to say the least, but I'm impressed to see it's an entrance to a flight of stairs leading down to a basement. Adryan lifts his eyebrows as if to say I know, right? And I nod my head in acknowledgement while leading the way down.

Each stair is lighted with its own LED strip, but I can imagine it's still not the most comfortable thing to walk down with human eyes. I offer my hand out to stop him from tripping and falling on me at one point, to which he just gives me the middle finger and overtakes.

I hear the voices before I see them and at the bottom of the stairs, there is a stainless-steel door that opens into a wider room that is extremely well-lit.

The ceilings are tall, which explains the long descent and it actually looks quite cool. There's a lot of blue lighting dotted around with comfortable-looking chairs and tables. It's almost like a modern office, rather than a meeting place for criminals.

"Not what you expected?" Adryan asks over his shoulder and I shake my head, not wanting to compliment him out loud and make his head any bigger than it needs to be.

"After I joined, I was able to funnel some of my paycheques to upgrade the place and while it wasn't much, it's made a big difference." He goes on as if I asked.

"You're not the only one that paid for this place." The man with the glasses calls over and he blanches instantly when seeing that it's me walking behind Adryan.

"You can relax you know?" Adryan says to him, and I raise one eyebrow in question. "What? Do you intend to kill him?"

"No," I admit, and he turns to the man as if to say *'See'*?

"His approach is wiser than yours though." I can't help but add but of course, he ignores me.

"I'm James." The dirty blonde from before says and I realise I'm going to have to use my real name with these people too. I should have said another fake name, I knew I should.

"Camilla."

"This is David and Paul," Adryan adds, pointing to the others that are still hesitant to speak in my presence.

Paul is the brother of the dead guy and David is the one with the glasses which is how I'll have to remember it. Neither of them makes eye contact and nobody seems that keen to speak.

"Is this it?" I ask and it comes out sharper than I intended but I leave it be.

"What were you expecting?" James asks and I'm impressed that he responded.

"More people." I simply reply, I wasn't expecting much to be honest. I just wanted to know if there was any more to expect before we get to the point.

"We have spies, but it doesn't make sense to call them all here just for meetings," Paul says, and I nod in understanding.

"Don't let me hold you up, I'm just here for my marks. You should probably be the one to tell me though." I direct this part to James, and I see him wince slightly at my addressing him specifically.

"Why?" Adryan asks and I mentally kick myself.

I should have kept it to myself in case I want to make a point. I'm starting to have a habit of thinking out loud and it's probably because I'm not used to being around people I have no intention of killing.

"You're tainted." I answer, and James looks almost insulted.

"I mean your soul is tainted." I sigh and it doesn't seem to have helped matters so I turn to Adryan to see if I'm making any sense at all. I can see the cogs turning in his mind.

"I see what you mean now." Adryan finally says in my direction and turns to James. "The rest of us aren't, which means if we order the kill, we'd taint too and risk the lovely Camilla here murdering us."

I stare at the ceiling, begging for the strength not to slap him. I know I let it slip but this wasn't something I wanted to make known and the more they have an idea about this, the more the idea can spread and cause me problems.

"She can't kill us?" David asks like I'm not here and I don't know if I should be offended or not that I am now labelled as she.

"No, she can, she just doesn't want to. We don't taste as good apparently." Adryan snorts and I exhale loudly to indicate my irritation. He's far too relaxed about this and I can tell his colleagues don't share his attitude.

James has paled considerably and it's more useful to me if they all just forget what I said already and get on with it.

"I wouldn't worry, if anyone here's getting murdered it's Blondie." I say to James while jerking my head in Adryan's direction and he smiles slightly.

"Here's me thinking we've bonded after you bought me coffee." He places a hand on his chest as if physically wounded and I grind my teeth.

"Maybe we should get started?" Paul hesitates to butt in, and I nod my head in agreement, ignoring Adryan completely now.

"So, the removal of Roland opened the spot I needed to get my guy into position. The whole Craig thing has distracted them enough to not look into it too deeply and the method really helped us out there."

I gain a nod from Adryan as he starts and it's like looking at another person. In the space of ten seconds, he's transformed from a man-child into a serious game player, and it doesn't take a genius to guess which version I prefer.

"Chrissy needs to lie lower from where she is because I've heard talk and I'm conscious we can't risk her being a person of interest again." He finishes and nods to Paul.

Apparently, this is an around-the-circle kind of thing where they report and indicate for the next person to start. It's oddly informal but I like it.

"Thanks for that, I'll pull her out tonight and put Murphy on the job. They've been touching base in case we needed to make the switch, it shouldn't delay things too much in the long term." Paul says, and it's strange to watch him talk and not think of murdering his brother. The fact the neck tattoo is missing helps keep me grounded though.

"Myself, Michael, and Bess are still on the payroll and they're approaching Sarah just now to see if she'll be open to it. It must mean that they're moving on something, if they need to increase their reach. Michael and I already hold most of the power in the sector and Sarah would make the majority." David's face looks grim, and I assume from that that he is a person of influence, a judge maybe?

"Special Agent," Adryan answers my thoughts before we all turn to James, and I don't like the idea of being readable, so I scowl to myself slightly.

"Very little from my side, we've mostly been told to keep our heads down and ears open. Having Mark and Craig killed in a short space of time has got them working us around the clock and I'm hoping I get assigned someone that actually talks." James shrugs and I don't have time to question his role before Adryan turns to me.

"James is a bodyguard rented out around the key players as an incentive and Paul is our technological lead. His team has been slowly accessing the security systems around known locations, but someone got a look at Chrissy last time she was planting a bug and they tend to remember faces." His voice is still low and once again I'm reminded of the man in the cellar.

I nod processing it all before contributing. "It sounds like I need to kill off Michael next."

Nobody speaks right away, and I don't miss the fact that a few looks are exchanged in the process.

David's jaw drops slightly, and his eyes widen before he finally replies, "You'd kill an agent?"

"Please, he can't be that great if he's on the payroll," I reply and I get a surprising nod from Paul in agreement.

"Plus, it sounds like with Michael out of the picture, it might spook Sarah into hesitating and the power won't be theirs anymore." I look to David for his reply, and he hesitates for a second.

I suppose it's easier for me to think this way, I'm an outsider and know none of these people. But then again, I can't imagine that I would care that much anyway, it's not my thing.

"He is a bad man." David sighs and bites his lip, considering many invisible options. "I think you're right, ultimately it's the best way to block them." He finally gives in, and I can see why he's so pure.

"I'll make it quick," I promise, and I can see that it calms him almost.

Unfortunately for this one I'll need to make a bit of a show to successfully spook Sarah, but David doesn't need to know that ahead of time.

"Anymore?" I add looking around.

This will last me a couple of days at most and then I'll be bored again. I'd rather not be forced to go looking for more abusers as that only frustrates me and I doubt any of them will be the cure that I need.

Paul hands a piece of paper to James and James then passes it to me which makes me smile.

"We've made a list of smaller bottlenecks. None like Michael though," James says and swallows, probably imagining that I'm salivating at the idea of eating his soul.

I don't know why I told Adryan that I eat them, I don't, but I wanted to scare him. I don't think it's something I'm going to be able to take back now though.

"Just remember what we're here for," Adryan says, slapping David on the back and holding eye contact with each of them in the circle.

"Peace?" I mutter under my breath sarcastically, unable to help myself and he catches it.

"Yes Cam, peace. A city where kids aren't dragged into selling drugs, where men and women aren't whored out against their will and where deaths aren't more numerous than births."

"Deaths exceed births here?" I ask in disbelief as I didn't realise it was *that* bad.

"A lot gets covered up and there are natural ways to die Cam." He reminds me and it sounds more realistic in my mind now. Shitty, but realistic.

The meeting ends there and after a series of rushed pleasantries we start to disperse, Adryan and I being the last to leave and he walks me home after my half-arsed refusal.

He's probably already guessed my address after seeing Elisabeth's ID in my purse and I don't really care.

As long as he leaves when we get there.

Chapter 11

"You're starting to become predictable," I say while not looking up from my book.

I could hear him as he entered, the half step he made as he turned around trying to find my seat, the low voice he used to order his coffee and the quick inhale he's just made as he approaches me.

Adryan places himself into the chair across from me and the blur of colour in my field of vision makes me look under the table.

"Why?" I simply ask, looking at the fact that he's wearing blue jeans under a light grey blazer. This is very unlike him, and I have a feeling he's done this on purpose off the back of all my comments.

"You said I overuse the suits, I figured this could be a compromise." He bobs his eyebrows indicating how smug he feels and I just sigh.

"What's with always wearing a blazer? You know I have to ask now." I lean back in my chair and fold my book around the library card to keep its place. I've been back a few times since I last saw him and I'm enjoying the escapism.

This book is about Alexander the Great and if for nothing else, I'm enjoying the piece of history that comes with it. I've never paid attention to the time of his reign. It's always been Caesar or Cleopatra that has attracted me to the 'BC' era and while I have heard of him, he should be spoken of more.

Adryan pulls at the end of his blazer as if checking it out himself for the first time and turns to me with a grin. "I like to look smart."

"You looked smart on Sunday," I say automatically, and I hope he doesn't take it as a compliment.

"Yeah well, I want to look like I've got my shit together and this does it for me." He shrugs and I decide to let it drop.

The jeans are a nice change, and it complements the navy jumper and white shirt combination. I've never seen him look out of place since we met, aside from coming out of the shower and I wonder how he developed this sort of taste.

It's more natural looking compared to the average broker that walks the streets and it's something that must have developed over time. If I cared more, I'd research the Ambrose family, just so that I can see what his father looked like and whether it's him that he got it from.

Then again, I doubt there'd be much available. If I was the Lord of Ashes, my first port of call would be to remove all traces of my face from the internet, just on the off chance that someone found out my real name.

"To what do I owe this displeasure?" I ask with narrowed eyes.

He rolls his in response. "When will you admit that you really love my company?"

I wait, not even bothering to glare at him and I start to pick up my book once more to spur him on. I'm not here to feed his ego, in fact I'm not here to see him at all. I'm here to sit on my own and unwind a bit, I deserve it after the week I've had and is it too much to ask to be left alone?

"It's been five days and Michael is still alive, call me curious." He finally speaks, getting to the point now.

"I've been busy," I say while casually reaching into my pocket.

I want to see how long I can stretch the suspense out for. I was going to contact him later today anyway as I decided to go a different way in the end, a more amusing way that will cover my tracks better. I feel like I'm in a TV show where I get to watch my plotting unravel in real-time.

"I know that look." He says, sitting up slightly as if he's excited.

"I have a look?" My face is unreadable, but I'd love to hear about this supposed look.

"You're up to something, would you care to share?" He grins and I can't help but return the gesture.

It's a nice surprise to know that someone else finds my schemes exciting as I usually have to appreciate them on my own. Not wanting to spoil the surprise, I check the time on my phone and purse my lips while doing the mental maths.

"I suppose word will be out by now," I mutter more to myself and turn to the waitress walking nearby. "Can you put the news on please, something's happened" I try my best to sound worried and she scurries to go and get the remote.

I like the fact that it's the same waitress from last time and she's not so much as looking at Adryan. It's nice to see that my glare can have a lingering effect and he should be careful before I use it more often.

The television in the corner is flipped to the news and there are sub-titles turned on for us to see what the crowds of police cars and news reporters are standing around for. They're all surrounding what I now know to be David's office and a fat ugly man is being escorted out with a rather red-looking face.

"What did you do?" Adryan whispers with an open mouth and I let myself take the sight in, it helps boost my ego a bit and I'd like to remember this moment.

Instead of replying I take my hand out of my pocket and hand him the piece of paper that James gave me on Tuesday. Every name had been crossed off and the words Suspicion of Murder are now being displayed across the TV screen in bold letters, as if the public wouldn't know how serious that is without the font.

Adryan's eyes bulge when reading and I flip my hair over my shoulder as a way of saying that I take it as a compliment. This was just what I needed, and my mood is considerably improved now.

When thinking about my task, I figured that something as public as this would be enough to spook whoever this Sarah was, and I doubt the Lord of Ashes will let him live much longer after this. It also means that all 7 murders have an answer to them, and nobody is sniffing around in my or Adryan's direction.

"He's just going to deny it," Adryan says, not looking back over from the TV as he takes in the report. I expected this and I take a second before deciding to break the news.

"They have witnesses," I say sweetly and sip at my warm coffee in a casual movement.

I decided that the cinnamon wasn't that bad in the end and I'm giving it another go. I didn't expect him to show up and I'm hoping he doesn't clock my order. I'm never in the mood to explain myself and he's bound to have questions.

"You're insane." He pauses, before turning back to me. "It's absolutely genius."

"I wear a size five shoe, anything Chanel or Louboutin will work," I reply, tilting my head to the side.

I may or may not have rehearsed this response to his reaction and I'm always open to a new pair of shoes, especially one of my favourites as he still owes me a pair from the day we met.

He chuckles. "I had something else in mind, but we can do that too."

"What did you get me?" I narrow my eyes because there's nothing on him and there is a strong part of me that perks up when hearing this. I've not had a gift in years, and I didn't expect him to take me seriously.

"I was going to offer you the control of fixing up my apartment, yours is far better decorated and you do love to complain about it." The coffee he ordered upon arrival is placed next to him and I try to contain the venom in my voice as a result of the unexpected witness.

"You've been in my apartment?"

"It's only fair, you broke into mine." He takes a sip, unfazed in appearance but I can hear his heart beating in panic.

I pause. "I'm impressed."

"I aim to please." He releases a breath and I'm surprised I didn't just rip his head off, but the truth is that I am impressed.

It's a crappy gift though. "Decorating is boring," I complain.

"How about one splash of colour, come art shopping with me?" Adryan adds and I narrow my eyes.

"Why do you want me to come with you?" This doesn't sound like a gift.

There has to be some sort of angle here.

"I figured it would be fun." He notices my look and adds. "A few people may have noticed us together and it would help with suspicion if they thought we were dating."

"I'm not fake dating you." I scowl and drain my cup. "This isn't a romance novel, and I don't have time for this shit."

He sighs, "Okay, what about a friendship then?"

I inhale sharply, considering the options.

I'm going to see him around either way, I just need to be pleasant about it. I suppose it could also benefit my cover as well. I'd rather people not recall what I look like and associate it with suspicion. It ruins the allure, or at least I assume it would.

"Fine, fake friendship it is." I stand abruptly. "There's an art dealer around the corner, let's go."

He struggles to finish his half-filled cup and I'm already out of the door.

By the third art dealer, Adryan looks like he wants to kill himself and it's almost worth the effort of sacrificing my Saturday to be here.

"What about this one?" He points to another painting with lots of dark blue and purple, so I frown.

"I say this as a *friend*... you need therapy." I mock the word friend and he scowls.

"What's wrong with it?" He insists and I pull him away, further into the collection to where the hidden gems tend to be. I've been here a few times before, so I know my way around well.

"It's depressing," I call over my shoulder, not caring if the owners of the place hear me because it is.

"*You're* depressing." He whispers under his breath, and I turn to face him, making it clear that I heard that.

"Regretting the whole thing already?" I fake sympathy and he just rolls his eyes.

I look around the next section and find something that has lots of red, yellow and gold worked into it. It's abstract so it's not a painting of anything in particular but if he hangs it above his bed, it may do just enough to salvage the room, so I nod to indicate that I've finally chosen.

He pulls a face. "Why this one?"

"I thought the gift was control, not being questioned." I turn around to face him.

He looks at the painting again, squints and sighs dramatically.

"Touché."

He waves over to the assistant and indicates that we want to buy it. "Where's this going then?" He asks, pulling out his card and walking us over to the desk.

"Above the bed," I say, still looking around the room but with myself in mind this time.

"Above my bed?" He replies, almost in horror.

"Are you deaf?" I say sweetly and he scowls.

"Is the room really that bad?" He asks, now signing the receipt and giving the gallery his address.

"Let's just say, I'm surprised you've not exited via the balcony at this point." I raise my eyebrows and he just laughs.

"You're a dramatic little thing, do you know that?"

I ignore the name as the purchase is complete. With my job finally done, I have to admit that it was more fun than I expected, the whinging and moaning aside, he's fair company when he wants to be.

"Let me know when it arrives and I'll hang it."

It's not an excuse to see him again, I just don't trust him to do it properly and I want to make sure he puts it where I tell him to. The control aspect really appeals to me.

"I've had the fridge stocked." He comments, remembering my complaints of no iced coffee and I nod my head in thanks. I'm surprised he remembered, as I didn't.

"Right well, I've got stuff to do. Try not to get killed and I'll see you tomorrow." I turn to leave without waiting for a reply and walk out the door.

There's another meeting tomorrow and just like last time, we're walking there together from the coffee shop.

Apparently, friends do that sort of thing and I wonder if it's worth buying a wig just so I don't have to bother. Then again it wasn't that bad today, so I'll just keep it in mind for the future.

Chapter 12

I look in the mirror as I am due to walk out of the door and rather than focusing on what's missing for once, I laugh at what's there.

Just because I know it will get a reaction, I am wearing loose blue jeans, a simple white T-shirt and a dark grey blazer. I've seen the look on women a few times when out in the city and I've never tried it before now because I'm sick of seeing them. I have to admit, a blazer feels powerful.

My heels are the same colour as the jacket and my hair is tied back in a loose and messy chignon. It's a fun look and I could see myself using it again.

I spray on the perfume I bought this morning and still can't decide whether I like it or not. It's unisex and you can tell that from the musky undertones but there's still a grapefruit side to it that is very joyful and fresh. Not like me at all but that's as close as I could find as everything else was too sweet and pure.

My nails are also redone and my appointment with Sacha was fun as, while I didn't say much, I could tell she was visibly more relaxed which made me feel good about myself. I don't care if that makes me selfish.

The sun isn't out but the overcast is too bright, so I use that as an excuse to wear a large pair of black sunglasses which compliments my style nicely. It's been a while since I've felt so comfortable in what I have on, maybe it's because it's more modest than my usual attire and the purpose is to annoy, not attract my victim.

As I walk across the street to the coffee shop, Adryan has to do a double take to make sure it's me when looking over and that amuses me to no end.

He's in black jeans again which is a nice surprise and a white button-down shirt that is thrown on top. I think he could already predict the comments should he attempt to wear his usual clothing choice.

"What happened to no suits on Sundays?" He looks me up and down and I smirk.

"I make the rules, I don't follow them." I move to stand next to him and I can see he has two coffees in his hands.

"It doesn't even fit you." He complains and he's not wrong, but the idea was for it to be baggy.

"Give it here." He puts both coffees on top of the window ledge and rolls up the sleeves for me so that they fit better.

I didn't think to do that because it looked good either way, but it helps and I thank him quietly. I don't know how I feel about the fact he just touched me, and I have no intention of killing him in the immediate future to mitigate that.

So I go to take the coffee from the ledge with my name on it and he softly slaps my hand away which makes me inhale sharply and raise my eyebrows at him.

"What?" I hiss.

"It's not for you, it's for Camilla." He says sweetly and I roll my eyes taking it anyway. "She's due here any minute, usually wearing a dress and scary heels." He continues and I start walking.

"You do love to hear yourself talk, don't you?" I say, holding back a smile because it was amusing, I'll give him that.

"You're welcome." He says slowly, tilting his head in my direction and I nod in thanks as saying it out loud would be like conceding and I don't do that.

"What did you do today then?" I ask, taking a sip and admiring the sugary taste of the caramel against the bitter espresso. I wasn't going to get one this time but I'm glad I have it for the walk again, it's way too good to resist.

"Are you... are you instigating small talk?" He puts his hand on his chest as if he's in shock, a gesture I've noticed a few times now and I merely look away from him, walking faster.

"I was waiting for the picture mostly and signed for it not long ago, I figured we could hang it after this." He catches up to me and smiles.

It's a nice smile, I can't deny that, but it's hard to think that someone with a similar smile might run the whole city.

"How'd you know I don't have plans?" I ask as if he shouldn't have assumed and he just laughs.

"Please... you have the same social life as me. Would you rather go out and find someone to kill or come and save me from a depressing bedroom?" He laughs.

I don't have plans; I was going to note down any new targets and relax for the night. Have a bath and read a book maybe as I don't need to hunt as much anymore and it's losing its appeal to be honest.

"What drinks do you have?" I don't say yes but he takes it as one anyway.

"I can order whatever you want." He promises and I swerve to face him.

"Drinks and a coffee." I muse. "You're wanting this friendship thing to be real, aren't you?" I mock him.

"You roast me for having no friends and now you roast me for attempting it, can I ever win?" He asks dramatically and I laugh as he has me there.

The bakery comes into view, and I drain the cup and throw it into the nearby bin. I can see the fake baker from here and can't help but wonder how many packs he must go through to keep up with this smoking routine. Does he actually know how to bake? I'm tempted to ask him but before I can, Adryan ushers me inside.

I make my way down the stairs with my heels clicking against each step and if it was just me, I'd go back up and down again just for the acoustics. It's one of the reasons I always wear them.

The lights are on already and I wonder if they made sure to get here early so that they can discuss things without me. I wouldn't blame them if they did, it would be the smarter thing to do. The stupid thing is Adryan insisting on walking me here and missing out. Nobody has followed us and surely he can walk somewhere on his own?

They all turn to face me when I walk through the door, and I lift the sunglasses onto the top of my head feeling like I'm in *The Devil Wears Prada* or something and I could get used to this. Adryan nods his greeting to everyone and once again we're stood in an awkward little circle.

"Do we have rules against chairs or is that too informal?" I can't help but say, eyeing the chairs to the right of us that look extremely nice right now.

"I promise I won't make anyone share the couch with me," I say with a grin and only Adryan thinks it's funny which doesn't surprise me.

We make our way to the chairs and it's instantly more comfortable but despite this, there's still a look of worry on Paul, David and James's faces that I don't miss. Adryan notices it too but he'd have to be blind not to.

"Out with it then." He almost snaps and the serious persona is back again. I like it.

"There's an opening tonight," Paul speaks as if he's still considering it while doing so.

"That's great," Adryan says, looking around for confirmation from the others.

"It's going to need to be one of us though," David adds, and I don't know why they're stressing about this.

The tension in the air is practically electric, and I have to narrow my eyes, wondering what I'm missing here. I mean, isn't this the exact reason why they brought me in?

So I clear my throat just to remind them of my presence before offering the services that I thought I already had, "Just send me then?"

"They'll clock you because you're not one of them," James answers as if it's something he wishes he could consider, and I don't know if that's an insult or a compliment. He doesn't know how indestructible I am, does he?

"And it's dangerous, I guess? What's it an opening for?" I ask around because no one seems to be talking.

"To see my brother," Adryan replies grimly.

"I thought I was going to kill him?" I half complain because I was starting to set my hopes on killing it all at the root.

Adryan only laughs. "Love the enthusiasm Cam, but there's no chance they'll let you in if James is saying no." he pauses. "I'll go, I don't mind."

But David hesitates, "I knew you'd want to, but someone needs to be higher up to know what happens if one of us is caught."

I can tell he means to know if one of them breaks under torture if they fail and that would mean they'd all have a target on their back and now I get why they're so stressed.

"Who is it then?" Adryan asks, clearly pissed off that he isn't the one to risk himself and I can't help but respect it.

"Me." Paul says, nodding to himself as if he's confirmed it.

No one contradicts him and silence falls. The tension is thick in the air, and I do the mental maths to try and picture it.

"Have you ever killed before?" I ask, already knowing the answer.

"I'll be able to." He says firmly as if I'm questioning his commitment, but I'm not.

"I don't doubt you'd try, but it's not as easy for someone like you." He frowns so I add. "A human, I mean."

"No room for weapons." James puts in numbly and I wince as I don't see this going well at all.

"How are you planning to do it then?" I ask anyone who will answer.

"Poison." Adryan replies, stirring from his thoughts. "He has a thin piece of plastic in the palm of his hand, you shake hands and the poison is transferred."

Wow, it's been so long with my powers that I'd almost forgotten how hard humans would have to work to get away with such things and my head is running a thousand miles per hour to try and think of each scenario that they might find.

"And what if he closes his palm?" I can't help but question when the risk hits me.

"The antidote is tied to a tooth; you bite and swallow before going in and it'll last about an hour." He looks to Paul to ensure he's okay with this and he only nods in reply. They've clearly thought of this before.

"Let's get you set up then," David says grimly, and they all walk over to the table.

"Do you have a list for Cam? I'll set off home and text the burner if anything comes up before, he's always changing things at the last minute," Adryan says. I don't like that I've got to leave just because he is. It just got interesting.

"Sure," James says mechanically, pulling out another list and I place it into my pocket.

In any other circumstance, I'd probably kick up a fuss at having to leave just because he is, but I get it, I came here as his cover and if he leaves without me, it's not going to work.

So instead, I stand up and wish Paul luck. Something that surprises both of us before making my way towards the stairs.

The sun is starting to set now and it's reflecting off the windows of the buildings. It's rather beautiful but we don't say anything, and I don't know why it bothers me.

Probably because I'm used to it now and I know that if he's quiet there's something bothering him. I shouldn't care but it's on my mind while Adryan is lost in thought, and I wonder if he knows how likely it is that his friend will die tonight? I hope for his sake that I'm wrong, but I know these sorts of things all too well.

I manage to hold it in until we're a block away from my apartment until I finally snap, unable not to speak which is odd for me.

"He'll be fine, you'll all be fine," I say automatically, wondering if I really mean it and why that was my go-to statement.

I mean, the poison trick is pretty clever but somehow, I doubt anyone but me could kill a man like that. If they've thought of it, he's probably got five scientists pumping the antidote into his every meal as he strikes me as the sort to not take any risks. I mean look at the fact that nobody knows his name or face, save for Adryan.

Maybe I should ask but I've not really felt the need to know to be honest, Lord of Ashes, Steve, who gives a fuck what he's called as long as he ends up dead? It's not like I could use it to ask around for him anyway.

"At least whatever they do to me isn't half as bad as what you will... eventually." Adryan winks, recovering himself fully now.

And I don't know why, but I feel the need to tell him. To remove that thought from his mind as a possibility and I'll blame it on the shard of the real Camilla that is still inside of me, as it can't be *this* me, can it?

"I can't hurt you," I confess, trying to keep my tone light as if this is a casual conversation while it's anything but.

"Wait, what?" He turns around to face me, eyes wide.

"I can't hurt any pure soul. That's my catch." I shrug and I swear it's like I've blown his mind.

"Why tell me?" He scrunches his eyebrows and it's a great question to be honest, why tell him?

"I figured it's only fair to even the playing field,"

Chapter 13

For some reason, I couldn't sleep last night, as if I cared about the outcome and I don't like the feeling.

The sheets felt heavier than usual, and the air felt thicker. It was suffocating and while I don't even need to breathe, I struggled with it. I keep telling myself that I don't give a crap about what happens but that's a lie.

I know that if Paul falls tonight, then it will be another innocent gone and just another dark mark on the soul of that bastard hiding behind an army of guards.

It infuriates me and when I finally crawled out of bed at 5:00am, I ran a rather large bath to stew away my feelings as this usually helps me. I lit candles, threw in a bath bomb and put on some music, the whole shebang but it hasn't done much for me to be honest.

Not long after getting in, the burner phone that Adryan gave to me the other day vibrates against the porcelain of the tub and I can see a text notification on the old Nokia. It's been days yet the thing is still on full charge, and I need to second-guess this whole smartphone idea.

Holding my breath, I unlock the screen and read the words sent to me by Adryan.

Paul is dead. Meet at 12 in the Coffee shop.

Is all he types, and I answer swiftly.

Okay.

I know he'll not be in the place for banter right now, none of them will be. So, I refill the hot water of my tub and stare at the ceiling. The bubbles have long since gone now and the candles smell more burnt than vanilla.

I focus on the emotion running through me, the energy it's building and try to put a name to the feeling. It's hot, dark and all-consuming, I hate it but unfortunately, it's familiar.

Rage, that's what it is, and I have no outlet for it. I need an outlet for it.

After this round of warm water goes cold, I emerge from the bath and splash everything around me while I yank my robe from the hanger with so much force that I put out the candles in the process, I don't even bother to drain the tub before walking into my wardrobe and I subconsciously pull on a black dress.

I had already texted the list of names that James handed over to me to my tech connection, Derek and I have since received the addresses and last known locations within the hour, feeling grateful that he's able to use street cameras and facial recognition. With him, I've found that once he's got a positive ID in the system, it's only a matter of time before he's sharing results, and this time he's really impressed me.

Blood blends in quite well with black and I smile at that fact when I leave my last victim's place of work.

It's 11:30am, and I've just finished hanging him from the building stairwell. He's lucky that at this point my mood has dulled somewhat and his end was quicker compared with the others.

I don't care if I get caught now, I welcome it. I welcome the Lord of Ashes to invite me to play.

I don't know why I didn't try this sooner, surely the way to get his attention is to make myself known and to wait for him to come to me? They can pull my nails out all day long if it takes me to him and I won't even invoice him for the trouble.

The screams from all six of them echo through my mind but I embrace them, I scream back, telling them to do it louder because that's all I want to hear before I take out their leader.

I can't do shit to stop the evil in the world, but I can put a dent in it, in my city, and that's what I'm going to do. If I find my freedom then it's a bonus, but I've got my sights set on the prize now and there's not a lot that's going to defer me away from my target.

When I arrive at the coffee shop, I order a coffee and sit by the windows so I can see Adryan when he comes. I'm glad I'm not human at this moment, purely because caffeine is the last thing I need and just imagining myself right now on caffeine is enough to bring a smile to my face though it falls sharply when Adryan walks past and notices it.

He probably thinks I don't care, and I can't blame him.

Instead of greeting me as he has before, he goes straight to the counter and orders a drink, even from here I can hear that his voice is deflated, and I swallow hard.

As he sits down opposite me, in his black suit, I don't say anything, I'll let him be the first to talk if he needs to, and I realise that this is the most cautious I've been in the last four years of someone else's feelings.

"He didn't talk." Adryan's voice is rough, and I grind my teeth to keep my face neutral, needing that pressure to hold it together.

My respect for the man known very briefly has risen and while I can't feel pain, I imagine it'll be hard to hold out against it. Do we know if they tortured him? Fuck, of course they did.

"He was brave," I speak tentatively, trying to find the right words and I am so out of practice for things like this that I almost feel bad.

Adryan winces at my words, "Don't pretend you care."

His voice has an element of disgust in it, and I bite my tongue to keep from retorting. I might be a monster, but I know better than to kick an animal when it's down where I can help it. Especially an innocent one.

"Does he have any family?" I ask, not as softly as before but still more gently than my usual tone.

Adryan laughs coldly. "You killed them, his brother was the last."

I take that hit but I know I can't promise myself to stomach another. He might be suffering but nobody speaks to me that way and this isn't a time to start making exceptions. After all, I didn't kill Paul, did I?

Though I don't know why, but it stings more than I thought it would, to have him address me this way.

"I'm sorry." He sighs, looking up at me with his head in his hands and I exhale knowing I won't have to hurt him.

"It's just, he's a friend... Was a friend." He corrects himself and I nod.

But it's probably better for me to stay quiet and to let him speak as I don't want to provoke another outburst.

"I said I had no friends, but we were friends. David and James are too." He sighs and takes a deep drink out of what I assume to be tea. I've never seen him drink tea before and I wonder if he's avoiding caffeine for the reasons I would have.

"That's why we're here anyway, I wanted to tell you that he didn't talk." His eyes are glued to a random spot on the table as if that's what's holding him in place.

His face is crumpled and if I had a heart it would break at the sight. I can't see the annoying arsehole that's always laughing anywhere behind those eyes, and I almost miss him.

Feeling anything like this isn't something I'd wish on my worst enemy, I know that because I've felt it before.

"I lost someone too once." My voice is quiet, and I think it's the weakest I've sounded in years without doing it on purpose.

I don't know why I said that, or why I opened my mouth at all when it's the last thing I ever want to talk about. It's in my mind, it's always in my mind but usually, I can keep it at bay long enough to distract myself from it.

"What?" He lifts his head up to ask.

My chest aches to let it out, to just speak about it for once, so I do as I feel like I'll never be able to stop the pain until then. Emotional pain is far worse than physical, and I know which one I'd rather the curse had removed.

"Four years ago, I had a lover. We'd bought an apartment, planned a life and it was the happiest I'd ever been." I breathe, reliving the memory that I try to bury down each day.

"The week before our first anniversary I was meant to meet him in the apartment, we'd closed that morning and I brought us some champagne because that's all he ever drank." I close my eyes and I can almost see the bottle before I dropped it.

"Go on..." Adryan says to indicate that he wants to know more, and I can see that it's helping somehow, so I do.

"When I got there, I found him dead, someone had killed him and left him there for me to find." I sigh. "Other than that, all I can remember is the pain, the pure emotion running through my veins as I begged anyone, anything to bring him back... And something answered."

Adryan swallows before grabbing my hand and I can't remember the last time someone touched me like that though I'm partly glad of it when thinking back to that day.

"I remember the deep voice echoing around the room, asking me if I really meant it. Would I give anything to bring him back?" I laugh coldly at myself.

I was an idiot. I didn't phrase it right and just said that I'd give them anything. I didn't say to bring him back that time which must have been my mistake and the next thing I knew, I was waking up a mile away. Alone and without him.

"I said yes, and it took my soul, not bringing him back as payment."

He breathes in sharply and I grimace.

"By the time I got back to the apartment, he was gone, and I was so empty." My voice catches and I wonder if I might actually cry, I haven't done that since being changed.

"He must have taken pity on me, whoever he was because he offered me a deal. He'd let me have my life back if I killed my lover's murderer and with the limited options I had left, I had no choice but to accept and he turned me into this, to help." I turn to him. "The only catch is that I can't harm those pure of soul and the only thing that can kill me is the person I seek to kill myself."

"I had no idea." Adryan croaks and I shrug.

"I've never told anyone."

"Did you... Do you have any ideas? Leads?" He sits up a bit and it's nice to see that it's distracted him even if it feels like it's breaking me.

"Nothing. I was new to the city when I met him, and I knew no one. He was all I had." I run my free hand through my loose hair. "I went to the police station which is where I learned to compel for the first time, and nobody had been brought in."

"So, you just kill any of them." He says, not a question but as if he's understanding almost.

"I don't have a choice." I exhale sharply before laughing to myself. "The worst part is that I enjoy it now, hurting those that have hurt others. If I can save one person from feeling like I did, then maybe it will be worth it."

We both sit staring for a few minutes, processing my reveal with him drinking his tea and me looking at the crowd outside the window as if one of them might hold the answers.

"Thank you for telling me." He breaks the silence, somehow knowing that that's probably the best thing to respond with, rather than more questions.

"I do care," I answer his previous accusation instead. "That's why I did this," I say as I hand him the piece of paper with six names crossed out in blood.

Each line is made from the specific person it names.

Chapter 14

Adryan and I have had lunch every day this week and for the most part I was the one who instigated it.

After the shock of losing a friend, naturally he's healing slowly, and I think seeing what he's going through helps me do the same. I've had four years to get over my trauma, but I've buried it and only now am I realising that it's still there.

We didn't talk much at first, there wasn't a whole lot to say and there wasn't a whole lot that we *wanted* to say. It seemed unfair to the ones we were grieving for to think about something else, but by Friday most of the silence was comfortable.

After seeing a change in him over the past few days, I think it's fair to say that he's finding his way back to his normal self and it's good to see.

Today's Saturday so I was more than happy, if not expecting to let him do his own thing but he texted me earlier with a location for somewhere new and before I could even look it up, we'd agreed to meet at 3pm.

I can't help but admit to looking forward to these little outings because in the meantime I'm left to my own thoughts, or worse still, feeling the urge to hunt. After talking about it for the first time in years, I've started remembering so much more and I've found that one minute I could be in the salon and the next I'll have a flashback to the night we met.

Sitting and talking with Adryan gives me something to focus on. I'm getting to know a new person, not remembering my old lover and it helps that they are so different.

For one, Nolan was quiet. He was reserved and more subtle with his humour. I remember that I used to be the one to order the meals and ask for directions and he loved it. He grounded me and I brought him out of his shell.

Every day he wore these thick-rimmed glasses that matched his dark hair, and he basically drank nothing but champagne in the evening. He would try to introduce me to the weirdest foods and it's sad in a way because it wasn't until it was too late that I finally understood what he was going on about all that time.

It didn't make sense to me, and it still doesn't, why someone would want to hurt him. How someone could do that to the man I loved and while we'd known each other for such a short time, he was all I had, and I was the same for him.

The raw pain of it has gone now. The life before me is more like a dream than anything else but the memories keep resurfacing and it's all I can do not to go out into the streets and kill every dark soul I can get my hands on.

Killing and Adryan; that's what keeps it at bay, and I think he can tell that from how open he's been to meeting with me during the day.

If I didn't know any better, I'd suspect that he pitied me.

I avoided the last meeting with James and David because I couldn't promise how I'd react in a confined space with them. I know James is a good man; tainted or not, but I see myself as too unpredictable to trust myself. So instead, he's just been giving me a steady stream of names over text.

He's made sure to give them one at a time now or else it'll be more suspicious, so I've added it to my usual hunting. I find that I simply can't sit still any more or stay in at night. The plan I made still stands, kill all I can to get the Lord of Ashes' attention.

That's all I had until Adryan said something the other day, half to himself and half as a comment and I was awoken to a new idea that changed nothing but also everything.

"What if the Lord of Ashes could be the cure through a technicality?"

"What the hell are you on about?" I replied instantly as it was so strange to have another person know about the curse, never mind having their own theories on it.

"He orders most of the murders in the city, even if he didn't make the final blow there's a good chance he's still the real murderer, right?" He looked over at me and I felt my jaw drop in shock, not just because it was a great idea, but because I'd never thought of it before.

Adryan didn't realise that that was probably the last thing he should have said and if anything, it doubled the craze running through me. That day I'd gone from a few people a night to double digits, all the dirtiest souls I can find and all working for the Lord of Ashes.

They didn't know this, but I don't need their lists anymore as I can compel my victims for names and by Friday morning it was on the news. Adryan didn't say anything, but I can tell it was on his mind and I was shocked that he didn't bring it up to be honest.

I walk up to the restaurant and realise that this is new for us. Usually, it's just a cafe or something that he can walk to in between lunch hours, and I think I might have been here before.

Today I've worn my usual black dress and I must have at least ten versions of it by now because of how well it helps me blend in. The shoes I have on are dark silver and my hair is plaited down my back, out of my face in a way that makes me feel younger than usual.

As I step into the entrance, I find that the maître d' is expecting me, and I'm escorted to a table in the far corner where Adryan is already sitting on his phone. Just like me, his suits are always dark now and it actually makes me sad to see because I've noticed that it tends to be a reflection of his mood, rather than a fashion choice these days.

I don't have the heart to tease him on it for once, so instead, I try something else. "I'll wear jeans tomorrow if you do?" I ask as I sit down.

I don't particularly want to wear them, but this may coax him back into some colour as I know he'll be surrounded in gloom back at his apartment and anything will make a difference in that place.

"What are we doing tomorrow?" He asks, putting his phone away and looking over towards me.

He must have been here early because the breadbasket is empty and whatever is in his glass is long gone by now. I'm sure we agreed on 3pm but I'd rather not ask in case I was wrong and I'm the reason he's been sitting here all alone.

"A garden centre... you need plants." I say as I reach for the glass of champagne that's already in front of my placemat, but I then hesitate when I realise what I'm doing.

Since all of the memories have come back, I haven't been able to touch the stuff and all I can see is Nolan in front of me telling me the brand and encouraging me to try it. But whenever I go to taste it, I just keep thinking of the smashed bottle on our apartment floor.

I sigh subtly, willing the image to fade from my mind, "Thanks for ordering, but do you mind if I have something else?"

I don't know why my voice has come out so quiet but rather than correct it, I hold my breath, hoping he doesn't say anything as I'd rather not have to explain my thought process out loud.

"Sure." He waves to the server and asks for them to take it away. "What do you want?"

I pause because I have no clue to be honest. I've not had any other 'going out' drink since turning and it's all I am used to by now.

"I don't know." I finally say.

He laughs and turns to the server. "We'll take a Bellini please."

"But that's the same thing." I start to complain, and he rolls his eyes at me while the man is already walking away.

"You can't cut it out completely just because of a memory, this way it's different." He pushes and I leave it be for once, partly because I'll miss the bubbles and mostly because this is the most sass he's ventured all week.

I miss that sharp tongue of his as when I'm the only one being sarcastic, I feel like an arsehole and while I'm used to it, it gets tiring after a while.

"Okay," I say, raising one eyebrow and nodding to the server for the drink now placed on my side of the table.

"I'll go to the garden centre if you hang the picture for me after this." He takes a sip.

I notice that he ordered one for himself too and I watch as he drinks it which makes me inhale sharply though I couldn't tell you why.

"Can you not hang it yourself?" I ask and he purses his lips as if that reply wasn't what he wanted.

After a pause he looks at me, tilting his head, "Do you trust me to listen to your orders?"

He knows how to speak to my inner control freak, and it would annoy the hell out of me if it isn't placed where I wanted it. It's just that I planned to go out tonight and now I'll have to make up for the numbers somehow.

"Fine but if there's no iced coffee, I'm throwing it from the balcony," I say sweetly, and he raises his glass in acknowledgement of the threat.

Adryan now picks up the menu that I hadn't thought to glance at yet and asks me, "Can I order?"

I wasn't expecting to order as I haven't been eating with him this week and I wasn't expecting the question because really, nobody has offered to do that before.

"I'm not really in the mood," I say casually and slide the menu now in my hands into the middle of the table. At the moment the ritual feels too human for me, and I've been trying to isolate myself from that where possible.

"Humour me?" His eyes lock with mine and for some reason, I nod.

I blame it on not having the energy to argue and I have now remembered that this place is nice. One meal isn't going to change the fact that I'm not human I suppose, and he knows what I am at the end of the day.

The big thing for me is that I no longer lose sight of who I am, what my mission is and why I am here. I've been pushing the full picture out for too long now and no wonder I'm handling it badly.

He orders us steak and I smile when remembering that it's the meal I mentioned to him once as one of the reasons I still eat food. I have it rare and the fries that come with it are topped with truffle oil and parmesan which are a lovely addition to the rich flavour.

We sit in silence while we eat and I can't help but look around the room, sizing up if anyone in here is worth trying to go after when I'm done. There are a few and I lick my lips in indecision, running the pros and cons of each through my mind.

"You're coming to mine, remember?" Adryan doesn't look up from his food, but he seems to have read my mind anyway.

"Can I not make a pit stop?" I ask innocently while finishing the last piece of meat and swirling the cocktail around in its pretty little glass.

He finally looks back up at me with narrowed eyes. "If I'm buying plants and wearing jeans, you're hanging a picture and behaving for one night."

I clench my teeth at the behaving comment as he doesn't need to know that I've already knocked off seven people today and I'm sorely tempted to burst his bubble. I don't sleep so well lately and I'm out of the apartment before 6:00am most days, trying to get a head start and trying to feel useful.

"Fine," I say firmly, feeling the irritation fade as I finish my drink and hand my card over to the server to pay for the meal.

"I'm a big boy you know, I can pay for myself." He frowns and I laugh.

"If you're so well paid, you'd not be having sandwiches each day and going to delis for dinner," I answer and the corners of his mouth twitch.

"Fine, but I'll be getting us a takeaway later." He raises his brows as if to challenge me and I bite.

I don't understand why he's always trying to force food down my throat and I half wonder if there's a reason behind it or not.

"Are you trying to get me fat?" The sarcasm is rich in my voice, and he laughs.

"I was going to ask; can you even control your weight now that you're... you know?" He swallows, wondering if I'll bite his head off for another intrusive question but he knows the worst now and there's no point in playing it coy.

"I don't think so. I can't starve to death, and I haven't eaten enough to know if I'd gain weight." He releases a breath at my response, and I grin. "Worried about that pure soul of yours?"

"I'm sure you'd find a way around it if you wanted to." He replies and I chuckle.

I'm not so sure about that but I have thought about it a couple of times when he's been particularly outspoken as he brings out my more creative side in those moments.

CURSE ME

"I have considered burning down a few buildings, it wouldn't be my fault if the doors were locked." I pretend as if it's a serious consideration and he just shakes his head.

"There she is." He comments, almost to himself and my eyebrows raise in question automatically, challenging him to expand on that weird little statement.

"You've not been yourself this week. Nice almost... it's unnerving." He comments, not looking at me but thanking the server for my card and handing it back across the table. "Come on, the longer we wait the sooner I might jump from the rooftops."

Chapter 15

The sun is out today, and the garden centre is alive with colour.

As agreed, Adryan and I are wearing jeans but of course he has a button down on as well and I have my black spikey heels with me too.

We look out of place, as everyone is wearing earthy colours while here we are, still looking like we could go out on the prowl. It makes me laugh when I first see us enter through the glass doors and I don't bother explaining why.

After hanging the painting last night, I took photos around the apartment to flag places where a plant might help and we have at least ten that we need to buy, and all of them large enough to grab the eye.

CURSE ME

As we walk around the various aisles of foliage, Adryan can't help but repeat over and over how hot it is and when I spot a hose running a few yards away, it takes all my control not to spray him with it just to keep him quiet.

In the trolley I have added two Philodendron Fuzzy Petiole which are basically giant leaf trees and three Yucca pots because I like the shape and have a few at home. These are big enough for me to now look at the smaller plants, ones we can hang from the ceiling, and I order him to go and look for pots while I browse.

The green from these will make a difference and while the red in the bedroom helps, I still hate to be in that apartment. Everything is so dark, and I want to start clawing at the walls from the moment I enter to the point where all the iced coffee in the world won't be enough to lure me there if I don't add a bit of life to the place.

By the time we finish, Adryan is grumbling at the price tag and I'm pushing the trolley to the hire car. This place is towards the edge of the city and for whatever reason neither of us has our own vehicle though there's no need really when I can run anywhere just as fast, and Adryan could hail a taxi.

I insist on driving because it's been way too long since I've been behind the wheel and it reminds me of my hometown, back to when I had my first jeep and drove everywhere. When moving to the city I had sold it and it took a few seconds this morning to remember how to get the clutch right, especially in heels.

The fear on Adryan's face when I hit the accelerator is hilarious and I don't feel kind enough to remind him that my reflexes are probably better than anyone else's so it doesn't matter if I break the speed limit.

When we pull up to his apartment complex it takes two trips to get all of the purchases into the elevator and I can't even see him over the leaves as we pile into the lift to ride all the way to the top.

He chatters the whole time as we start to migrate the pots in through his door and as we are close to done, I go to the fridge to get myself a drink while he finishes moving things in. Despite me being the strongest of the two, I leave him to take on the brunt of the labour because he insists and I'm not in the mood to challenge that. It's not like I want to lug his things about and ruin my shoes anyway.

"Don't rip the leaf." I scold when he grabs one the wrong way and I lift the pot from his hands as if it was no more than a teacup.

I don't even have to think of using my strength anymore and it's not until he says "Show off." that I realise that this one must have been heavy.

After fifteen minutes of adjusting the pots and spritzing water, the apartment doesn't look so gloomy anymore and it actually looks quite nice to the point where I feel jealous of it again. I could see myself taking over the place if I was tempted enough.

"It looks ridiculous." Adryan comments from the couch and I shoot him a dirty look.

"It's ridiculous how well I've done with the material I had to work with." I reply sharply, and he just rolls his eyes.

I can tell that he likes it, or at least I think he does as he seems more relaxed now and he's even got his feet up, shoes and all which I haven't seen him do before.

"I'm ordering food, what do you want?" He pulls out his phone and starts scrolling through a food app.

"I'm good," I reply, looking back to my work while remaining seated on the floor by a terracotta pot.

This one is my favourite. The container's colour is bright but relaxed and I have several of these plants in my apartment.

"What. Do. You. Want?" He says each word slowly and I scowl.

"Watch the attitude Ambrose," I call over to him.

He laughs. "What? Are you going to set the building on fire after all this effort?"

I clock how he remembers my comment from earlier and I don't even know if I would be able to set the building alight with innocents in it. I can't say that I've tried it before, nor have I really been tempted to be honest. I have a temper but when it comes down to it, I like that there's a limitation that leaves the good ones off-limits.

So I just sigh. "I don't like you."

This makes him laugh even harder. "That's the best you've got?"

"It's the best you deserve." I scowl and walk over to the couch, plonking myself down into the soft cushions as I could fall asleep right there.

I stayed out late last night after leaving here at 10:00pm. We'd had Chinese food and bonded a bit which was weird for me. I ended up not coming home until like 6:00 am to make up for lost time as I figured I'd be missing a lot while out today too.

It's annoying how I still have to sleep after being cursed. I don't need food, water or even to breathe I don't think, but my body automatically shuts itself down when it's too tired and it can be a real pain in the arse.

"Would you like a blanket over there?" Adryan teases and I give him the middle finger.

"I'd like quiet, but I doubt I'll be that lucky." I bite out but the yawn that comes from my mouth reduces the sting.

"I'm ordering sandwiches and I'm getting you one." He replies, ignoring my comment and I groan dramatically.

Him and food, honestly. You'd think he grew up starving or something.

"Can you not make a sandwich yourself? Or is that only something poor people do?"

"Right." He stands up and I open my eyes to watch him. "Just for that, I'm going to make something."

I laugh in the direction of his face and curl my legs up to my chest. I love this sofa and it's exactly what I need just now.

The loud pounding of a heartbeat wakes me up with a jolt and I see Adryan standing over me with creased brows.

"What the hell are you playing at?" I snap and sit myself up higher.

From the noise coming from him I look around the room, fully expecting an invasion or at the very least a large wasp or something but there's no apparent threat which annoys me more. I was right in the middle of a dream, and it can be trippy to be brought back to consciousness like that.

"You don't breathe in your sleep." Adryan replies and his heart is only calming down slightly now that I'm awake.

"Really?"

"Believe me, I'd not want to wake you up otherwise." He seems serious and I smile.

Nobody has told me that before but then again, I've never slept in someone's presence since being cursed and I'm surprised that I let that happen, exhausted or not.

"How long was I out?" I yawn again and it can't have been long.

"Only an hour, food will be ready soon." He says as he's already walking back to the kitchen. "How come you're so tired?" He asks in a tone that tells me he knows fine well why I am.

"Being around you bores me too much and this is my natural response." I bite out, as I stretch my legs and rise to my feet.

"Good one." He replies sarcastically and I give him the middle finger for like the fourth time today.

Usually, I'm a lot better with comebacks but I can't be bothered, and he knows I can be quick when I want to be. Plus, sometimes the middle finger is all that needs said and I'm conserving energy here.

"I'm sure I said I'm not hungry," I call over as I walk into the kitchen and can smell meat cooking.

"I'm pretty sure I don't care." He doesn't miss a beat in throwing back and I swear sometimes it's like talking to myself with him.

"What are you making?" I ask, ignoring the comment.

"Roast Dinner." He looks quite proud of himself, and I can't remember the last time I tried it.

"And you just happen to have had all the ingredients lying around?" I question, dipping my finger into the boiling pot of sauce to taste it. It's good.

I can't remember the last time I cooked something. No wait, I actually can... it was never.

"That's so weird." He comments on my finger dipping before shaking his head and actually answering. "I nipped downstairs while you were out. You can get them delivered."

I dip my finger in again and ignore his motion to swat my hand away. "I suppose I could try some."

Now that I've tasted it, it's triggered something and woken up my hunger with a jolt.

"Go set the table." He hands me a cloth and some cutlery, and a snarl rises from my throat automatically.

"Please?" He adds and I smile coldly before turning around as I don't care if we've bonded slightly, if he orders me around, he's going to end up with this cloth wrapped around his neck.

From here I can see the condensation feeding into the leaves of the plant hanging from the cupboards and I have to say that I've done a good job. This place doesn't depress me nearly as much as it did. and the next step would be to introduce a rug like mine as this place is gagging for more detail.

"No." Adryan says as he carries two hot plates to the table.

"Either you're hearing things or reading minds, but I didn't say anything," I reply while grabbing my knife and fork to dig into the smell causing saliva to pool in my mouth.

"I know that look, you're not changing anything else." He laughs while doing the same.

The meat is perfectly cooked as I slice into it, and it just melts apart like butter making me sigh at the sight. It takes skill to get it prepared that well and I wonder how he managed it.

"I'm sure I was promised control?" I recall, answering his statement and pretending to care as he can't exactly stop me from bringing more things in here if I wanted to.

"Yeah well, I'm calling take backs. This place is basically a jungle now."

The roast potatoes are crisp, and the carrots have been cooked perfectly with honey drizzled over it. The gravy has red wine infused into it and when noticing, I stand up to go raking around the cupboards.

He has one dedicated completely to booze and behind all the Whiskey, Bourbon and Scotch I find a bottle of red and snap off the cork before pouring two very large glasses that use up the whole thing.

I walk back to the table and place it down roughly on a coaster as I'm eager to eat some more of this. He nods as he sees the liquor and doesn't even comment at my rummaging around his things. I think he's used to it now and if I wasn't too busy, I'd comment on how that removes most of the fun.

The wine is bitter and the veg is sweet which is a great combination, but by the time we're done, my eyelids are drooping, and it seems as though the nap has done nothing but highlight my need to lie down properly.

"The guest bedroom is free if you want it." Adryan says out of the blue, after watching me try and fail to swallow down a yawn, while pointing to the room across the hall from him. It didn't look very well used and was more of an office than anything else, so I only bothered with a cactus in there when planning my plant invasion earlier.

The idea of standing up right now feels like more effort than it's worth and it's fair to say that this is pushing the limit on what this new body can last on.

"Do you need a carry?" He croons over at me after I fail to reply, and I snarl in his direction.

"Fuck off and paint something else grey...For all I know you've tried to poison me." I grumble as I stand to start walking down the hall as my way of accepting his offer.

Chances are I'll regret it in the morning, but I doubt I'd make it home, never mind stay there and give my body what it needs.

"The thought definitely crossed my mind but unfortunately, you'd survive." He jokes and I flip him off one last time before slamming the door behind me.

ELLE CHIPP

Chapter 16

I leave his place at 5am and as suspected, I kick myself for staying the night, though I can't deny that I needed it.

There's not a chance in hell that I'd have stayed in if I was home alone, and my body was catching up with me quickly. The past few days have been exhausting, physically and mentally and I'm sort of glad that I've had that chance to take a break.

It was nice as well to have some home cooked food and while I won't be making a big deal of it or anything, I appreciate the fact that he took the time to make us something. Even if I did tell him not to bother.

When leaving I become aware of the fact that I'm growing fond of Adryan, especially after this week. He's good company and I find myself enjoying it, sometimes even more than when I'm alone which is new. What he said wasn't wrong the other day, I have been nicer and it's almost as if I can't help it.

    I don't know if it's the fact that he's the only constant person I speak to or the fact that we're both going through something similar but he's a friend now and I can't deny that. From the start, he wouldn't tolerate any of my bullshit and it kind of makes me feel good, the fact that someone pure doesn't absolutely hate me after all I've done, as I know I would.

    From his place, I go directly to mine to get ready as these jeans are too light and I have started to wear a wig this week as part of my hunting routine.

    I'm out most nights now and I tend to look the same with all of my black dresses. The idea of someone recognising me when at lunch with Adryan made me a bit nervous to be honest as his friend just died and the last thing he needs is to be caught up in my shit as well.

    Plus, it'll let me try out the look to see if I like it or not and I could make it permanent if I really want to as I've not tried dying my black hair since I turned. I don't know why but the thought never crossed my mind to try and change things, but now it has and maybe it'll be a good thing.

    I have a few targets off the back of my last trip out and I hope things go quickly. Really, it can't be that hard if they're all still half asleep, dragging their sorry carcasses off to work on a Monday morning, and when thinking of this, part of me is glad that I don't need to work anymore. After all I've seen and done, 9:00am-5:00pm would seem ridiculous.

My first stop takes me to a woman named Sarah-Jane Huxley and I know that a few blocks over from here I could find the cellar where I first met Adryan. I'm guessing this means that I'm getting further into the organisation and that I'll have some luck later on, but maybe it's just wishful thinking.

The house I enter is small, but expensive when considering the fact that we're in the middle of the city. The walls are colourful, the carpets are worn and for the first time in a while, a place actually looks lived in when finding one of my targets.

I hear four heartbeats when I enter and curse silently, guessing that she must have a family. I hate doing things like this when innocents are around, especially kids and it's a bad way to start the morning.

I look around the house, more out of curiosity than anything else and can see wedding photographs as I climb the stairs. Seeing two people look at each other so happily makes my stomach churn and I focus on my mission to stop from thinking of Nolan.

But much to my surprise, there are no children in the bedrooms, not even an adult and I'm getting more confused the further I travel in as there's clearly someone who lives here, I can hear them.

When finally walking into the attic room, I find them. All four humans are asleep and bound in the corner which summons anger into my chest. Two of them are kids and from their tear-stained faces, they've clearly been traumatised.

I walk over silently so as not to wake them and untie the ropes with my nails. The woman stirs and I place my hand over her mouth before dragging her into the hallway, leaving her husband behind.

"What happened?" I hiss at her.

Knowing that I should probably be nicer, but I have it on good authority that she's been working with the Lord of Ashes to help distribute his weapons more easily.

"Please, leave my children and just take me, I'll be quiet, please." She instantly starts sobbing and I grind together my teeth. It's the worst insult that she could have given me, being mistaken for one of his goons.

"I'm not here to kill you." I lie as I technically was but now's not the time. "What happened?"

"I can't tell you." She trembles and I try not to roll my eyes while she can see.

I summon ice into my eyes and repeat the question for the third time. They can't have been here longer than the night or she'd be in far worse shape and maybe I can find the people who did this.

"I tried to stop but he punished me. Punished us. He was going to leave us here to die." Her nose is running, and I rip a piece of felt from my dress to hand to her so that she can wipe it.

"Who punished you? What did you stop?" I feel for her, what she's gone through is horrible, but I need her to use her words better while I can still keep my rage under control.

"The Lord of Ashes. He kept threatening me, making me work for him and I found a way out, but he heard and now we're dead." Her hands go to her hair in panic, and I instruct her to calm down as I know that without the ice in my eyes, the instruction would be useless.

"You're not dead. You're just..." *Fucked*, I want to say, because if I was a human in her shoes, I'd be shitting bricks too and this gives me all the more reason to hunt him down.

"What was your plan? How were you getting out?" I ask her, praying it's something half useful or it's going to be a long morning.

"Witness protection." She whimpers and I nod in disappointment as he's got spies all over the place so that's not going to work.

I try to think but I can hear the kids speaking through the walls, they're starting to wake up and the last thing I want to hear is them crying when there's nothing that I can do about it.

"Do you have savings? Fake IDs? Anything we can use?"

I don't know why I'm saying we, but I'm not going to just leave them. I can't really blame her for what she's done, and she's made the effort to get out. The least I can do is put my resources to some use where I can and I half wonder if it's worth calling Adryan, but I'd rather handle this on my own.

"No." She's staring into space, and I sigh.

The next thirty-minutes consist of packing up all their stuff, booking a hire car, four plane tickets and transferring a hefty amount of cash over to them in Elisabeth's name.

I'm hoping that if they can get out of the city, they'll have better luck and after she described a familiar-sounding ginger, they won't be tracked for very much longer if I can help it.

I wait until the car pulls away before I turn back on the house and wonder what sort of a person could tie up a child? I mean, I thought she was a bitch, but I didn't take Abbey for the type, to be honest.

If my sources are correct as I stand texting them, she was last seen at her apartment and I'm quite curious now to see where she resides and if it's as ugly as her personality.

My heels click as they trot along the quiet streets as people are getting up for work now and a few are already commuting. I'm quite pleased though when I find myself going into a poorer neighbourhood and I hope the bitch gets paid pennies for what she's done as she doesn't deserve even that.

After three flights of stairs, I find her door and I make a show of banging on it, hopefully scaring her into thinking it's the police or something, and it would be nice to get her adrenaline flowing before I end her.

She opens the door with wide eyes that grow further when she sees me, and I bob my eyebrows in greeting as I walk past her and into the room. It's small, clean and has about as much personality as a prison cell.

I expected more than just magnolia from the lip piercing to be honest. The carpet is brown, the walls are practically bare, and the curtains look like they could barely block a streetlight from how thin they are.

Abbey is still dressed in pyjamas and they're a simple black and white striped set with a vest revealing the bare skin of her chest. She's pale, but then again, I suppose her complexion could be from the situation that we find ourselves in.

"You've been a busy girl," I call over to her as she stays next to the door.

She doesn't reply and I sit myself on her white leather sofa. There are no books, no magazines and I'm bored to tears just imagining living here. I wonder if Mark Burnley lived here too?

"What do you want?" Her voice is strong all things considered, and I grin over at her.

"I want a world where children aren't manhandled by vicious idiots, but unfortunately I can't have that, can I?" I ask, tilting my head and glaring at her with a look that brings many to their knees.

To her credit, her legs just wobble though her breathing increases with the fear.

"How'd yo-" I cut her off with the wave of my hand and signal for her to come and sit, knowing that the ice inside my eyes is not to be disobeyed.

The sun is fully up now, and it shines into this pathetic room. It radiates off of her red hair and I wonder how she would look if she were actually on fire.

I'm tempted to find out.

I stand now that she's sitting because I want her to feel my dominance of the situation, to fear it and to dread what is to come. I hope her imagination is going crazy and I regret that reading minds wasn't a gift I was presented with when turned.

"We're going to have a little talk."

Is all I say before I bare my teeth and begin.

Chapter 17

When I'm done hunting for the day, I look at myself in the mirror of my apartment and realise that I don't even look human. My hair is like a bird's nest, my skin is stained with blood and my eyes are rabid. I look like I should be behind bars at the local zoo, scaring the children on school visits.

It feels almost criminal that something as bad as me could be friends with someone as pure as Adryan. So much so, that I don't reply when he texts to ask where I went as it's none of his concern and I'd have preferred it if he didn't notice at all.

I run a bath and soak for a good hour, watching the colour turn red and the water go cold. I use two different hair masks to get the knots out of my hair and carefully plait it down my bare back as I stare up at the ceiling in thought.

The heat of the steam tickles my skin as it flows over me and the quiet trickles of warm water echo in my ears as I pour more in to heat myself up.

I've heard nothing from the Lord of Ashes, and I've made the news twice now which worries me.

No one has dared to interrogate me about it, and nobody seems to be scared when finding me sitting there all alone. People are just as attracted to me as they were weeks ago and if possible, the blonde is even more of a hit. I just hate the way it messes with my hair when it's tied up under it.

Looking over my hands, I can see that my nails are in absolute shambles from this morning's activities and it's only my thumb that is still painted and complete. I can't really be bothered to go back to Sacha, so while lying there I rip it out myself to allow it to grow back and leave them all bare and natural.

Usually, I like to watch them grow back but I'm distracted right now as I found something out this morning that really set me over the edge. My reaction was even more extreme than it was originally which is really saying something when kids are involved.

It turns out that my dear friend Abbey was looking a little too closely in Adryan's direction, and while she hadn't voiced her suspicions, I saw them. So, in a rage I took her to the cellar and got it out of her by force.

It felt rather poetic to tie her down where I was once held, to play with the orange light bulb like she was and to tease her about Mark. It was cruel and I enjoyed it.

But I think it's because it felt personal for the first time.

As the water reaches a level where it threatens to spill over, I drain the tub and run it again rather than get out. There's nothing to stop me from staying here all day and the smell of lavender is helping to cool my temper that keeps flaring up at the thought of red hair.

I just hope that the family got away okay and that's the only reason I keep checking the news. Apparently, it makes no difference to the Lord of Ashes and through the anger I can tell that I'm starting to lose hope.

The burner phone vibrates against the porcelain, and I wait thirty minutes before even bothering to rise and check it as there's only one person with that number and I'm not in the mood to respond.

I can't do lunch today; I have a meeting. Dinner instead?

Adryan texts me and I frown at the small screen. After my incident this morning, I don't like how close we are getting, and I wonder if it's best to nip it in the bud before he really gets caught up with his brother.

I don't plan to stick with his incognito/spymaster approach anymore and I want the danger to come to me now.

If Abbey was already sniffing around, who's to say that there aren't others, and it might take a lot more than a wig to put them off the scent?

I'm not hungry.

I reply, not bothering to give an excuse and I hope that my blunt words will put him off. But unfortunately, not even 5 minutes pass before I feel the vibration again and I roll my eyes as I pick it back up in my hand.

I don't care, see you at Salvatore's at 6 - I have news.

I hate being told what to do and he knows that, so after reading the words three times, I throw the phone across the bathroom in a rage.

It's not until I get out of the bath again to walk and pick up the pieces, that I find it survived and the only reason behind it is because it's a Nokia brick.

At least now I know why he insisted on giving me that one.

As I walk up the steps and into Salvatore's, I have a scowl on my face that could curdle milk.

I tried hunting before I was due to arrive and unfortunately, it didn't help as I picked up more leads than answers, so this only adds to the irritation as I have to stop what I'm doing when I've made such little progress.

I can see him across the room as I enter, and I spot the Bellini and food at my place already. It seems he's taken the liberty to order again, and I bite my lip so hard that I break the skin in irritation, but unfortunately, it's healed by the time I take my seat.

"You're becoming foolish." I say as a way of greeting, and he looks over to me as I sit before giving me a smile that I do not return.

"And you're becoming even more charming." He replies sweetly and he pushes the plate of pasta closer to me before I have a chance to bite back.

"What part of my demeanour indicates that I like being told what to do?" My voice is sharp as I cut to the chase and his eyes go round, probably realising that I meant what I said.

But despite the shock, he recovers quickly. "And what's wrong with you today?"

The sarcasm and tone behind his voice grates at me and I swear that it's the worst question you could possibly ask someone when they are mad at you.

Any idiot would know that.

"Aside from being bossed about, nothing at all," I say while picking up a fork and stabbing one of the small parcels.

I can smell the truffles and these just happen to be a weakness of mine, or I'd have been tempted to repeat the fact that I'm not hungry, but it would be a crime for such a meal to go to waste, a crime I actually care about.

The flavour is strong, and the sauce is creamy. The Parma Ham and truffles blend together very nicely, and I can't help thinking that I might come back here again.

Most likely without him.

The restaurant is busy and I'm pretty sure that it's only just opened up. There is a very faint smell of paint in the air that nobody else but me would pick up on and there's not even the hint of a stain against the white tablecloth.

"Why'd you leave so early?" Adryan pushes through the silence and I swallow before answering.

"Why do you care?" I don't blink when levelling him with my gaze.

"I thought we were past this." He sighs, putting down his fork and crossing his arms which only raises my irritation. I'm doing this for his own damn good and he's acting like I'm a petty child, but little does he know that this is me behaving.

"Tread carefully," I warn in a low voice, and I hear him swallow hard as he takes a drink from his water.

I wish I could ignore the pulse thumping inside of his chest as it keeps ringing through my ears, but I can't, to the point where I almost wonder if he's doing it on purpose.

"You were fine yesterday and now you're acting like you were three weeks ago." He frowns.

"Maybe I've come to my senses," I reply while continuing to eat and ignoring the look on his face.

"Is this about Abbey?" He asks, leaning forward and I breathe in sharply at the name.

Just remembering the woman makes me want to turn back time and relive this morning all over again. She deserved what she got and really, she got off lightly when considering what she could have done to him with her theories.

I've also heard nothing from the family and while she promised she was working alone on that case, I don't believe that nobody will go to check in on them, expecting to find a body in the attic. This adds to my stress, and I take a drink from the cocktail in front of me to distract myself.

"Good news travels fast I see," I say with a forced smile.

"I knew she was on my tail, but I'd decided it was a good thing." He shrugs and now he really has my attention.

"Why would it be a good thing?" I drop my fork now.

How the hell did he know? She assured me that she told no one and there's no way that she could have found a way to lie through compulsion so fast. Loopholes take time to think up and she wasn't that smart.

"Because that's what I was aiming for, the only thing that's going to get my brother to show up is when he thinks there's a threat that needs to be dealt with" Adryan seems annoyed, and I know that he's thinking about Paul.

"What do you think I'm doing?" I snap.

He shouldn't be so stupid as to think he could survive that. The only reason I can try it is because I'm literally indestructible which nullifies the threat.

"Yeah, I guessed that but if it's me he'll probably care more... no offence." He adds and doesn't break my eye contact.

"If it's you, he'll kill you." I say through my teeth, "Very easily might I add, and he won't need to show up to manage it."

The idea annoys me quite a bit and I'm starting to panic now, how many am I going to have to kill? What has he done?

"I can't just do nothing." His voice almost cracks and I close my eyes to process that for one second before answering.

"You can survive and let me do what I do best." My voice is firm, leaving no room for negotiation.

If he's smart, he will accept this and realise how stupid he's being, but Adryan doesn't tend to be smart when it comes to his brother, and I fully expect his reply.

"Who named you a dictator?" He snaps and I smile.

He may not be as big of a control freak as I am, but he likes his power and we're quite similar this way, it's probably why we bonded so fast.

"Dictators aren't given power, they take it." I laugh arrogantly and continue eating. "Why else did you partner with me?"

"Because we were struggling and running out of time." His voice hesitates and I try to keep my face neutral.

"Look, I've made the news a good few times now and it's only a matter of time before he bites. If it makes you feel better, I'll text you if they take me, how's that?" My voice is borderline condescending, but he ignores it.

"I need to do something!" He sounds determined and I close my eyes to roll them privately.

He's stubborn like me too and I realise that it's not always a good thing when you're basically arguing with yourself.

"You want to die?" I say as if repeating what he just said.

"If that's what it takes to be involved then yes." His nostrils flare.

The voice is back, the leader's voice and I can't deny that this is what convinces me. It gets me every damn time and I've missed it to be honest.

"Fine. If I get caught, I'll call you, how's that?" I don't hide the irritation in my tone, and he just smiles.

"Perfect... Now eat up." He says and I throw a piece of pasta on his forehead before he can even blink.

I might have let him convince me, but he needs to watch his mouth. I'm not a saint and my patience has a limit.

"Good to see we're friends again." Is all he says, ignoring the scowl on my face.

"You're on probation," I reply and for the first time today, I let myself relax.

Chapter 18

Another week passes and there's still no word from the Lord of Arseholes.

Adryan is just as on edge as I am as he's constantly barking down the phone to David and James. If they really meant it when they said they are all at an equal level, I'd have told him to do one by now, but they tolerate it with good sport.

Nobody has suspected any of them yet, but they have each heard whispers of a crazy blonde with a terrifying dedication to wiping out the organisation. So much so that something like pride runs through my veins when I place on the wig now.

ELLE CHIPP

My shift pattern has adjusted recently and rather than patrol at night, I leave during the day. Too many things can be covered up in the dark and I want to be seen.

Most evenings are spent with Adryan, either at his or mine which I never thought would happen, but it has evolved quickly. He has an annoying habit of making sure that I eat something and despite telling him that it makes no difference, he's a force to be reckoned with.

Monday was the first time he had come to my apartment with my permission, and it was very weird to see someone there and expect them to walk out again on their own two feet.

When walking through the door the first thing he saw was all of the colours, candles and plants. I think it's fair to say that he understood his apartment's assault better after that and to be honest, I actually felt quite self-conscious having him there in my space.

He even made a point to bring a dark grey throw blanket on his next visit, as if to say that if I can complain about his gloom, he can complain about my vibrance. It's now permanently laid on my bed and I have to say it complements the decor.

I don't have a guest room, Elisabeth converted it into a closet, and I was quite pleased with that fact up until recently. So, whenever it's my turn to host, he sleeps on the leather sofa, and I don't hear the end of how uncomfortable it is.

It was different, having him sleep at my place compared to accidentally crashing at his and I kept waking up during the night to look out of the door and see if he was still there. It was like I couldn't get the sound of his breathing out of my mind, and it felt odd.

It felt odd but good to have someone around.

It's my turn again tonight so I've actually bought a pull-out bed, something I've never needed to purchase in my life, but I have. I'd rather he not wreck my sofa by sleeping on it and if it's becoming a more normal thing, I'd prefer it if he were comfortable.

It's a side table by day, but you can pull it apart and it lets someone sleep on it as and when needed. I was just going to go for a blow-up bed or something at first, but they're too easily popped and they're a pain when they deflate. I surprised myself with how fussy I was being when picking it out and I finally settled on this one.

It is a pretty blue colour, and I may or may not have seen something similar in a victim's house when perusing one morning. It is like a strange version of Pinterest sometimes, getting inspiration from the oddest of places and I will definitely not be telling him where the idea came from. Not that he'd ask.

We've been getting on quite well and I'd forgotten what it's like to have a friend. I like being able to actually talk to someone and not just play with them for my own gain. It's nice and probably just what I need right now.

Adryan's still not pleased that I'm the one laying the trap for his brother, rather than him. It's something that I may or may not rub in his face from time to time when he needs taking down a peg or two and I'm working my arse off to get somewhere with this already. It's harder than I thought to get this human's attention and my patience is wearing thin.

To throw it back, Adryan has started to mock the fact that I cannot cook. My defence is that I have never needed to cook. I live in a city, and I have always had a job that funds my eating out habits, even before I moved here.

I don't know where or how he learned, and he won't tell me, but because he knows how to do something better than I can, it gives him great joy and my teeth are starting to wear away from grinding them so much.

So, tonight I have hired a caterer. Something Adryan will remain in the dark about and they will be here very soon to cook a meal and promptly piss off so that I can take the credit.

It's not the most honourable thing I've ever done but I kill people, so it's not the biggest sin on my list.

Today is Sunday which means we wear jeans like some depressing version of 'Mean Girls', and I've managed to find a floppy bow tie that goes with my outfit. The blazer thing was fun, but I can't use it too often like he does, and it has got this preppy vibe to it that I like.

The food is cooked and laid out to perfection. I may or may not have micromanaged the presentation, but the tip was more than generous, and she was leaving with constant *'thank-yous'* being thrown over her shoulder.

As I close the door behind her, I smile to the ceiling, willing Elisabeth's ghost to appear so that I can see her face. I'm consciously trying to be more generous where I can but it's getting harder to believe that this monster is salvageable at this point.

Adryan is ten minutes late when he finally knocks and the scowl on my face increases when I see a bouquet of black flowers in his hands. He's never done that before and the colour makes my eyes widen in shock.

"What the hell are those?" I ask through narrowed eyes as I drag him into the room.

There are pretty much no formalities now and I don't even know why he knocked this time. He usually just walks right in because that's what I've always done with him.

"I saw them downtown. I thought it would be funny." He says, smiling as he puts them down on my coffee table. They already come with a little box around them for presentation and I stare at it for a second wondering what to think.

"Why?" The dark colour throws everything off and it's like Elisabeth has possessed him to get revenge on the tip.

"It's too bright in here. It's depressing." He mocks and we go over to the pre-set table to eat.

With the plants in the centre, the colours of the food and the hardwood table, it looks like it's been staged, and I have to take a second to appreciate that this is in my apartment right now before it's ripped to shreds to assuage my hunger.

"What's all this?" He questions while looking at the pots of curry, rice, poppadoms and chutneys dotted around the table.

"Food?" I sarcastically reply while loading up my plate, not even bothering to wait for him to be seated before starting.

Rebecca, the caterer went with Indian as it's better to share and I could probably get away with claiming the credit if I said I followed a recipe. I doubt I could have managed this well, but it was a decent excuse and I *love* Indian food.

He takes a bite from one of the spoons and eyes me with suspicion. "You didn't cook this."

"Are you calling me a liar?" I threaten sweetly but it doesn't work anymore. I miss the reactions to be honest, they were half the fun and I wonder what it would take for him to think I was scary again.

"I certainly am, you burned the pot noodle on Wednesday." He laughs at the memory, and I kick him sharply in the shins. "There's no need for that." He frowns rubbing them.

"If you want to question me, you can do it out in the hall," I say, using my naan to scoop a portion of curry-soaked rice into my mouth. The flavours are exquisite, and I'll be using Rebecca again, that's for sure.

"The hall will be better than that sofa." He pretends to rub his neck and I roll my eyes.

Here we go again, it can't be that bad.

"I've found a solution for that." I say, waiting for him to ask.

I like interior design, but he doesn't, so dragging interest out of him can be like getting blood from a stone most of the time. In fact, I could probably get blood from a stone far more easily.

"You have?" His eyebrows raise and his pulse jolts for a second, but it's not until I notice the flush that I get the assumption.

"Not *that* you pervert." I scold, throwing a poppadom at him. "I've bought you a bed."

"Really? You didn't need to; I was only messing with you." He laughs though the flush doesn't go away which I try not to notice.

"If I have to listen to you insult my beautiful couch one more time... I'm going to cut it open and sew you in permanently." I reply and he rolls his eyes.

"Wouldn't that ruin the couch?" His mouth is half open with food as he says this, and I narrow my eyes.

"It'll be worth it for a fitting punishment." I cross my arms.

"Well, if it's as good as the meal, I'll be asleep within the hour." He laughs and takes another bite.

We continue to eat in silence because the food deserves our full attention when it's as good as this. Rebecca has really outdone herself with this meal and I don't know why I don't eat this more often.

I try to place a smug look on my face when he's clearly enjoying each bite as I know that that's what I'd be doing if I really did cook this. There's not a chance in hell I'd have gotten anywhere close, but he doesn't need to know that.

By the time the food is gone, I start to wash the countless dishes because up until now I've never needed a dishwasher while Adryan dries them next to me, which is nice. My kitchen has always just been for show and it's odd to be in here while actually using it to have food cooked.

I doubt Elisabeth used it either, I found a box of shoes in there like she was trying out Carrie Bradshaw's idea and I bought all the plates and stuff so that I had something to use if I got takeout and coffee.

CURSE ME

I didn't own these particular dishes before today but there's room in the cupboards and Adryan doesn't say anything about it, as it's not like he knew what was in them before now.

When done cleaning up, the side table is pulled into the middle of the room, and I make sure to have his full attention when I demonstrate its shapeshifting abilities. He looks bored but claps at the end when I gesture that it's required, and I drag it to the corner window easily, so it'll be like he's falling off the building if he turns around.

My couch will be a lovely alternative in that case, won't it?

By the time I sit on the sofa, Adryan has the TV on, and I extend my hand to demand the remote privileges. I've never really used the TV until now and Adryan has connected his various streaming apps that let us watch more shows.

I don't even know what the show we're watching is called, but parts of it are funny and there's a lot of gore that keeps me interested. I like to comment on it sometimes to let him know if it's realistic or not and that's where I can get a reaction out of him, when he's able to imagine it better.

Aside from that, we tend to go quiet at this point and I just pass the popcorn he insists on bringing between us as we snack.

"What'd you do today?" He asks when getting me another coffee from the fridge and a Coke for himself.

My mini fridge has been moved from the door to the kitchen now and it's stocked up on coffee for me and soft drinks for him. Caffeine after 5:00pm is apparently a no-go, not that it matters to me, and I've had to provide alternatives to live up to my hosting potential. It was annoying when he kept bringing his own drinks for himself, as if he thought I'd not bother.

"I cooked a delicious meal, and yourself?" I lie convincingly, as I don't need to tell him who I murdered.

"Bit of shopping, I saw James and David. They're doing well, all things considered." He says as he sits back down, and I nod my head. Paul is still a sensitive topic and we have been avoiding it recently.

"And you decided to buy those abominations?" I say while nodding to the coffee table and he grins.

"They're lovely, what are you on about? They really liven the place up a bit." He's using the words I've said when dragging in more plants and rugs into his apartment.

It's turned into a really nice place now and I'd like to use it to take the credit for his improving mood. He's graduated back to light greys this week which is something.

"Don't expect to see them when you return, I hate fake flowers." I say sweetly and he scowls.

"What roses do you know that grow black naturally?" He asks with sass rolling from his tongue and I turn up the TV to ignore him. It's becoming a go-to move of mine lately.

By the next episode, there is a brilliant plot twist and I annoy him by constantly asking a thousand questions, as if he's seen it before. To give him credit, he handles them better than I usually do but just now he's made the mistake of physically putting his hand over my mouth to quiet me.

Unfortunately for him, this ends up with him flipped over his shoulder and onto his back. He's still on the cushions though, as the intention wasn't to break his back this time.

"Be careful there. You almost hurt yourself." I say innocently as I put my head over his.

I can smell his cologne and can't decide if it's sandalwood or cedar that I can sense. It's almost as if he smells like a library and if it wasn't weird that I noticed, I'd have teased him about it.

We're facing opposite directions, and I see his eyes adjust to where he is and what he's looking up at, or should I say *who* he is looking up at?

Again, I hear his heart jolt and his face flushes which makes me sit back up and shift in my seat. I wonder if my reaction was too extreme. It's my automatic response when someone touches me out of the blue and I'm not used to it.

"I didn't hurt you, did I?" I ask, turning towards him as he sits up again.

"No, just shocked me a bit." He laughs, running a hand through his hair to try and fix the damage the pillows have done to it. Strands are pointing in every direction and the pale shade suits him well.

"You sure?" I push, I don't like how my voice sounds, it's not the usual sarcasm and venom.

"Forgive me, but I'm not usually flipped onto my back like a sack of potatoes." He laughs again and I drop it. The flush is still there and it's probably from the physical contact.

We don't tend to do that and while it was in retaliation, I shouldn't have touched him. I'm a lot stronger than he is and I keep forgetting that he's delicate.

Chapter 19

I wake up with my head on Adryan's shoulder and jump to my feet as if I'm a human sitting on an electric wire. My heart beats dramatically, something that I am not used to, and I look around the room to try and ground myself in the current moment.

It's still the middle of the night and I realise that we must have fallen asleep while watching the TV. There's popcorn sprayed all over the couch where we sat, and I have a nasty feeling that my coffee has spilt over the rug from the caffeine smell rising from the floor.

I make my way into the bathroom with the strong urge to be alone. It doesn't matter that he's asleep, I need the space and I turn on my shower to drown out the sound of his breathing. While stepping in, I leave the temperature on cold, and I shampoo and condition my hair thoroughly while I try to count the tiles as a distraction.

After nearly always taking a bath since living here, I've never noticed how the colours inside are a blended shade of blue and green and as the soap pools at my feet, I imagine what it would look like if I got some vines in here to hang from the door.

My body is completely awake now despite the time and even after the near ice bath, I can't stop thinking about what I just let happen. I've slept in the same apartment as him before but never next to him. The idea of being comfortable enough to touch someone while asleep is insane and I feel sick at the thought of Nolan being the last person that happened with.

It's been four years, but it still feels wrong. Like it's crossing a line and friendship doesn't equate to sleeping next to each other. He shouldn't feel comfortable enough to do that with a thing like me. It's dangerous and he needs to be more careful, I need to be more careful. I don't care if it was an accident, it gives the wrong impression, and I can't allow it.

I pace back and forth, and I decide that I might as well start my day now. I can already tell that trying to sleep again would be a lost cause so from there I towel dry my hair in the bedroom before pulling on the wig. I can't deny that it's starting to annoy me now with the itchy lace as night after night with this thing on is getting old and I have serious respect for people that do this more regularly than I do.

    I'm on my hands and knees when I come out of my room, and I move around the den quietly as I try to clean up the mess from the night before. I pull on my shoes while rising back to my full height and it's only when I turn to the door that I see that Adryan hasn't moved yet. His head is lying there at an awkward angle at the end of my couch and with a low sigh, I know that I'm not letting him complain about my sofa again.

    I have no intention of hearing his moans about a painful neck, especially after buying a damn bed to shut him up, so I carry him from the sofa and onto the mattress.

    I know from our similarities that he'd hate the idea of me carrying him anywhere and it makes me smile when doing so. Maybe he'll think he was too tired to remember hitting the hay and we can leave it at that, if I'm the only one that knows what happened, it should be fine right?

    The last thing I do before I leave is place the spare key on the counter (in case I'm too long) and then I lock the door behind me. Nobody has ever dared to break into my apartment before but him, but it's times like these that I wish I had a guard dog, or something similar, to leave behind.

    I step into the street, and I can see that the stars are out with the night still young. The fact that it's a weekday means nothing in the city and the bars are bouncing with plenty of people to sink my teeth into, literally.

While making my way downtown, I notice that Roland's place is still open and it's a nice surprise to see. I go in there first to check it out and while there are whispers of what happened, nothing is close to the actual truth.

I'm so happy that I actually buy the informant a drink before I start planning to rip him to pieces as I recognize him as one of the men that locked me in the room with his boss and I can't help but imagine how many other men and women he's done that to.

After doing a quick once over, ignoring the leather jacket and bare torso, I can see that his soul isn't clean at all, and it just takes a suggestive wink to get him to follow me outside like a lost little puppy.

His meaty arms would be intimidating to anyone but myself and every time he flexes, I have to fight the urge to laugh. I eat men like him for breakfast and if he knew the monster he was messing with, well, he wouldn't bother trying to flirt.

I leave him behind a dumpster and before I can get back onto the open street, I hear voices from the window above that makes me stop.

You can tell a bad voice when you hear one, the same way that you can tell if a plant hasn't had sunshine in a good few days. They're dark, dry and void of any form of life. I could write a book on things like this from all of my experiences and all three of the voices I can hear, apply.

Without a second thought, I scale the brick wall with my nails before hanging from the ledge. The window is closed but that doesn't matter to me, they might as well be shouting with my increased hearing.

"We're to go to the estate." One of them grumbles and another person inhales sharply before letting it go as it sounds as though wherever he meant isn't ideal news.

"Are you sure?" Someone else asks and I cringe when I hear a punch being thrown.

It's fair to say that one of these guys doesn't like being questioned and to be honest, I kind of see where he's coming from. Does he sound like the type of man you'd talk back to?

I mean, maybe for me but certainly not for anyone else. Just from the pitch, I can tell that he's huge and it sounds like the other guy has had quite a few punches before to explain the lack of brain cells.

"I'm sorry Hank." I hear a mumble and I have to bite my lip from laughing at the submissive tone. They're no better than a pack of wolves.

"Tell that to his lordship, it was his instruction." A growl says and this really has my attention now.

Could they be talking about the Lord of Ashes?

"I'd never question him, never." The idiot says and there's only a cold laugh in reply.

This guy is good, and I wonder, what sort of a fight will he put up? I ask myself that as I use my hands and pull myself up and onto the ledge easily. It's always a shock when doing that as I could barely do a push up in my human form and now it's like second nature.

I kick through the glass and land on the carpet, brushing the fake hair from my face before I start to survey the room. It's nicely decorated with modern furnishings and the only annoyance is the smell. Something must have died in here and after looking into the corner, I spot whoever it is that is rolled up in a rug.

Really? How many times have I seen that one before?

"Good evening." I say politely as if I haven't just barged right in.

"Fuck off." The one I assume to be Hank spits at me, I use a candle stick to smash into the side of his skull without a moment's hesitation.

He's not dead but it'll keep him asleep while I play with the others. I want to set the standard early to show that disrespect will not be tolerated with me, and I kick his limp body to make sure that he's down for the count.

"Is that any way to treat a guest?" I shake my head while looking over his comatose body and the other two are basically awe-struck.

"How did you...?" The smaller of the pair trails off, too busy looking between us and I summon the ice to my eyes while I take a seat on a red armchair before motioning for them to do the same.

"Who is this lord that you're talking about?" My voice is cold, and I can see the sweat on their brows.

"The Lord of Ashes." They stutter at the same time.

It's all I can do not to whoop out loud now that I finally have a lead, and I calm myself with knowing that I need to gather some more information before I can celebrate.

"And he's going to be at his estate? Where's his estate?" I ask and the grin on my face must be unnerving them because they almost don't hear me this time.

"In the city, just on the outskirts."

"Interesting. Do you know anything else to do with his whereabouts?" I pick at my nails and their lips start to tremble.

"No, he'll kill us. Please." One begs and the other is losing the colour in his face fast.

I wonder if he'll pass out? The Lord of Ashes must be good if he's able to invoke fear like that from so far away. I'd like to think that I have that effect, but then again, I don't leave loose ends lying around.

"No he won't, silly." I croon and walk over to him to boop his nose like you would a child.

His dark greasy hair looks like it hasn't been washed in days and his red eyes have me wondering if it's from the punch or if he's on something. The other guy is blond and skinny, and I can see the bones on his arms all too clearly. When was the last time he ate, or is it an illness or something as that doesn't look normal to me?

"He won't?" The dark-haired one questions, and Hank was right, it is annoying when he does that.

"Of course not." I snap his neck. "Because *I* will."

I let the other scream before I end him too and it takes an hour before Hank wakes, but I don't bother tying him to a chair or anything else as equally useless. The second I see life in his eyes, I compel him to sit still and that's far more powerful.

He looks around to see the bodies of his colleagues and I raise my brows, welcoming a comment.

"What are you?" He asks through his teeth, and I'm tempted to pull one out, just for the lack of imagination.

"Now now, surely you've got more to worry about than that?" My voice is condescending, and I can tell that this pisses him off more than any old threat.

His type is so easy to mess with.

"Fuck you." He spits again and before he can blink, I have broken his left leg.

To his credit he doesn't scream that loud, I've heard worse and by the second time around he actually manages to swallow it. He deserves a pay raise and I bet it would be a lot harder to get his cooperation without compulsion.

It's a shame he ran into me.

"Are you going to be my friend, Hank?" I use the candle stick again and trail it down the side of his face in a light caress, his heart rate speeds up, and his eyes widen as he tries to fight the fear building up.

But after a minute I remove the choice and ice fills my eyes.

Chapter 20

It's not even 6:00am when I bound back into the apartment, my heels sound like horses galloping against the hardwood floors and I roughly shake Adryan awake when I reach the bed.

There are dark circles in his eyes that make me wonder if he hasn't been sleeping well lately and he's managed to cocoon himself into the blankets while I've been out as if he's cold. While I wake him, he reacts as if falling from a twenty-story building and I have to bite my lip to stop from laughing out loud.

As I pull the wig off myself while he gathers his mind back together, I end up frowning at the blood I find staining the edges and I suppose that's why my hair went darker with the curse because up until now I've never had this issue.

It kind of puts a damper on my plans to change myself to be honest, and I wait for him to speak first while studying it. I didn't realise how much of a mess I can make.

"I didn't order a wake-up call." He grumbles.

"You didn't order a lead either but here I am," I reply with a grin, and this instantly gets his attention.

"You have a lead? How?" He spews out and I laugh in response.

Handing him a cold coffee, because that's all I have, I make a mental note to buy some more soft drinks.

"I obviously do have a lead and I think you know how." I smile as he narrows his eyes at me. "Does your family have a house on the outskirts?" I ask.

"Yeah, if you can call it that. The thing is huge." He mutters, rubbing his head and I wonder if he needs a couple more hours before he can process this properly. He looks shattered.

"Well, he'll be there on Friday apparently. I spoke with some thug called Hank about it." I shrug because I didn't bother asking the names of the others.

"You saw Hank? Hank Dawson?" Adryan sits up slightly.

"Unfortunately, I didn't bother asking his full name, but he was telling the truth." I say smugly.

I know that because I asked very nicely, I don't bother to add on the end because I think he gets where this information came from.

Adryan swallows hard and I tilt my head to inspect him. "He's part of my brother's inner circle. If he's around it must mean it's true."

He looks rather shaken up and I thought he'd be more excited than this but it's not until a second later that I realise that he's probably thinking about the last time we had a lead and what happened to Paul.

"I can go alone, you know. Just give me the address." I say, half expecting the reaction to follow.

"Piss off. I'm coming with you" He scratches his head considering something. "I just need to get the week off first."

He stands up and fishes his phone out of his pocket, ignoring the expression of worry in my voice. The tight jeans can't have been comfortable to sleep in and he looks slightly dishevelled compared to usual.

I zone out as he dials his office, complaining of Covid or something along those lines and I go into the bathroom to run a bath as an automatic reaction. It's the only way I know how to relax myself and while I'd rather he wasn't naked in my own personal bathroom, I'm out of ideas.

As if on autopilot I put the usual oils and salts in before cringing when I see the bubbles form. He's probably not going to want this now so in response, I decide to go full tilt as I might as well do it to annoy him.

I light my candles, put on some whale music and turn off the lights as I need to get myself a new wig anyway so he can have the place to himself. It should give him the space he needs to relax a bit and we can put a plan together when I'm back.

When I walk back to the kitchen, he's raking through my 'food' cupboards, and it takes me a second to realise why that's something I might not want him to do after the ruse last night.

"I knew you didn't cook." He calls out. "There's nothing in here that could make up a meal."

Shit, I got the pots and pans to keep up the image but forgot that actual food which is non-existent in this apartment aside from the leftovers. So much for outsmarting him then.

"Took you long enough," I say casually but kick myself for forgetting. "Anyway, I need to go out to get something, but I've run you a bath, you erm... Looks like you need it." I look him up and down mockingly and he scowls.

"Is this your way of saying that I look like shit?" He folds his arms.

"Yeah, pretty much. Clean towels are on the rack, and I'll wait out here if I'm back before you're done."

I don't wait for him to say anything else before I'm walking down the stairs and out of the front doors of the building. I have a habit of walking off and he's used to it by now I should think.

My feet make their way to the place where I originally bought the wig and I replace it with one similar, only this time it's a shorter cut which I'm hoping means that it'll last longer. If I'm having to replace it every other week it's going to become more trouble than it's worth, but if Friday goes to plan it won't matter.

When I walk back out, I realise that the wig shop isn't far from the nail salon and really, it would be rude not to go there too when my hands are in the state they're currently in.

As I make my way over, I see myself in the reflection of the shop windows and my hair is a complete mess from being tied back under the mesh. I smooth it with my fingers and tie it in a knot on the top of my head as I walk, cringing at how I must have looked like a scarecrow when in the last place.

Sacha is in good enough spirits when I sit down, and I zone out a bit when she starts her usual routine. My brain is buzzing with details and reliving this morning on repeat, trying to remember anything I could have missed.

I think she can tell I am more distracted than usual when I don't hear her the first time she asks a question needing an answer. My gaze flicks back over to her direction and she swallows hard.

She hesitates to repeat that they are out of my favourite shade, and I clench my jaw in reply. She's clearly terrified now that she's noticed, and I scan the shelf behind her to take in the other reds that are too vibrant and orangey for my liking and how the closest purple is a plumb.

But when looking over the outfit that I have on and will likely be wearing for the foreseeable, I agree to a matte black and it's not a bad change in the end.

I'm not the same as I was a few weeks ago and the darker colour fits me better anyway. It's simple, bold and threatening like me, and why shouldn't I do something else different. Clearly change is a good thing after the lucky break I had last night.

We manage to finish up in under an hour with her a lot more at ease within herself and as I walk slowly back to my apartment, I gather a black coffee and Frappuccino en route. I can't deny the excitement I'm still feeling about the lead, but I'm concerned about Adryan's reaction.

As I walk through the door he's sitting on my sofa with the fold-out bed once again a side table and I'm impressed that he knew how to right it again as I could have sworn he wasn't listening.

"Getting your nails done was the urgent errand?" He asks with eyebrows raised as I hand him his cup.

"It was on the list." I say casually, holding up the wig and pulling the dirty one on the counter down into the bin.

"I've been meaning to ask, what's with the wig?" He takes a sip and I see how his hair is still wet. The curls are more profound this way and I can smell the oils from here.

"I figured if the woman hanging around someone's brother is similar to a murderer attacking his people, it might be too easy to put two and two together." I shrug, sitting down.

His face hardens, "You're protecting me?" He sounds disgusted and that only makes me laugh.

"And that is so terrible because...?"

"Because I don't want you to, give me that." He stands up, going over to my newly bought accessory and I'm in front of him within a matter of seconds.

I hold up my hand to indicate that I've managed to hide it in the same space of time and tilt my head "It's cute that you think you can stop me."

He doesn't really stand a chance here. If I want to do something, I'm going to do it and causing his death isn't on my list funnily enough.

"Why?" He scowls.

"Why what?" I reply with a calm voice, sensing the building frustration.

"Why bother?" He's serious and I smile playfully to defuse the tension.

"If you get caught, they'll torture you and I'd rather my apartment remain a secret as I'm rather fond of it." I explain, sipping my drink casually.

If I make the reason selfish, I'm hoping he won't react as badly, but I have to respect it though, I'd do the exact same if the roles were reversed and the last time someone tried to help him and his group, they ended up dead.

So, he only narrows his eyes at me.

"What? You've seen the bathtub, ones like that are as rare as rocking horse shit." I joke.

"I don't need to be protected." He says through his teeth, and I sigh, he's not going to drop this without a fight.

"Fine, how about I promise never to do it again? If I find you hanging from a cliff, I'll assume it's what you want." I offer my hand to shake in jest, but he actually takes it which annoys me.

As much as I understand it, he needs to get used to my looking out for him. That's why he brought me onboard after all and I need him to stop thinking of me as a person and instead as the monster I am. I am here for a purpose and I'm doing what I'm meant to.

"Just for that reaction I'm going to tell you, I wasn't going to but now I will." I tilt my head in amusement.

"Tell me what?" He's chilled out a bit now and sips his coffee while he can.

"I carried you to your bed this morning. Someone couldn't even make it over from the couch." I ensure to omit the part about my making the same mistake though.

"Did you remove my balls while you were at it?" He barks but takes it better than the protecting thing.

I can tell that he hates things like that and it's fun to wind him up to be honest. I like to remind him that I'm the alpha here, lest he forgets what I am.

"I tried, but couldn't find them." I wink, not able to help myself.

"Well, that I know is a lie."

He looks smug now and I roll my eyes. Such a typical male answer.

Rather than argue further I'll take this chance to get us out of the apartment and fix the hunger I assume he's feeling. I want to get out of the building and see him wake up a bit faster so that we can plan already.

"Well, as fun as this is, let's get you some breakfast. I'd rather not add hangry to the list of reasons you're pissed at me." I tease.

He laughs his agreement and I usher him out the door before he can say anything else. The last thing I see before locking up is the dark flowers on my coffee table and I can't help but think that they now match my nails.

Chapter 21

For breakfast, we both order an obnoxiously large pile of pancakes that are smothered in various berries, bananas and syrup. I can't remember the last time that I've ordered something like this and the sweetness of it all tingles against my tongue.

Since Adryan is faking an illness, we've had to find a place that is lesser known to the public and we have ended up stumbling into this gem. It's around the corner from The Grasshopper and because it's in a run-down part of town, Adryan's acquaintances aren't likely to spot him at this time in the morning.

The waitress is an older looking lady with long grey hair and deep brown eyes. It was a nice surprise when we first walked in to find that the cafe was empty aside from a man in the corner on his laptop. He appears to be nice enough and I've compelled them both to forget they saw us anyway so it's not like it matters.

After ordering it became obvious that she was the cook as well as the server and she was extra cautious when bringing our order out to us. She even takes the compliments to heart when Adryan says that they're the best he's ever had, while I on the other hand just smile and say they're fine. It's becoming a habit for us to sit in silence while we eat and I look around the room in the meantime, taking it all in. The wall to our right is filled with blackboard paint that illustrates the menu in elegant handwriting and the wall to our left is a simple cream colour, covered in mismatched frames and black and white photos.

    The windows are locked in by a grey set of wood and from the slight chipping, I can tell that it used to be a baby blue shade before that. Each of the tables dotted around the room is finished with a red and white chequered cloth to protect the original surface which gives it a quaint Parisian vibe while the floor is made up of light pine wood.

    There's evidence of a lot of foot traffic from once upon a time and aside from the wear, it is very well maintained. Noticing that particular detail holds my attention longer than the rest and it makes me wonder why this place is so quiet. If this is a regular business, then I can't imagine how the discolouration appeared and surely it would be busier now if people are on the way to work?

"Do you get many people in here?" I ask as she fills up my mug and her eyes widen as I speak.

I've only said about three words to her since coming in, leaving most of it up to Adryan and now I'm making small talk voluntarily which must come at her as a shock.

"We used to, but not lately." She hesitates to answer, and I sigh, knowing I'm not going to like the reason why just from instinct.

"Why not?" Adryan beats me to it, and I sip my coffee, expecting a vague answer. That would be the smart choice if my suspicions are correct.

"Oh, you know, things change. I'm sure it'll pick up again soon." She forces a cheerful look to take over her face, but I see right through it.

"Who was it and what have they done?" I ask, still drinking when tunnelling into her face with my ice.

Her mouth falls into a small frown and the sad gleam in her eyes resonates with me and I hate that this is an expression that I have seen all too often.

"My nephew. He makes it well known that he doesn't like visitors here and threatens those that enter." Her face is glazed now, and I clench my jaw.

I hate hearing things like this, and my temper increases as I process her words. While I don't have any family, I still can't imagine treating a member of it like that, especially one that is so pure and innocent.

"Why?" Adryan asks and I repeat the question with my power after she hesitates again.

"He wants me to give it up, retire, and hand the shop space over to him."

Worry clouds her eyes as she comes back to herself, and I demand that she relax about it straight away. I have no qualms about taking him out to solve her problem and will not see her stress herself over it.

"Why does he want your space?" Adryan asks, tightly holding the knife in his right hand and I clock the anger on his face.

The woman bites her lip, clearly knowing she shouldn't say anything but is already in too deep for this to make a difference now.

"He owns a business next door and wants to expand." She hesitates on the word 'business' and I can tell it's going to be shady. Smuggler? Dealer? Worse?

"Tell me his name and I'll sort it," I sigh, draining my cup and gently taking the jug from her hands before filling it up again while she blinks.

"Jason Easton." The words come out and I can tell that she didn't want them to.

I wonder if even after all he has done, does she still love him? Family is such a strange thing and if I had the time, I would study the concept more.

"Forget we had this conversation and do not worry about your nephew anymore." I say firmly before changing back into my usual expression and handing her back the jug with a small smile.

She walks away as if she's just woken up from a nap and I can tell that the man in the corner hasn't noticed a thing, but he'll forget this when we leave anyway.

My thoughts are interrupted by Adryan, "You're not going to kill him, are you?" He asks, looking at me with creased brows.

"Why shouldn't I?" I shrug, it sounds like he deserves it to be honest.

"People do things like this all the time, you can't just kill him for it." He looks at me with an expression that is somewhere between confusion and frustration.

It's far too early to be having the morality conversation with him and I was expecting to spend my morning planning his brother's demise, not having my actions questioned.

"Says the one who sat clutching a knife the whole time?" I throw back at him, picking up my utensils to start eating again.

I don't care that he's judging me, it was just a matter of time anyway. Maybe it's what's needed for him to take me more seriously. I'm not some innocent girl he met on the street, I am a murderer that happens to be damn good at her job.

"I said don't kill him, not let him get away with it." He murmurs as if he's worried about someone overhearing and I tilt my head.

"What would you have me do then?" I whisper to mock his reservation.

"Compel him, tell him to stop." He says it like it's obvious and I roll my eyes.

"I can't compel the world away, Adryan." I sigh.

"You can't kill it either." He hesitates to point back, and I purse my lips.

I can tell that this is bothering him from his facial expression and while I want him to understand that this is what I do, I don't like seeing that look on his face.

I swear he's going to make me regret this whole friendship.

"Compulsion can have loopholes." I say after a minute of thinking.

"What do you mean?" He asks, equally as distant and lost in thought.

"If I compel him to stop, there are always ways around it. Like he could get someone else to threaten her, he could harm her, hire someone. It might take a while but there tend to be ways around it for things like that." I bite my lip, trying to think of all the different things I could use to block him off.

"Just don't kill him, if you don't have to." He winces, predicting my response and I only nod.

"Okay, I won't." I shrug, taking another bite of my food and one of the berries is crushed against my tongue, creating a symphony of flavour.

"You'll agree, just like that?" He questions, narrowing his eyes in suspicion.

"If he's just a stupid nephew, I'll compel him. If it's more sinister than that I'll play with him a bit but if he's really bad, he's dead." My tone is serious, and he nods.

I can live with going easier on the morally grey so to speak, but people that are murderers and rapists are on another level and taking them off the streets is a service I pride myself on doing. People get away with shit like that far too often and I am sick of feeling powerless to stop it. I have the power and I'm going to use it; I don't care what he thinks.

"Do you want to help?" I ask sweetly now that the worry on his face has gone.

"I'd rather get a root canal to be honest." He confesses with a sliver of humour laced in.

"I recall you reacting quite well when I was being tortured." I pull a face and he grins.

"I vomited after you left." He replies and I burst out laughing.

I would never have guessed that in a million years. He seemed so tough and firm until I compelled him and that's why I was so shocked when I saw his soul.

"No wonder you're so pure. It's a good thing I'm killing your brother and not you. Are you sure you want to come?" My voice is playful, but my question is valid. I'd rather not have him there if he's going to freak out.

"I can handle it, I was fine with you, wasn't I?" He's serious now and I nod, knowing it's not worth arguing with him.

Jason is a minor drug dealer so I figured that warranted a clear command to leave his aunt alone (via any method I could think of) ...on top of a broken leg.

He's a chartered accountant so it's not like he's risking it all to put food on the table and because of that, I felt significantly less sympathetic compared to what I could have. Naturally, I also shut down the whole operation while I was there, scaring each of his partners well enough to wet their pants and solidly adjust their career paths in the meantime.

Men like him disgust me, but I hope that doing this will prevent him from getting any worse. It's never guaranteed though, truly bad people have a way of making sure they stay down that route once started.

CURSE ME

So I'll just need to keep an eye on the area.

Chapter 22

"Fun question, if someone points a gun at you and I have the chance to stop it, would this count as breaking our deal?" I say as Adryan and I drive through the city and towards his family estate.

I've searched it online and he wasn't kidding when he said the place was huge. Its parameter is basically the size of my hometown and with it being so close to the city, I really don't want to know how much it's worth.

Adryan doesn't answer as he's focused on the road instead, and I'm guessing that's why he insisted on driving this time.

"Come on, you can't be that stubborn that you'd rather die than let me stop them?" I pout and he sighs, drumming his fingers against the wheel as an obvious sign of frustration.

He turns to look at me with a face that forces me to bite back a laugh. "Why do you always assume it's me that'll need saving? What about you?" He narrows his eyes. "I'm serious, if my brother is the one you need, then he can kill you, right?"

He's not wrong but the idea still amuses me. I'm faster and stronger than anything that he can imagine, all while being able to control his mind if I really wanted to. I doubt his brother can hold a torch to what I'm capable of and if he wasn't so pissed off with me, I'd say I was offended.

"Okay, new deal. If we can help each other, we do?" I offer, trying to keep a straight face.

"Fine." He snaps and I smile.

We've spent the past few days under the bakery with James and David. I've been fine when being around James and his dark soul which is nice, and David has proven to be quite useful when showing Adryan how to cover his back.

I almost feel bad about snarling at him when he offered to show me too. He should have known better than to try to teach me how to suck eggs and it's fair to say he won't be risking that again.

James has managed to score us a few details on the guards that will be there tonight, and Adryan knows this place inside and out. Apparently, he lived there from the age of five and it's hard to imagine growing up surrounded by so much wealth. It's a wonder he's not as full of himself as he could be and that's saying something when coming from me.

The car we've hired is under Elisabeth's name and I insist on playing obnoxiously loud music that eventually gets Adryan to sing along. It's a fun role reversal where it's me being the loud one to get him out of his shell when it's almost always the other way around but he's in his 'leader mode' now and I wish I didn't find it so attractive.

I think he's stressed about the fact that he's going home, as from what he said it's been years and I imagine that there are a lot of memories there. I don't feel the need to ask anything else because, unlike him, I know when not to probe with continuous personal questions and I'll just bank my curiosity for later.

The roads are pretty clear for a Friday and the roof is down which makes my hair go wild in the wind. There was no point in wearing a wig and it's fair to say that it would have flown right off at this point.

Our faces are full of smiles, laughter and singing and I'm really starting to like Adryan. I see a lot of myself in him and if it wasn't for the fact that he was so pure...well, I don't know what I'd think.

I keep turning to look at him every so often, to study his face and try and remember what it was like before I knew him. Part of me wonders if I've managed to block it all out already because I'm struggling and he's now fully a part of my routine.

On top of all this, I've been trying to stop the feeling of hope but unsuccessfully, it's all I could contemplate while we've gotten ready for today and who knows, Adryan might be right, the Lord of Ashes could be my cure.

What would that mean?

Obviously, I'd have some questions. Was it a direct kill? What was his motive? And if it was one of his armed dogs, who the fuck was it? Because with the curse broken or not, I'm still getting my revenge.

I keep shaking it from my mind as there's nothing useful that will come from thinking about it and part of me, the cynical part, is whispering 'What if it's just a joke?' What if this deal was something put in place to keep me killing off the darker souls, to punish me further and keep the hope alive?

I can't deny that if this doesn't follow through, it's going to hurt badly. I've forgotten what it's like not to have any leads and to just imagine going back to mindlessly killing anyone feels exhausting. None of this has ever made any sense and I don't know why I expect it to start doing so any time soon, but the hope is there, and the damage will be done if this fails.

After about an hour's drive, we pull into a lay-by that is a mile south of our destination and from there we proceed on foot. There is a lot of forestry on these parts of the grounds, and we are slowly making our way through the foliage in silence. Luckily for us, I can spot where the telltale red lights are flashing which gives away camera locations, and we're able to avoid them quite easily.

I can feel the tension rolling off of Adryan's body and I almost want to give his shoulder a squeeze of reassurance, just to calm him down. "It'll be okay, you know?" I whisper and he smiles weakly.

I don't blame him; his life is on the line here and I can't stop thinking about that fact either. If his brother finds out that he's the one who betrayed him, I can only guess his reaction and I'd rather not stick around long enough to find out.

Secretly, I've already decided that I'm going to compel him to get to safety if anything happens. I don't give a fuck about deals anymore; I care about survival. At least with Adryan, there's something I can do to prevent his death, even if he'll never forgive me.

To be honest I'd rather never speak to him again and know that he's alive than have him be okay with me and watch his throat get slit open.

The image of the blood on my kitchen floor is raw in my mind and my screams from that day are still echoing in my ears along with that voice, that horrible voice offering me a deal and it makes the hairs on my arm raise in recollection alone.

"You okay?" Adryan asks, squeezing my shoulder and I laugh that his comfort response is the same as mine. Of course it is.

"Yeah, I'm fine." I clear my throat to refocus on the task at hand and we pick up the pace.

By the time the house is in view, I disappear from his side to go and pick off the guards facing our direction before they can sound the alarm.

All of them are tall, meaty and tattooed. A terrifying front to most, but to me it only means that their reflexes are slower, and I can hide behind them while doing my thing.

As I make my way back again, I notice how Adryan's face has paled somewhat and his eyes are wide and alert. I raise my eyebrows in question now that he's close enough to read my expression and he swallows roughly.

"I know you said you were fast but..." His voice trails off, looking at the building I've just scaled and bodies that have fallen in a matter of minutes.

"Don't tell me now that you doubted my skill." I pretend to be insulted and he rolls his eyes.

The joking helps both of our nerves and I wonder when the best moment will be for me to send him away. Maybe it's not worth waiting for danger but better instead to get a head start? Still, the idea of unforgivably ruining our friendship is a tough one, and even though I know the choice I'll make, I hesitate.

Interrupting my dilemma, he points to a door towards the back of the house, "If we go through that door, we'll have a path straight through the kitchen." I nod and we lightly make our way over.

While doing so, I make sure my eyes are filled with ice to deter any cameras looking our way and I figure that it would be far more suspicious to destroy them to which Adryan agrees quietly when he gets what I'm doing.

The kitchen is below the main level, which is really strange for me but apparently, it's normal for Adryan. The meals are prepared by paid (and unpaid) servants and are brought up from there, which sounds oddly formal for a lord of crime.

We enter through the door, and I successfully manage to compel the whole room to not notice us which makes the expression on Adryan's face nothing short of awe. I pull a cocky expression which defuses it into an eye roll, and he only makes me laugh.

The evening meal is being prepared but nothing is leaving the room yet which gives us a clear space to walk up the connecting stairs and into the main hallway.

As we make our way further in, I can hear voices and I signal Adryan to be quiet. His steps are a lot louder than mine and I'm ashamed to admit that I find it more irritating than I should. I'm used to working solo and I swear that my senses are going into overdrive here.

The door to what appears to be a banquet hall is closed but the voices behind it aren't muffled very well at all. With all the security I imagine that they're not expecting strangers to be sneaking around here, so there'd be no point in changing that fact, up until now.

A faintly familiar voice is talking and what can only be described as a shiver runs down my body like a bucket of ice. My legs go rigid at the sound, and I swallow the excess saliva building up in my mouth as an automatic reaction.

My hands actually shake as I turn the doorknob gingerly and I gently push it forward a crack to try and see the face behind it, praying that my instincts are wrong.

But they aren't.

I feel my heart physically drop in my chest and my breathing catches. Before my knees can buckle Adryan's arm goes around my waist quickly, pulling me and the door backwards and down into the stairway from which we came.

"What's wrong?" He whispers, his eyes frantically checking my face that's frozen in a state of pain and anguish.

I try to speak but my breathing keeps catching and for the first time in four years a tear rolls down my cheek. I didn't even think that was still possible, as what use is tear ducts in this form?

I'm not used to this but then again this is far from what I ever expected. My chest actually burns from the pressure building up and it's all I can do to keep swallowing down bile.

"Cam, what's wrong?" Adryan's tone is desperate now, both hands are on either side of my face, forcing me to look at him.

But after what I've just seen, it's as if the physical contact stings me and I pull away before I dare to speak.

"Nolan." I croak out and more tears follow.

Chapter 23

"How do you know my brother's name?" He asks, momentarily forgetting the danger.

"Your brother?" I practically yell and my mouth hangs open like a fish once I put two and two together.

No. No. No.

That would mean that Nolan; my perfectly innocent, quiet, sweet Nolan... is the Lord of Ashes.

I swallow down the shock and feel a sense of anger rise in its place. In a second, I have Adryan's shirt balled in my fists and I've pressed him against the wall, lifting him into the air.

There's not a chance in hell that he can escape me, and my list of questions has grown considerably in the last few minutes. If Nolan was his brother, how did he not know about me? Does that mean that he *knew* about me?

"Tell me you're not in on this." I grit out between my teeth. "Tell me you didn't know." I almost sob.

My trembling lungs rattle through my chest as I take in deep breaths to try and calm myself. I don't know who I'm kidding though, that's never worked, and I doubt it'll start doing so now.

"Know what? What is wrong with you? Cam!" He rushes out and my grip only tightens as I hear the threads starting to tear. I half consider if it's worth ripping it from him to dangle in his brothers' face, but the ignorance on Adryan's expression is something I can't ignore.

"Your brother!" I let go and he drops down to the stone with a thud. "Your brother is my Nolan." My voice cracks when I say the name and his eyes widen in realisation.

"No!" He whispers, both hands go up to his hair and I let more tears fall.

There's no point holding them back at this point, the relief is needed, and I can't think straight enough to be bothered about them. If he has an issue with it, he can get in line because I have more pressing matters to focus on right about now.

"Why didn't you tell me his name?" He asks after a few seconds of us both staring at the floor, trying to understand what this means.

It's a good question and I have to think back to why I never told him. Then again, he was never that forthcoming with information and I could just as easily turn it back to ask him the same thing.

"Your last name is Ambrose and his wasn't." I whisper because I'm not in the mood to argue and all I can feel at this moment is the betrayal. How is this even possible?

"What was his name?" Adryan pushes gently and I grind my jaw as it's summoned into my mind automatically.

"Emerys." I force myself to get it out. I've not said it in so long, hell, I've not thought it in so long to be honest. I've been too busy searching for the Lord of Ashes this past month, who is apparently the same fucking person.

Adryan sighs and puts a hand on the back of his neck. "They mean the same thing."

"What?" I ask sharper than I intended for him but I'm past caring at this point.

"Ambrose and Emerys, they are both surnames meaning immortal." He laughs coldly. "It's the last name my father used when courting my mother."

I feel sick and swallow what has to be the last meal I ate. I don't think I'm ever eating again as long as I live at this rate as I can't imagine this feeling ever fading.

"I thought you said that the voice didn't bring him back?" Adryan asks and my attention is snapped back to him.

"I saw him, he was lying on the kitchen floor with his throat slit... and then I made the damn deal." My voice shakes and he places a hand on the middle of my back in comfort. "By the time I came back, his body was gone, and the blood was still there. I assumed whoever killed him came back for the body."

I can't help but flinch at his touch as it feels too wrong, too familiar for us.

"And this was four years ago?" Adryan sighs, biting his lip as if he's realised something.

"Yes," I reply.

Four years of my life were spent on someone who didn't bother to come looking for me, who spent his second chance killing people for no good reason and who has no qualms with hurting children. Never in a million years would I have guessed that that would apply to my Nolan, a man who must no longer exist beneath that monster's shell.

"Five years ago Nolan went underground. Nobody saw him for over a year and when they had him cornered, well, they said he killed himself." He shakes his head in disgust. "By the time they'd dragged his body back to my father and they'd all met up in the morgue to confirm it was him, he was gone."

"He killed himself?" I repeat, unable to believe the words entering my ears.

"Nobody understood how he faked it. They saw him do it, they said he did it right in front of the window while staring down at them, some last attempt to regain control of the situation." Adryan shakes his head at this, and I process the words.

The realisation hits me like a shot, he means the window of the kitchen where I found him. It fits what I saw, what I found, and I can't deny the likely truth behind it. I just never took him as the type to take his own life, no matter what situation he found himself in.

"Cam, where are you going?" Adryan chases after me as I walk back into the grounds and towards the woods.

I can't kill Nolan. I can't, I know I can't.

I gave up everything for him and even if he's abandoned me all this time, he's still Nolan. He's still my person and I can't do that, can I?

"Cam." Adryan is out of breath as he finds me where I'm pacing in place.

I've not moved any further because I can't decide if I should stay or if I should go. If I go, I'm stuck like this forever but if I stay, I have to kill the only man I've ever loved.

I mean, if all I've heard is true, have I ever even met Nolan? Or did killing himself change things? Did it damage his soul and the reason he's like this is because I brought him back when he was meant to stay dead?

What if that means that all of his evil behaviour, all of the agony and the murders are because of me?

I start hyperventilating and it takes a slap from Adryan to distract me. I feel no pain but the touch of someone else is too much for me right now and I flinch away from him as if mortally wounded.

"It's all my fault." I keep muttering over and over again.

All those souls, dark because of me, because of what I started.

"What's your fault? Cam speak to me." He almost yells in my face, desperate for a response and I shake my head.

"I saved him, what if I did this? Made him like this?" My voice is small and as human as it's sounded in a long time.

But Adryan laughs coldly as he clocks onto my meaning. "Cam... he has been like that since he was a child."

I look up, desperate to believe him but it's too easy to give up, too easy to believe my own innocence in something so big and Adryan must sense this because he keeps going,

"Cam, he used to pull apart butterflies. He'd pluck the feathers from live birds just for fun and, fuck...he did this to me when I was seven." He pulls up his shirt and shows a thick scar near the bottom of his rib cage,

"What's that?" My voice is high and outraged at the thought of anyone hurting him.

It's at least 6 inches long, 2 inches thick and what appears to have been a deep burn if my experience on *healed* injuries is anything to trust. For a human, I imagine the pain would have been unbearable.

"He tried to brand me." His voice is hard, like it's simply a matter of fact and this time I can't hold back the vomit as it rises.

He rubs my back, and I don't have the strength to beg him to please stop touching me. Every part of my body screams at me that the contact is wrong, and I want to curl in on myself the second I feel the surface of his palm.

"Appreciate the concern, Cam." He smiles sadly at my reaction, and I wipe my face.

I hate feeling so weak while standing in front of him. I've not been like this since the night Nolan apparently decided to kill himself and I never thought that he'd do something like that, but then again, I never saw *this* coming either.

"What do I do?" I look up at him to ask, once I've caught my breath.

"I can't tell you that." Adryan sighs and I pull a face as if to say that was far from helpful.

"I can't tell you. As much as I'd love to, you're the only one that knows what you can live with." He looks sad, disappointed even and I hate that he's feeling that way toward me.

"I could be human again." I say, not sure if I want to ask him for his thoughts or if I just want to say it out loud for the first time.

Adryan's face breaks out into a small smile. "I know you could, but would you want to be?"

What sort of a question is that? Of course I would.

"I've always wanted to be. I never wanted this." I stare at my hands, the hands that have taken the lives of so many people before me and I try to remember what they were like before.

They were soft I think, more tanned and delicate. You could never describe these things as delicate, not now.

"Do you still love him?" His voice is quieter, and his face is unreadable as he looks down towards my eyes. Of all the things he could ask, I'm not sure why that is at the top of the list, but I think about it anyway trying to find a way to answer.

"No...I- I don't know." I conceded truthfully. He abandoned me, he's a monster but... so am I.

Doesn't that mean we're suited? Didn't I always know that I'd never be good enough for a pure soul after all of this? Isn't it fitting that the man I loved ends up being the only thing worse than me?

After all of the killing, the hunting and the fighting, it ends being that the person I needed to kill is the one I was sacrificing it for all along. I bet the voice is howling with laughter wherever it is right now.

Kill your lover's murderer.

Yeah well, it failed to mention that they are the same fucking person.

I'm right, I have to have been right all along, this is hell. I am in hell, and I am being punished for something bad. Something I can't recall, it's the only reasonable explanation.

But after all of that, if I am really in hell why would they bring me Adryan?

I laugh out loud at the naive question I ask myself.

They probably did it to make me learn to care again, to heal slowly and then rip the carpet out from under me all over.

Well, not for much longer, I don't care if they won, I really don't anymore.

I'm going to die and I'm going to be free of this. I'll kill him and then I'll turn on myself right after as if there's a small chance that this isn't hell, well, it can't be worse than where I am now.

Chapter 24

"Cam, where are you going?" Adryan follows me and I turn around sharply to face him.

His hair is messed from running after me and the blood has rushed to his cheeks from the exertion. The concern in his eyes is comforting to see, but I know that it won't last much longer.

"Take the car and leave." There is ice in my eyes and there is pain in my voice as I order "Keep your head down and live well, Adryan."

It takes a second for the compulsion to kick in and I watch the betrayal show on his face as he realises what I've just done but now that it's out there and in place I can breathe again.

His feet turn him in the direction of the car, and I know that there's nothing that he can do to stop himself. There's no loophole for something as simple as that and I look at his face for the last time as if to try and remember as much as possible.

But is there any point? Is there any point in memorising the shape of his nose? Any point in holding onto the green shade of his eyes? Now that I know, I can see the slight similarities between him and his brother, but Adryan is brighter, warmer and I hope that I won't be awake much longer to dwell on it.

"Cam don't do this!" He shouts over his shoulder and before any more emotion can stir in my chest, I bolt for the house.

He doesn't need to see this side of me. The true monster that I can become and the violence that's about to ensue. It would be nice to be remembered as something more delicate than how I plan to go out, and even if he has only known this side of me, I'd like to think that he saw something more than just the curse.

The woods pass me in a blur and the air on my face is refreshing, blowing away the flush on my cheeks and removing the remaining dampness from my eyes.

The second time I see this house, I ignore the sinking feeling in my stomach and keep going. This time I won't care about the kitchen, and I head straight for the front door. It takes half a thought to rip it off its hinges and I then smash it to ribbons off the top of my raised knee.

The noise echoes off the walls around me and as if summoned, a swarm of people rush into the entry hall. Weapons are raised all around and there is a cold laugh that emerges from my chest that sounds as if it's from another being. It's too low and rough to be mine but I can feel it leave my throat, confirming the owner.

With the power that has never left my eyes, I order them all to stand down and to part the way to where I know he is. I can hear my own heart thundering in my chest, and I don't know if the screams are coming from the crowd running away, or if it's from me as I walk through the door.

It's a small blessing, the fact that my hands aren't shaking this time and I think that the shock is gone. Only anger remains and I honestly don't even know where it's directed. To him? To the voice? To me? I mean, I suppose it doesn't even matter at this point.

My gaze searches around the room and I was right, it's essentially a banquet hall. The high ceilings are filled with wooden beans and perfectly carved roses. Such a luxury seems odd in here, it feels too old for the plain furnishings and simple walls filling the space below and I might as well have stepped into a museum.

With barely any effort my eyes find him, as if drawn in by a magnet. There, at the front of the room he stands and it's as if I'm looking at a ghost. I feel my limbs tremble at the second sight of him, as if I half expected to have imagined it all or for him to have disappeared like a wisp of air.

But no, he's there and my jaw clenches so tightly I think it could very well snap in two.

"Cami?" He looks up and the word hurts more than any punch to the gut ever could.

"Don't." I say with a low and dangerous voice. It sounds like how Adryan's can be, and I wish I could have lived the rest of my life without being called that name again.

"Wh-How?" His voice is high, and his eyebrows are halfway up his forehead.

"Oh, it's a fun story." I say with my mouth turning up into a smile.

He abandoned you, I keep thinking over and over to myself. The face in front of me is like a thousand daggers to the heart and I need something to cling to, to keep me going.

He abandoned you! He abandoned you! He abandoned you!

"I- I thought you were dead?" He says and there's something like pain in his voice.

I can't care, I shouldn't care. Every life I took, every person I hurt, and every soul I delivered was for him. He didn't even bother to give me the heads up that he was still breathing.

Part of me wishes he wasn't, just so that I don't have to be the one to stop it again and I may hate him at this moment, but he was still my person and now I have to kill him. If for nothing else, I'll hate him for that.

"You thought what?" I ask, my voice is still cold, and I don't know how I'm managing it to be honest.

In one hushed breath, I order the rest of the bodies from the room. I don't want witnesses for this and it's going to be the hardest thing I've ever had to do in my life.

"I thought you were dead." He says more evenly now, and I narrow my eyes.

"Why would I be dead?" Not a part of me believes him.

Why should I? The Nolan I knew was sweet, he was innocent. I remember the night he felt sorry for the mouse that we trapped in the apartment, and I had to be the one to take it outside for crying out loud. There's not a chance in hell that that man could have branded his little brother, right?

Just the thought of Adryan's scar urges me on, and I mentally thank him for that bit of information. It might just help me enough to summon the rage I need to actually go through with this.

"When I woke up, you weren't there." His voice shakes and I study his face.

His eyes are the same, dark and wide. The creases around his mouth are basically carved into his face from the way he used to smile, and I notice deeper lines have now worked their way onto his brow. As if he's stopped smiling so much and stress has taken over. Good, it's what he deserves.

"No shit." I finally say.

I know I wasn't there because I was a mile away, waking up empty and alone. I stayed that way for years afterwards and it was only until I met his brother that I started to feel less so. How fucked up is that?

Did he even care? Does he even remember what it was like after all this time?

"I escaped from my father's house the second I knew where I was, but by the time I got back to our apartment you were gone… There was blood everywhere." The eyes on mine are unmoving and I can't tell if that part is in earnest or not.

I know there was blood everywhere and I know I was missing, because when I came back, I saw the same thing and it broke me. He broke me.

"Cute story." I drag a chair loudly over to where I am standing, blocking the entrance and I lie back on it comfortably.

I don't want him to know how stressed out this all makes me feel. I don't want him to know that every glance in his direction is like a knife in the back, and I certainly don't want him to sense any weaknesses.

"You don't believe me?" He questions.

"Why should I believe you?" I tilt my head to the side, wondering what sort of explanation he can possibly think of.

"Be-Because you're mine." He stutters and a cold laugh escapes me.

"I stopped being yours the day you left me."

A lie but he doesn't need to know that.

He doesn't need to know about the pining, the pain or the emptiness I felt after he slit his own throat. He doesn't need to know about the guilt I felt as I got closer to Adryan, just because it felt dishonest to his memory to be moving on. All he needs to know is that the act is up and that it's time to pay the piper.

"Left you? I thought you were dead!" His voice raises ever so slightly, and he swallows when seeing the look on my face. He might not know of the powers I possess, but it would go against the most basic of survival instincts to ignore it.

"What? A bit of blood, no body and you assume I'm dead?" I snap.

Anything could have happened, anything! I could have been taken, attacked, lying hurt in an alleyway bleeding out somewhere and apparently, he'd have been none the wiser.

Funnily enough, *that* sounds like the Nolan I know. The timid, soft man that avoided conflict like the plague and if that's who I still thought he was, maybe I could forgive it.

"What about you then? Did you see a body?" He pushes back thinking he has me and my breathing hitches.

"Yes." I hiss through my teeth. "Yes, I fucking did."

He blanches slightly before gaining his momentum again. "And what did you do? I ended up in a morgue under my father's house, you didn't think to call for help?"

The anger in his voice boils my blood and it takes every bit of strength I have to be able to reply in a semi-calm voice. The ungrateful bastard.

"How do you think you survived? How do you think I ended up like this?" I spit.

"Like what?" His face is blank, and I smile.

"Look out of that window there and just see what happened to that heavy door of yours."

He does and when he sees the splinters lying on the gravel, his face pales several shades.

"I'm sure you've heard of my work; the blonde hair really suits me." The arrogance in my voice is fake but he can't tell the difference as I never spoke like this before the curse.

"How did you do that? You have no weapons." His eyes are wide as he speaks.

I lift my feet up slowly to place them casually onto the tabletop and I'm starting to feel more in control now.

The fear in his face is calming me and if I stop looking into those eyes then I can maybe forget who it is. The fact that the glasses aren't there really helps and for all I know they were just a lie too.

"I am the weapon."

"What happened to you?" He whispers and for some reason, I feel the need to swallow.

What did happen to me? Why has all of this happened when all I wanted to do was to move to the city, have a better life and maybe fall in love?

"You."

Chapter 25

A woman walks into the room by using a door hidden by the panelling that decorates the walls. She almost drops the platter that she's carrying from the shock of seeing me there, alone with her boss.

From the amount of food that she carries, I can only assume that he was meant to be alone at this point. Is it likely that the rest of the crowd have now left? I doubt it, their leader is in danger and any subordinate worth their weight should be fighting against my compulsion by now.

I wonder if any of them have it in them to get back in. I've only seen it once in my four years and the man that achieved it was a slippery little snake to say the least.

"Eat with me?" Nolan asks as he motions for the woman to keep walking and she makes sure not to look into my eyes while doing so. Does she know what I can do? Has news already spread to below decks?

Of course it has, nothing travels faster than the speed of gossip, but then again, why would she be so shocked to find me here?

"I don't eat," I reply numbly, not even looking at him.

I push the thoughts of this woman aside as I need to figure out what I am going to do. If I can't decide what to think, then how the hell can I kill him? I'm so close to freedom and yet I've never felt so far.

"What?" He looks shocked and I crack a small smile at his question, will this be my last reaction like that?

"I don't need food to live anymore." I sigh and wave a hand in front of me as a dismissive gesture.

He watches this and processes the statement before loading the food from the platter onto his plate quietly and I bite my lip in thought as I try to think of a plan for myself.

"Stay with me anyway. Ask me anything you want, and I'll tell you the truth." He promises and I move to a seat that is placed under the table already, trying not to growl aloud at the fact that he's trying to tell me what to do.

But it's not like I can leave now as where else can I go after something like this?

The woman hurries to leave and I play with the spoon on the table by my placemat. Spinning it around by pressing my index finger to the centre of the curve and moving it in a circle. The motion is childish but it's comforting, and my eyes are glued to it for a good few minutes before anything changes.

"Cami?" Nolan asks, looking at my face with honest eyes and I leave the cutlery alone.

"You were bad before I met you, they say that you were evil," I whisper the last word while knowing it can just as well be applied to me. "Do you deny it?"

He releases a breath and cuts the piece of beef that is on his plate, it's covered in gravy and resembles the meal that Adryan once cooked for me. This doesn't smell as nice though, but I might be biassed, and he dips his meat into the potatoes before facing me again.

"I was." He admits and takes a bite.

He chews it slowly before swallowing and then takes a sip of the champagne that was already set on the table. Some business meeting this must have been if that's what's on the menu and maybe getting a job wouldn't be that bad when things go back to normal.

But I have no plans to go back to normal, do I?

"When I met you, I changed." He faces me again. "I thought I got out, I thought we were going to have a future together." His voice catches but I make no acknowledgement with my face.

Nothing about this is easy and I'd rather keep my cards close to my chest for now.

"After I thought he took you from me, I didn't see the point. A world without you in it was a world that deserved to suffer." The words are bitter as they escape his mouth, and my chest actually warms.

That's the same thought I've had many times over the years, and it makes me feel something to hear him say the same thing. It makes me feel less alone which is what I've needed for so long.

"I know what you mean." I concede and continue to play with the spoon to defuse the emotion I just let slip.

I don't want him to think that it fixes everything because it won't, it just means that we felt something in common and I don't recall ever feeling that between us. We were like chalk and cheese before, and I loved that. He made me see things differently but it's not so terrible to know that we also share something every once in a while.

He breathes heavily when I say this and tries to contain a smile as he takes another bite.

"Why?" I ask again, curiosity getting the better of me. "Why were you like this to begin with?"

To this he only shrugs. "Because I could. My father was the same and power was something that was always on hand, expected even and it wasn't until I was forced to live a life without it that I considered it as even being a possibility".

This I can tell is true from the way his eyes keep flicking up to me from his plate, as if he's waiting for judgement and I wait for it too, but it doesn't come.

For me though, it's different. I have no need for power, it's taken and thrown back the second I have what I want and from there I move on. What is power anyway? With this family it just looks as if power is money. To be able to pay people under you to do bad things and to build an empire off the back of it.

My motivation comes from the curse, as since it took over the anger inside of me has become more intense. It flares up so much more easily now and everything is heightened. Over the past few years, the only emotions I've ever really had were negative and the positive only started to come out when spending time with Adryan.

I wonder if that's why I let him in so quickly?

"Why did you hurt Adryan?" I can't help but ask. It's one of the offences that I know I can't forgive.

"How do you know Adryan?" His brows furrow and I tilt my head, approaching irritation as I see his brother in him again with this response, always asking questions in the worst possible moments.

"Answer the question."

"We were kids, we were fencing with the fire set, and I lunged at him with the poker." I hear him hold his breath and I hate that suspicion rises in me.

"He said you branded him." I hide my clenched fist under the table and the less he knows about my friendship with his brother, the better it might be for him if this ends badly.

"I did it on purpose if that's what you're getting at." He sighs. "He'd have done the same, his was just as hot." His face is remorseful, but I take it with a pinch of salt.

He admitted to doing it on purpose but that was after I pushed him. Then again, I don't really know what I want him to say. He doesn't know how well I know his brother and he could have said a lot less.

I just hate the fact he did it in the first place. Did he mean it when he said that Adryan would have done the same? I mean I can't exactly go and ask him after sending him away like I did.

"I've never laid a hand on him since." He adds, after noting my silence for a few minutes.

"Will that remain the case?"

The Nolan I knew valued his word above all else, and there have been some reports of the Lord of Ashes caring about his honour now and again, despite being an arsehole. Having his guarantee will rest my mind a bit and I probably shouldn't have even mentioned Adryan, but I had to know why.

"You have my word." He places his hand on his chest and I exhale discreetly.

Adryan is safe... Or as safe as he can be.

"You said before that you didn't know if life without power was even a possibility...what do you think about it now?" I hold his gaze this time and he drops the loaded fork to the plate, contemplating his reply.

"I don't know." He confesses. "I don't want to be bad, but at this point, I don't really know how to change."

I feel his response in the sliver of my soul that is remaining. I don't want to be bad either, but with the anger and the urges, sometimes it's hard just to turn it off.

I reach over and take his glass from the coaster. I swirl it around and inhale the scent before emptying the contents down my throat. I wish there was enough alcohol in this room to cause a buzz as I'd down it in an instant, being a perfect piece of distraction.

"You've done it before," I say.

"I had you." His hand is under his chin as he looks at me, the food is forgotten now.

"True." I smile, hoping that he can't see my bobbing knee below the table.

The conversation is so weird, so formal and yet it feels more real than any other we've had before. All of his cards are on the table, and I've never felt this equal towards him.

Before, I'd always wondered what he saw in me but now knowing his past and relating it to my own, the gap between us doesn't seem so far. Even if there are a lot of things still standing between us.

"Could I again?" His voice drops in volume considerably and his fingers shake as they reach for his things to continue eating.

My movement stops as I hear the words and my breathing ceases for a minute while I consider. There is nothing in this world I want more than to go back to how it was with him, to not know his past or future and to be myself again.

But it's different now. Now I know what he's done, and I don't know how I should feel about it.

My history since we parted isn't exactly squeaky clean but at least I've drawn the line at those that deserved it, or at least those I thought deserved it. I've not hurt any kids or innocents, but he has.

The Nolan I knew is a completely different person and I don't know if he even exists anymore. Nothing about this man seems shy or reserved but I suppose he doesn't have any more secrets to keep from me now, it's all out in the open.

"I don't know." I pour more from the bottle of Moet and down the glass without thinking.

"Is it what I've done?" He bites his lip while asking and I can feel the nerves that are radiating off him.

"Yes... No... Maybe," I pause as that response could only have come from my gut and it surprises me as there are a few things that still bother me. "It's who you are... I- I don't know you." I shrug.

I hate letting any of this come out of me. I'm so used to emotions staying inside and I'm avoiding any form of interaction with him that I could class as familiar to stop the pain.

"I'll admit..." He pours himself another drink now and takes a swig. "There's more to me than you knew, but I'm still the same person."

"Are you?" I ask automatically as it's a bold statement to make, especially when it was so long ago that I first knew him.

"Let me prove it." His voice goes low again, his eyes are pleading mine. "A day, give me a day?"

Chapter 26

When I wake in the morning I feel cold. It's meant to be the height of summer, but the air conditioning must be set to high and there are goosebumps all over my skin as I remove the sheet from me.

I half expect to see the cactus on Adryan's desk as confirmation that I crashed at his place again but I'm not there.

The room is large and bright with white walls and huge mirrors reflecting light around. Every detail is coated in silver, and it feels so strange knowing that last night I met Nolan again and this is where he lives and grew up.

Somehow, I can't believe it, even though I am here and am wearing the shirt and shorts he gave me. They smell like him, like French vanilla and tobacco showing me how all of the candles and wax melts are nothing compared to the real thing.

I crawl out of the bed and find my dress crumpled on the floor, pull it over my head and slide on the heels that feel suddenly strange to me now. They're so dark that they look wrong here in a place of light and does that mean I do too?

Looking back Nolan always liked simplicity, he was never cold but if he had his way, we'd have had bare walls and cream carpets as the only decoration in the apartment. I was the one that brought the colour.

I walk over to the balcony and look down to the grounds of green trees and an endless lawn. It's so extravagant that it feels out of place when remembering us in my tiny bedroom most of the time.

We spent most of our money on food, drinks and going out; it didn't seem to matter that we lived in what was essentially a box. Both of our jobs sucked and a lot of the time it felt like we were barely making it by, but neither of us cared as long as we were together.

When we managed to get somewhere of our own, he'd told me that an aunt had died or something and that's how he afforded the deposit for a bigger place. I should have realised how he never mentioned her before or how he got the taste for fine dining in the first place.

The door at the other side of the room opens and Nolan walks in tentatively, eyes going from the bed to where I stand.

His glasses are back, and I can feel my heart in my chest at the sight of them as if they're my old friends. If I turn around and forget where we are, it's almost as if nothing happened, but that would defeat the purpose of the day I've given him.

"Good morning." He smiles as he walks over and kisses my forehead.

He used to always do that, and it would melt me every single time so I cough to hide the jolt that runs through me at his touch as I can't deny that I've missed it.

"Morning." I smile as I turn back out towards the view, as I've not finished taking it all in. It's so beautiful and it's something I'm dying to explore with him if he's willing to show me.

"I've brought you a coffee and the paper." He says in my ear as I'm still distracted by the outside and my thoughts.

I can't help but grin at this like a schoolgirl and turn to him, tucking a loose strand of hair behind my ear. He remembers how I used to always read it over breakfast.

The coffee is warm and milky, and I swallow it down, almost wishing we could both crawl back into bed and lie together like we used to. I used to always have my coffee like this, and I can't remember the last time he made me a cup, as you never think it'll be the last time, so you never savour moments like that.

"Do you want to go for a walk first or have me give you the tour?" He asks after I place down my empty cup.

We're sat on the furniture set on the balcony and I've already handed him the sports section to skim over while I devour the news. Old habits die hard.

I'm not sure how I would have felt if I had been mentioned there on the front page again. All this time I wanted it to be noticed by the Lord of Ashes, but now the idea makes me blush and I'm glad he doesn't notice.

"No breakfast?" I say as I place the paper down on the table, putting the saucer on top so that it doesn't blow away in the breeze.

"I've already eaten, and I remember what you told me." He winks and I smile.

He listened to every detail of my curse before we parted ways last night.

I told him of my strengths and may or may not have failed to mention my weaknesses. I'm still undecided on him as a whole and the more untouchable he thinks I am the better, as far as I'm concerned.

"Let's do the tour first, I like looking at old things and the house looks like it could be too." I smile at him as I always used to tease him for being a couple of years older than me and it feels natural to bring it back.

He only rolls his eyes good-naturedly and offers the crook of his elbow.

I reach for it this time without hesitation, unlike how I declined last night and try to ignore how warm his skin feels underneath the shirt.

There is a lot of staff as we make our way along the corridors, and I have to wonder where his family must have gotten all of this money. Were all of them evil? Was there really a Lordship running in the family or is it a crime title that's self-appointed?

Nobody here dares to make eye contact with me and for that I'm glad. They'll have all seen me in my murderous rage when storming through the door, and it would be smart for them not to forget it, though it must be hard while currently replacing it out front.

He spares no detail when walking me through the house, teaching me the history he never got to share before and shyly hinting at the future I could consider mine for the taking. I don't know what to think when he does it the first time but after the third or fourth, I've mastered my *'That's nice'* expression to hide the inner panic.

So far, he's been my Nolan all morning, but before I make any decisions, I need to see the two together. I need to be able to trust him, which is going to be hard to be honest.

The only person I've trusted since the curse is Adryan, and that's after scaring him to death all the time with threats.

The rooms are all filled with glorious pieces of art, modern details and every inch of it is polished to perfection. What I said before still stands as it's almost like walking through a museum with all the statues and artefacts to the point where it's hard to imagine him and his brother growing up here.

After a quick lunch for the human, we tour the grounds, seeing how each blade of grass is freshly manicured and I can't help but wonder how many gardeners they have here.

Nolan finally works up the courage to grab my hand as we walk this time and I'm almost glad. It feels good, it feels normal almost, but I can't stop thinking about what still bothers me. The questions I still need answers to.

"Your day is almost up." I say as the grandfather clock strikes three, echoing out onto the lawn where we can still hear it a good few hundred yards away.

"How am I doing?" He asks tentatively.

"Nolan exists, but I've yet to meet the other side." I hint towards the Lord of Ashes.

"Ahh him." He exhales.

"I'm struggling with it, I'll be honest. Even though I have a past... I can't get over the kids and innocents thing." I turn to him, feeling the need to lay it out on the table.

"Kids?" He barks at me in shock.

Part of me is dying to reply with '*Are you deaf*' but I don't with the expression on his face, as it's a bit more serious than it usually is when squabbling with Adryan.

"Do you deny it?" I test as unfortunately I bear witness to this unpleasant fact.

"I've never harmed a child a day in my life." He looks at me and then grimaces. "Aside from Adryan, but I was a kid then too."

I sigh, calling all of the day into question now, "I wish you wouldn't lie."

If he can't be honest then we stand no chance.

Not that we really matter in the grand scheme of things, but how can I give up my freedom for someone that does something like that? When my freedom could mean stopping him from doing it all over again in the future because he wouldn't be here.

Fuck, it's starting to get hard imagining him not being here all over again.

"I'm not lying." He practically growls and I return the tone.

"I saw them."

"What? How?" He looks repulsed but he can pull any expression he wants to; it doesn't change what I saw and compelled.

"Abbey Darnley. She tied up a family of four and left them in the attic for dead after you blackmailed them when they tried to escape." I stand with my hands on my hips, daring him to contradict me.

"I've never heard that name in my life." He raises his hands in the air.

"Yeah well I have, starting with the time she held me captive in your father's basement." I snap, knowing he can't deny the ownership of *that*.

"They held you captive?" He almost yells and I hold up my palm to him.

"One issue at a time please, as you've used up most of the day."

He looks well and truly flustered now and I wonder if it's because I've caught him, or if he's really telling the truth.

"Look, you can't expect me to know everything that goes on? The Lord of Ashes is the business more than anything else and when it comes to threats and actual strategy, Hank heads most of that stuff up... I could ask him over but he's dead."

I blush despite my frustration at the mention of Hank. "Yeah, that was me." I confess while I have the chance.

"What?" He yells again and I'm really going to lose my patience soon, Nolan or not, as he never used to raise his voice like this.

"He was a dick and I needed information on your whereabouts." I dismiss it with a wave of my hand, and he narrows his eyes.

"Why did you need to know my whereabouts?"

I realise that it makes sense for him to ask that, I have failed to mention the cure so far as either he'll use it to trick me, or it'll make him feel guilty and I hate the thought of either option.

"I was avenging the family... you know, the one you claim to know nothing about?"

It's not exactly a lie, it was on my list of reasons to hunt him down and I want him to focus on answering me. I can't understand how he wouldn't know about it, and I can't breathe thinking that he's responsible.

"I had no idea about that." He repeats.

"Are you telling me you've never willingly harmed an innocent?" A guilty feeling lands in my stomach as I call the ice to my eyes, but I can't help it though, I need to know.

If he's lying, then I can't go on with it. I get the whole 'the world deserves to suffer' thing when grieving but this is the big difference between us, I have a temper, I know I do, but I like to think I'm fair.

"Never." He says and there's a look of hurt on his face when he is released from my stare which almost breaks my heart. He was telling the truth and not only did I not believe him, I compelled him.

"I'm sorry." My hands go to my hair in disgust with myself.

I honestly thought the answer would be yes. He's the Lord of Ashes, how could he not harm innocents? He's not pure. I can see that he's not, but neither am I.

"I wish you didn't have to do that, but I understand why you did." His voice is shaky and I'm so angry with myself. I believed the absolute worst about him, and I was wrong, and then I compelled him on top of it!

"I'm so sorry." I repeat, reaching out for his hand and pulling away as how can I force my contact on him after what I just did?

"I understand." He tries to soothe me and grabs my hand with his anyway, running his other over the back of mine like he used to when I got upset in the past.

"How? It was a complete breach of privacy; I can't believe I did that." I feel my lips trembling and he pulls me in for an embrace that feels completely alien to me in this body.

"Do you believe me? Is it enough to forgive me?" He says as his chin rests on the top of my head.

I can't believe he's saying that to me, as if what he's said is true, which it must be, he's never harmed an innocent on purpose, he really did think I was dead, and he's vowed never to hurt Adryan.

How can I hold anything else against him after that? Haven't I done just as bad? Haven't I just crossed a line that should result in him turning me out?

"Yes." I breathe against him, and he squeezes my shoulders.

"Would you mind if I ask that you not do that again?... It felt weird." He sounds nervous when saying it, which hurts like a knife in the gut, but I deserve it.

"I won't." I promise.

Chapter 27

The stars are out as the twilight fades away into the night and Nolan has requested his staff prepare a picnic for us to enjoy out on the terrace. I mean, I say picnic when really, it's a few bottles of champagne and some nibbles that he can pick at while we sit and talk.

It's the most extravagant date we've ever had, but when considering the previous budget, we didn't do too badly before. I wanted to meet the occasion and I actually accepted when he offered me a change of clothes for the night, even if it did sound a bit over the top for just going outside.

When I walked into my room, I found three custom-made gowns waiting for me and I don't know how he managed it, considering I stormed in here yesterday evening.

Each one is perfectly sized and coloured to match my body and complexion to the point where there's not a chance that this would have fitted the old me, which leaves me to conclude that they are recent orders.

I bit through my lip a good few times when trying to decide between the dark blue dress made up of velvet that comes with a slit up the thigh or the blood-red number that came draped over its own mannequin and I swear that it could have stood up on its own.

But in the end, I surprise both myself and the woman allocated to help me get ready, by choosing neither of them, opting for the nude slip dress made of the smoothest silk that I've ever felt before. It is clinging to me like a second skin and despite having the sewing kit on hand, the woman is needed for nothing but to curl the back of my hair for me.

It's the brightest thing that I have worn in weeks, and it feels strange to look down and not see black materials covering me up anymore. Strange, but good. As I tie my hair out of my face, I can almost pretend that I am me again. Cami.

The peach-coloured heels that I wear are covered by the trail of fabric following behind me and I hold it up in my left arm as I descend down the stairs to meet him once dressed.

When I see him for the first time since changing, I notice that he's wearing a grey tartan suit now and just finding him there, waiting down at the bottom for me almost takes my breath away.

This feels scarily like a dream, and I pinch my nails right through my skin to see if I can summon enough pain to wake me up from it, but I don't, and instead, I take Nolan's hand as he walks me out into the night.

The staff have done a beautiful job, as there to greet us, are Edison bulbs hanging from the orangery roof top and wooden beams dotted around us. On top of this, the centrepiece of our table is covered in other little fairy lights to illuminate the scene further.

Nolan pulls out my chair for me which makes my heart beat faster than it should and then pours me a drink before sitting himself down. There is no one else around, just us and I can't help thinking that this is how it always should have been.

All of my worries and concerns have an answer and rather than listening into them battling through my mind, I zone it out and concentrate on the intricate details of my glass.

"Did you like them?" Nolan breaks the silence and nods towards the dress that I am wearing.

"They're beautiful. I just don't know how you managed it." I beam at him while running a hand over the material and feeling the softness of it once more.

"I ordered them the second you left the hall last night and had Marleen adjust them throughout the day as best she could." He explains.

Marleen is the woman who waited on me earlier I assume, though she refused to speak when I was there and I wasn't that concerned with changing that fact. Nolan is the only person I really feel the urge to talk to at the moment, for obvious reasons.

"They fit like a glove." I comment to commend him on his thoughtfulness.

"I can see that." He bites his lip, and I can feel his eyes roaming over my body.

For the second time today, I feel goosebumps appear across my skin and it's obvious enough for him to offer his jacket which is a sweet gesture. It's something I know that he would have done before all of this happened.

"What have you been doing with your time then, aside from the obvious?" He asks after I refuse it and he takes a bite from a cracker that is covered in caviar.

Personally, I've never really been a fan of caviar as the idea of eating fish eggs doesn't sit very well with me, and I'm not tempted to try anything on his plate right now.

Aside from the food I don't like, there's no point in pretending to be something that I'm not as he's fully accepted that I don't need food to live anymore, to the point where it's strange not having the constant pressure to order something.

"I go to the library, visit coffee shops and still love to people watch." I move my finger around the edge of the glass, listening to the sound humming through. "What about you? Aside from the obvious." I smile up at him shyly.

The Nolan I knew would love to attend the theatre where he could afford it, he'd frequent museums and even try writing from time to time. Now that I see that the lifestyle is vastly different from before, I wonder how different his interests have gotten.

"Unfortunately, I can't go out in public as much as I used to, I've recently started to shoot, and you've seen the library we have upstairs... Take what you want by the way, what's mine is yours." He takes a sip of his own drink, but his glowing eyes don't leave mine for a second.

"You might come to regret that," I smirk at him, remembering that our tastes weren't actually that different when it came to literature. Probably because we both liked classics and once you get into them, you can handle any theme.

"You're welcome to try." He laughs and tries a mini sandwich that looks to be filled with cheese and pickles, topped with brioche.

"No writing?" I ask.

I used to love reading his novellas. The suspense was perfect every time and I could never understand how he was able to plan so meticulously but I suppose it makes more sense now, given his day job.

"No writing." He sighs. "I've not had the time and I've not had my muse." He winks and I roll my eyes.

"Cheeseball."

He's laying it on thick tonight, but it feels good and after being alone for so long, I'll take anything he can give me at this point.

"Do you have a job? Where are you staying these days?" He asks casually and I think of Elizabeth's apartment currently sitting dormant.

"No job, I flit from place to place and crash where I can." I cross my legs and lean towards him while lying. I don't know why, but I'd rather he not know about my apartment.

Adryan could be there and while he's given his word to never hurt him, I think I'd prefer for Adryan to stay far away from the family business. They must have a lot of enemies if Nolan has had to give up his interests and I'd rather they remain in the dark about his brother.

They could use it against him, against me.

"Will you consider staying with me from now on?" He asks me and I don't know why I didn't see that one coming to be honest.

"I don't kn-"

He cuts in with, "I want you to." Which makes me laugh.

"I suppose it would be nice to make up for lost time." I confess and there is a flush of red raising to my cheeks from the admission. It's going to take some getting used to, this sweet talk malarky.

Nolan only chuckles. "There's no need to play it coy with me, I'll beg you if I have to." He reaches out for my hand and there's an electric pulse jolting through it at the contact. I could get used to this very easily.

"I'll stay," I promise, and I can't hold back the smile that breaks onto my face.

"We'll have to move on soon, but I'll make it worth your while." He grins and I scrunch my brows in question. Why would we have to move on? I can't think of any reason.

This place is huge and beautiful. Being so close to the city is a major convenience but without all of the congestion and loud noises to the point where I can't think of somewhere more perfect for us.

"Why?" I ask, the curiosity obvious in my voice.

"Well I'm not the most liked person in the world, remember? And it's part of the security protocol we have in place." He shrugs and takes another bite of a cracker.

"Who could possibly harm you here?" I laugh and it's his turn for the questioning gaze.

"You do remember smashing my front door, right?" His eyebrows are raised, and I pull a sheepish expression at the realisation.

I don't know whether to be proud or embarrassed about this anymore, but he knows what I am.

"That was me, I'm different... plus it's not like anyone can hurt you when I'm around." I run my free hand up his arm in reassurance and his eyes light slightly.

"You'd protect me?" He asks, as if not quite believing what I said.

"Of course I would. It'll be a welcome surprise to a new life of peace and quiet." I stick my tongue out and he lifts my hand to kiss the back of my palm.

"Thank you." He's serious when he says it and I brush him off as how could he imagine otherwise?

"I'm hoping you'll be less of a target now anyway..." I approach tentatively after a brief pause.

I've been meaning to find a way to bring this into the conversation organically, and what better moment than the present?

"What do you mean?" He asks without looking up from his glass, filling it again and then doing the same with mine. I don't know why but I suddenly feel shy.

"Well, now that we're here and we're together." I stumble slightly on the word. "The world doesn't need to suffer anymore and maybe you could, you know... behave again." I grind my teeth to keep my face neutral.

"I see." He looks at me and shifts in his chair nervously just like he did last night.

My pulse rises slightly at this response, and I start to wonder if his answer will make a difference to the happiness I have started to feel. Would I be able to stand by if he stuck with the Lord of Ashes title? I don't think so.

"Is that a problem?" I ask,

"Not a problem, just-" He takes a sip. "I need some time. I can't get everything on the books overnight."

"I get that," I reply, and I do.

I can't expect him to snap his fingers and be a model citizen. Just like I can't snap my fingers and ignore the anger that still bubbles in me from time to time.

But we can try together, right?

"Thank you." He smiles. "Give me a month? A month and then maybe you can respect me again." He jokes half-heartedly and I shake my head.

"I do respect you, Nolan, I know what it was like. We just have a reason to try harder now." I look at him seriously while I speak.

His fingers loop through mine in response and I squeeze gently, very aware of my strength compared to his. The last thing I want to do is break anything and it's odd to think of him as delicate in comparison.

"I like hearing you say that again." He says finally.

I stare at his fingers, taking pictures of the moment in my mind while studying the little details of him. The backs of his hands are so soft but there is the occasional scar that surfaces, and I wonder who did them.

"Say what?" I lift my gaze from our hands to his face, remembering his words.

"We." He whispers and leans in. "Cami?"

"Yeah?"

"Can I kiss you again?"

Chapter 28

He does kiss me, and I could cry from the relief I feel from the moment our lips meet again for the first time. The softness of his movement and the smell of his breath is like heaven, and I lean into him so much that without his arms wrapped around me, I'd have fallen from my seat.

When he touches me all of the air leaves my body and my heart thumps against my chest hard, screaming for more, for him. I don't think I'll ever forget this moment; how the lights twinkle around us, how the crickets are chirping in the background or the feeling of finally being back by his side.

I don't know how long we pass like this, but after a while, he breaks away and rises to stand. I wasn't expecting the interruption and I look up at him with round eyes, wondering what he could possibly be thinking before he holds out a hand to me.

I take it without a second thought, and he pulls me to my feet. before I can even think he swoops me into his arms and it's like we're in a silly little fairy tale. I've never related to the princess in those stories up until now, and it feels good to find my prince.

He carries me back into the house and makes our way up the stairs, I don't even care that I can walk on my own or that he's drank a full bottle to himself, I've just missed this feeling.

I can still taste him on my lips and my body is awake with the awareness of being pressed against his chest. This was once my happy place; my greatest comfort and it feels divine to be back again.

There is a click of a door before he sets me down on a bed and I don't need to look around to know that we're now in his bedroom, our bedroom. I don't even recall half of the journey up the stairs, I only know that his eyes never left mine and that I felt weightless in his arms.

The sheets are soft under my skin and the room is dark. Every inch of me is aware of him standing there and I'm dying to kiss him again, to feel him, to reassure myself that he's still there and not an illusion.

How many times have I dreamt of this? How many times have I imagined running back into his arms and finally feeling his body pressed against mine? Now it's real and I need him.

Everything is so different, and I hold my breath, thinking about how this must seem to him now.

My hair, my breasts, my skin, even my eyes have changed, never mind the brand now hidden beneath the fabric and I wonder if he'll miss my old looks like I do, if he'll care that I'm not the same anymore. He used to love my freckles and that's why I've always been so upset that they're gone. Before I met him, I was always so insecure about them, but he has a way of making it all better.

I glance over myself before making eye contact again, all to find him looking down at me like a hunter does its prey. But I'd gladly get caught up in his clutches right now.

"You're so beautiful." He whispers in my ear as he tucks a lock of hair behind it.

"You don't mind... How I am?" I ask hesitantly and he shakes his head rapidly, holding my face between his hands as he looks into my eyes.

"Never, you're perfect. Everything about you is so perfect, how could I mind?" His eyes search every surface and the way he's biting his lip has me feeling human again. This is almost just like it was.

His lips find mine and a sound somewhere between a sigh and a moan escapes me.

My hands move to his dark hair, and I can feel the thick rim of his glasses press against my cheeks. It's a feeling that was once so familiar and one that I'll never forget.

He pulls me closer to him as the kissing intensifies and the sensation is like ecstasy while his fingers trail up and down the skin of my legs. The fabric from the bottom of my dress is bundled up towards my thighs and I haven't noticed this up until now. When did he manage that?

Gasping for breath he pulls away after a minute or two and looks at the silk that's still separating him from my skin.

"May I?" He asks gruffly and I nod shyly.

His hands go to the material, and he lifts it over my head in one swift movement. I giggle at the sigh of contentment that he makes as he looks me over. When was the last time I giggled? Probably four years ago.

He's the first person to see this body naked and I almost feel the urge to cover myself.

"Perfect." He repeats as he leans down to kiss me again and I swear it's like all of my broken pieces are welding back together just from his touch.

My hands reach for his shirt. An expensive-looking cotton but he's so eager that he rips it in two for fear of waiting a second longer to feel my body on his. The contact is just what I needed, and my breath leaves my body in a low sigh.

"I've missed you. Every day I've missed you." He murmurs against my skin as he kisses his way along my collarbone.

I feel so bare lying here beneath him like this and my hands trail their way down to his belt. His skin is warm and smooth against my fingertips which makes me want to have him all the more.

A small yelp of surprise escapes me as his teeth graze the underside of my nipple. The feeling rockets straight down to my core and I can feel the dampness pooling there in an automatic reaction.

Nobody has touched me like this in so long and I ache for him, I need him.

"Where do you want me to touch you Cami?" He says against my brand as he sucks and licks his way back toward my mouth, not even commenting on the hideous mark left behind because of my curse.

I know the answer before he even asks me. I want him to touch me *there*, where even I have dared not to go since the last time we were together for fear of spoiling what was once his.

He's removing his trousers as he goes, and I grab his hand in a desperate motion to press it against my sex. There's only underwear separating us now and a moan escapes my mouth as he pushes them to the side to rub his thumb along my centre.

How could I have lasted so long without feeling like this? How have I survived all of these years without him? I could cry from the release threatening to break free from that motion alone.

"You want me to touch you here?" His mouth is against my ear, and it sends shivers down my spine.

"Please." I beg, and he chuckles. Lowering his head back down to my neck.

He nibbles at the part of my neck located between my ear and collar while he plays with me using his fingers. It takes all I have not to writhe under him and it's too much. It's too much but I can't possibly get enough.

My last barrier is removed in one swift tug and along with it goes his boxers, springing him free and I bite my lip at the sight of him so hard that I can taste metal on my tongue.

His thumb continues its movements as he circles the bundle of nerves between my thighs, and the tension building in me is so tight that I swear I could snap in two at any moment now.

"Have you missed me, Cami?" He asks and I cry out a *yes* in return as I get closer.

He slows his movements, torturing me with his delicate touch that fuels a fire across my body. His fingers are barely on me and yet I feel him so much. Every motion sends a wave of pleasure down and the noise that leaves my mouth as I climax can't possibly be human.

"Show me." He lifts me up gently towards him so that we are facing each other. "Show me how much you've missed me." He says through his teeth, unable to stifle a moan of anticipation as I lick my lips at the sight of him waiting for me.

The size and girth are even more than I remember, and I bend down to wrap my mouth around him.

The taste of him takes me home.

Lying in a king-sized bed beside Nolan with nothing on but a smile feels too good to be true.

A steady pulse of pleasure continues to echo throughout my veins, and I can't stop looking at him through my lashes as I lie with my head and arms on his chest comfortably.

"I've missed this." I break the silence and his chocolate eyes lock onto mine.

"I've missed you." He moves to sit up and places a gentle kiss on the tip of my nose as he always did.

"Was it always like this? It can't have been." I move my fingers in circles, grazing through the patch of hair on his chest.

"Trust me Cami, if it was up to me, we'd have never left the bedroom." He winks and I giggle again for the second time in years.

"It's not a bad idea, Ambrose," I smirk up at him. "I'm sure your staff can bring up any supplies you need."

His breathing catches. "How do you know my last name?"

I realise that I've not said that in front of him yet and it takes a second to force myself to understand all over again why he lied about his name in the first place.

He had to; I know that now.

"I know about Adryan, remember?" I remind him and a rush of guilt hits me like a train when mentioning him out loud.

I bet he hates me since I sent him away to protect him, but I suppose that isn't even needed now, Nolan gave me his word and he's never hurt an innocent since they were children, right?

"Were you mad when you found out?" Nolan's voice is gentle, and I move higher up the bed to kiss him again.

"I understand now," I reassure him, and I hear his raised heartbeat dilute slightly.

"How do you know Adryan then?" He asks and I can tell from the tone that he's been wanting to for some time now.

After what we have just done, I'd rather not be talking about his brother, but I can tell that it would be pushed further if I brush it off while he's so curious.

"I don't really." I lie instinctively and I don't know why but it bothers me that this is my gut reaction as it shouldn't be like that.

"He was there when Abbey held me in the basement, and I saw the similarities straight away. Once I realised that the name meant the same thing, it didn't take long for me to be able to put two and two together and compel him to find out more."

I hate how easy it is to do this, to lie to him and make it believable. Why can't I just tell him?

Do I feel guilty for getting close to another person when I could have been searching for him all this time? Should I have been mourning him and not making friends? Maybe if it wasn't his brother, it wouldn't be so hard to admit.

"If you hadn't killed her already, I'd have had her head on a spike before breakfast." He growls angrily.

My face heats at his words and I swear a part of my heart melts for him. I'm so used to looking out for myself and I don't think anyone's been able to protect me before.

The only ones that ever seemed to have cared are him... and Adryan.

Chapter 29

It has been a week since that night on the terrace with Nolan and *over* a week since I sent my only friend away from me, serving the freshly made bond with good intentions, not that he'll care. It's flown by and when I realised the date it felt like a joke played on me for a second or two.

I've not left the estate this whole time and each day is like another test of reality. I wake up next to him each morning with a shock and I find myself reaching for him during the night, all to make sure it's not just a figment of my imagination.

My dreams are filled with scenarios to explain it all away and the first few seconds of each morning are needed to bat away the various cries of paranoia deep in my mind. It's like I can't accept that something good is finally happening to me.

It's probably because being with Nolan again is more than I ever dared to hope for, I mean, I crave his touch like an addict does with their chosen drug. So much so that you'd think it was unhealthy.

The first few days were like learning to walk all over again but we've found a routine quite quickly which is helpful and each day he brings me a coffee (now iced) with a copy of the latest newspaper. We wake ourselves up together on the balcony and enjoy feeling the breeze on our faces which is always a welcome feeling against the flush of our cheeks.

After that we tend to walk along the green hand in hand, exploring our new home and making plans for the future. Sometimes he brings a shotgun with him as well to show off his skills and other days he brings a book so that we can lie somewhere while I ask him to read out loud.

Usually, he works from noon up until 4:00pm and then we can spend our evening sipping champagne and making up for lost time. I can't imagine how many bottles we have gotten through due to my high tolerance, but he doesn't seem bothered in the slightest.

The dining room we spend most of our time in is huge and yet it's always just the two of us crammed into one side of it, to the point where a cupboard under the stairs would probably do us just as well. I've found that talking nonstop is never a challenge and he's desperate to know everything there is to know about me.

Any detail I gloss over is a detail he wanted to hear the most and any second that we have spent apart is a second that he promises to make up for.

After the first few days, I realised how useless it was to try to sugarcoat it all, so I stopped. For some unknown reason, he thrives on it, and I don't know why I can't do that for him too, but I can't as I don't want to know what he's done.

Ever since the first night, everything that I wear now is new and fitted to perfection. It's something that he insisted on as a 'matter of pride' and it's 'his way of looking after me' as he likes to put it, which is something I'm getting used to.

I'm not used to being fussed over.

A whole new wardrobe has been bought and prepared for me here and I swear it'll take weeks for me to be able to try each of these. The skirts are floaty, the trousers are tight, and I've never felt so sexy and wanted in my whole entire life.

As if that wasn't enough, he keeps spoiling me with gifts and even I, the material girl, am in awe of it all. No expense appears to have been spared and it's a side to him I've never seen before. I don't know which version of him this originates from, Nolan or the Lord of Ashes, and somehow it seems rude to try and find out the answer.

My windows are filled high with roses, lilies and sunflowers and I never thought I would say the words 'too many plants' but I had to put a stop to it all after a few days because I was starting to lose the room for it.

He promises to build me a greenhouse soon so that I never have to utter the phrase again and it's strange to think that he cares so much about what I like. It makes me feel useless in comparison, as all that I can give him is my love and protection. He could get that from a dog.

I've realised this morning that the only colour I haven't really seen since my original clothes were taken away, is black. Nothing here is very dark and I find myself missing it at times. Even my nails are now a cute shade of baby pink from the stylist he brought in for me, and it's almost as if the monster inside of me has vanished. I just wish she could leave completely without the cure.

Nolan loves her though.

He loves her body, her skills and her history. I never expected anyone to feel that way about me, never mind the sweet man I used to know. But to be fair to the facts, he's different now too.

He's sharper and more alert. Through the walls I can hear his voice when conducting business and I've never heard it sound so assertive and strong. He's respected here and it's not just me that they are all scared of.

I find it hard to imagine that he could hurt anyone when he's next to me, but when hearing him in there, it's not so unrealistic. I've mentioned before how I'm good at spotting a bad voice, and he can put on a pretty good impression of it when he wants.

I need to keep reminding myself that he's not just my Nolan anymore, he's also the Lord of Ashes and I have a mental countdown on the go, waiting for the month to be up and for him to put a stop to it all.

While I wait for him as he works it's hard sometimes to keep busy, and I've been downstairs in the kitchens today while Nolan left on business. I had to force them to speak to me with the ice in my eyes because they were all so afraid and all I could feel around me was anxiety.

It was suffocating but it felt too intrusive to ask them why, plus it was kind of obvious when I remembered that they'll have seen the remnants of the front door I caved in. I don't really know what it would take for them to get used to my being around, but I'll file that one under future Cami's problems.

I'm in my happy place for now and the hard tasks can wait till later.

The reason I went down there is because I asked them to prepare the truffle pasta I had tried a few weeks ago. I've not been able to stop thinking about it and I know that Nolan will love that kind of food. I'm also conscious that I've not eaten since I've been here and it would be a nice treat for myself as while I don't need it, I miss it and I think it was silly to stop altogether. Just because I don't have to eat doesn't mean I shouldn't, especially if it's something I enjoy.

Today, I'm dressed in a long pink dress that hugs my breasts and hips but floats down past my legs like a waterfall of clouds. My hair is down and loose and I've even taken the time to curl it in the mirror to get it just right. Marleen hasn't really been needed, the idea of being dressed by someone else feels weird to me and I'm happy to go on as normal.

The shoes I have on are gold wedges, the sort of heels you'd expect a Barbie doll to wear. I stare at myself in one of the bedroom mirrors before making my way downstairs. He seems to like me better in brighter colours and I'm not ashamed to admit that I dress more for him now.

I've had to start stocking up on toiletries and I realised that I have no real use for makeup anymore, but I asked for it anyway. I have used the brown eyeliner bought for me to dot back on the freckles I miss so badly and I'm half tempted to ask Nolan to order thicker concealer for me to cover the brand on my chest but I'm too embarrassed. He makes no secret of the fact that he loves every part of me, and I know that he'll hate to think that I'm hiding away from it.

He keeps calling my curse, *my gift* in a serious way and it's the only time he really pisses me off.

It's not a gift, it's a burden and I suppose with him not knowing the catch, he won't see it that way. I was almost tempted to tell him about it to get him to stop, but with the way he's been acting, I just know that he'll feel horrible. He'd hate to stand between me and something I want.

I tread my way downstairs lightly and I can hear that there's a meeting going on inside the hall. I've not attended any of them yet and it seems that neither myself nor Nolan feels inclined to change that fact, since that side of the business will be over soon anyway.

The voices quiet down and I can clearly hear Nolan's pitch as he holds the attention of those around him. I didn't intend to at first as it seems like a breach of privacy, but I can't help it as my feet take me silently over to the door to listen in.

It resonates with me quite quickly how different his leading voice is from his brothers. Adryan tends to radiate power when he speaks, while Nolan evokes fear without even trying it seems.

The silence is deafening and I half wonder if they're all about to walk out and catch me here before he starts again, and I hold my breath so as not to distort it.

"The guard is dead, and Michah can take his place." He booms.

This causes a murmur of conversation now radiating against the wooden frame of the door and I can't help but wonder who they are talking about. Why kill just a guard? Isn't he supposed to be reducing these things down?

I didn't really want to know what he's been up to, but at the same time, the ignorance is killing me. I can't sleep sometimes thinking about what could be happening somewhere out there, thinking of what sort of actions he has ordered that will darken his soul further. It's pitch black already and a large part of me still feels responsible for it all, given the fact that I brought him back.

Nolan clears his throat to speak again, "He's given me the location and they made the drop last night. They both were there and they're now in the townhouse until I give further instruction."

The voices call out once again in reply and there are theories forming in my mind that makes my blood run cold. No... I'm being silly.

Why on earth would James come to mind when he says that? There are hundreds, if not thousands of guards under his employ and it could even be an outsider. I need to get a grip.

I'm about to walk away, shaking my head and cursing myself for questioning his intentions before he speaks again and my ear presses to the door automatically.

"Yes, he caved in the end. I'm going to see if I can push him further before we cut him loose. The more information about the cure, the better."

Chapter 30

Does he mean *my* cure?

My heart is thumping, and I bolt up the stairs and into our room before the door opens and the crowd can make their way into the hallway. It's so frantic that a part of me wonders if they can hear it from down there.

The words I heard prove nothing, it could mean anything at all. Nolan probably kills guards all the time, a disgusting fact but true and what does a cure prove? Someone could be poisoned, could be ill and need treatment is all.

But I can't convince myself. If he promised, why didn't I tell him about my friendship with Adryan? Why couldn't I trust him with that information? It fits too well to ignore it completely but how could I ask him about it without insulting him?

I've done this twice now, I've thought the worst, compelled him and been proven wrong. How can I possibly do this again? Especially after saying I wouldn't.

I can't, that's how. It's a coincidence and I'm relating what parts were said to what little things I know. I'm being unfair to him and I'm wrong.

But what if I'm right?

That would mean he's going to cut Adryan loose. Loose! That's what he meant, wasn't it? The location is the bakery and the two they are holding could be Adryan and David.

He could be going to kill Adryan. My friend, my Adryan whom I was meant to protect.

I pace the floor, running my hands through my hair and I hear Nolan's voice call up to me from the bottom of the stairs, so I breathe in deeply.

I take my time walking down the stairs and I swallow hard when my eyes meet his face. That beautiful face that I've loved for years, and I can't be right. I can't.

"Something you want to tell me?" He raises one eyebrow.

"No?" I question, finding the muscles in my face needed to appear aloof.

"Really? Because something on the table smells incredible and I sure as hell didn't order it." He smiles and presses his hand against the small of my back as he escorts me into the dining room but suddenly, I don't want to be alone with him.

I want someone there, a witness. Someone to give me the strength and the courage to ask what I want to know.

"I'm having some too." I try to sound cheerful before grinding my teeth back together. The pressure on my jaw gives me something to focus on and I almost wish I could feel the pain.

"Why?" He laughs as he takes his usual seat at the head of the table, and I take mine to his left.

He pulls my chair closer to him along with my placemat and I flush, forgetting for a second what I'm focused on. "It's delicious, why not?"

"Because you don't need to." He reminds me like I'm being silly, and it annoys me slightly as just because I don't need to, doesn't mean I can't.

"What did you do today?" I ask casually, ignoring his comment and placing a parcel on my tongue. It's just as good as I remember but with all these thoughts, I can't enjoy it.

"Do you not find it weird to eat?" He looks at me and I don't reply, I only place another into my mouth.

I don't want to talk about my eating habits. I want to talk about what he did and calm my screaming mind already.

"I went to check on some business. What about you, did you read the book I bought?" His fingers trace up the length of my arm and goosebumps rise in place.

How long have I craved this? Surely this touch can't have done what I think he has.

"Hmmm." I sigh. "Yes, I read it this morning while you were gone."

I hate that that's a lie. I don't read romance anymore and I didn't have the heart to tell him that when he bought me a clothbound copy of my old favourite. It's the thought that counts and I can't believe he remembered after all this time. I could have cried.

Nolan takes a bite now and I use this as my opening.

"Have you spoken with Adryan recently?" My face is blank, and I don't like that this act starts to feel familiar. Like I'm pretending again, hunting again.

But maybe if he answers this, I can drop it and relax?

Then again, what if he thinks that it's weird that I've asked? As far as he knows we aren't even friends and he's just a man I compelled to find him. Sweat starts to build on the back of my neck but he doesn't look suspicious which helps.

"No, we aren't close Cami. I know it's weird for you to imagine, being an only child and all, but we've never really spoken since my father died." He pats the back of my hand and I nod.

Since he killed his father, is what I think to myself automatically, but I ignore it. He's given me an out with the only child thing and I could leave it there, I could believe him and drop it forever.

A woman enters through a serving door, and I can see her trembling from here. She's carrying a bottle of Dom Perignon and looking anywhere but in our direction and this bothers me. I'm sick of being feared here and there's nothing either of us has done to the staff to cause concern.

I was fine with being feared before but if this is meant to be my home it should be different, I should be different.

So, I summon the ice to my eyes and call over to her as she turns to walk away. "Pour me a glass, please?"

I hand her mine with an outstretched hand and with the compulsion, her hands no longer shake as she takes it from me.

"And his." I point to Nolan's glass, and she obeys.

"Cami, you don't need your powers to ask that." Nolan chuckles and I smile.

"I want her to feel more relaxed around us, we're good people now Nolan." I remind him and he merely shrugs, though I'd have preferred it if he said more. Agreed with me even.

"I'd like to add to mine, can you bring me some peach juice please?" I direct my icy gaze to her again because I would like a Bellini tonight, I miss them.

"You can't be serious?" Nolan asks as she leaves, and I turn to him.

The brown eyes staring at me are nothing like his brothers, but the expression is. The disgust.

It shocks me, Nolan has never looked at me that way, but Adryan has. I remember it from the day I met him and it's like a bucket of ice water being poured down my back.

But it serves well as a cruel reminder of what I have not dared to ask.

"Where is Adryan?" I blurt out, unable to contain it any longer.

"In my townhouse." His glazed eyes widen.

The ice hadn't left my eyes yet and I can't believe that I have just compelled him by accident.

I've just made him confess my worst fear, that I was right but why the hell is Adryan in his townhouse?

"What have you done to him?" I ask as I tunnel directly into his face.

"I've taken him hostage and tortured him." This time his eyes don't widen, and I hold him there, trying to process his words.

My ears are ringing and for a second, I actually think that I've just heard him wrong.

"Why?" I whisper. Unable to speak any louder.

"He wanted to take my power. I couldn't let him live." The compelled Nolan still finds a way to laugh through it and I stifle down a snarl.

"You promised. Why did you lie?" My breathing is increasing rapidly, and I throw the bottle of champagne across the room as a way to release the anger.

"Which time?"

I bite my lip in frustration and can taste the tangy metal of blood against my tongue. Which time? What does that mean? He's been lying to me regularly?

"When did you not lie?" I almost yell, holding my breath now and aware of each one he takes.

"I've always lied."

The zombie-like person in front of me has no tone and no expression while within a matter of seconds, the few pieces of food I've taken down threaten to resurface to the tabletop.

"When we were first together were you lying? Why?" My voice shakes and there's no point controlling it right now, please tell me this isn't true. Please. Please. Please.

"Yes. I wanted a cover, and you wanted love."

Somehow, hearing it from him like this hurts more than if he was to say it with venom. There's no angle, no malice, just truth and it cuts through me to my core.

"Did you love me? Did you even like me?" I snap, pacing up and down next to the table, willing my heart to slow or there's a good chance it will crash out from my chest.

Even on the worst day, I didn't imagine it would be this bad. I thought that he abandoned me and was evil. I considered him lying about his feelings, but I never believed it, I couldn't believe it and now there's this.

"I liked fucking you."

He might as well have slapped me across the face. That's all he can say, after all I've done and gone through for him. After all I felt, that is his honest answer.

"Why lie now?"

I'm going to let him answer and then I'm going to bring him back, let him watch what I'm about to do to him. Let him feel what he's about to feel.

"Your powers, they'd be useful. I wanted to use them until I found out about the cure, and then I needed you to want me alive." He blinks at me, as if he's telling me it's raining.

I'd be useful? He needed me to want him alive? Are you fucking kidding me?

"Say only the truth to me," I growl, and I let the ice drop.

I watch as his face returns back into his power and his jaw falls open, trembling in fear.

"Cami..." He whispers, instantly holding his hands up in front of him and pushes his chair back, scraping against the wooden flooring.

"Nolan." My voice is cold, unforgiving.

"Tell me where Adryan and David are... before I kill you," I emphasise the last part and I hear his heart throb.

Good. I want to hear it before I rip that fucker out of its cavity, like he's just done to mine.

"They're at my townhouse, 21 Park Lane on 5th." He says through his hands that are clamped over his mouth, like that will make any difference.

"Any last words?" I ask sweetly, enjoying the sweat that's beading from his forehead.

To think I was worried about offending him a few minutes ago, to think I was sweating over this man. I can't believe it; I can't even let it hurt because I simply can't believe it yet.

How could this happen to me? How could I be so stupid as to believe him, to ask such vague questions before and have the idiocy to feel bad about it and believe him blindly?

Human me fair enough, but now? After all the evil I have seen and been, how could I not see this for what it was?

"You can't kill me." He stutters, holding the chair out and I'll be honest, I never took Nolan for a coward.

"And why not, pray tell?" I tilt my head at him, waiting for his reply.

He hesitates and I perch against the table, inspecting my nails before ripping them off, one by one. The pink isn't me, none of this shit is me and I shouldn't have been so foolish.

"Without your curse, you can't save them." He gets out desperately, still not calm enough to lower the chair.

"Calling it a curse now I see, what happened to my gift?" I mock through my teeth.

"It was a gift until I realised the cure." He spits out and I throw a glass at his head and watch it shatter off him and onto the ground.

He's bleeding along his cheekbone but it's not enough, I want more. I want justice.

He drops the chair, more confident now. "You can't kill me." He repeats and before I can rip off his head, I realise that the bastard is right.

My mind goes a thousand miles an hour, considering the different possibilities and I can't think of anything I like the sound of. I can't think of anything that will let me win.

If I kill him now, I have no power and I won't be able to help David and Adryan.

If I leave him here, he can escape on some bullshit technicality.

I could compel him to kill himself, but then there's the risk that it won't cure me if I don't give the final blow, and then I'm stuck forever.

He has me beat and he knows it so he's standing taller now, the colour is returning to his complexion, and I focus on the cut on his cheek to calm me down.

And finally, the solution comes to me a second later, if I can't just go ahead and kill him, I'm just going to have to hurt him.

Badly.

Chapter 31

As I run down the road, faster than any car could ever go, I can't help but wonder if I should be grateful for my sins, for the information it has given me to know that Nolan won't survive the night.

I left him on the floor like the pathetic mess he was when I was done with him, and my only regret is that I won't get to watch him die. I picture it as I go as a sort of comfort. The way his lids might close at long last and how that miserable heart will finally stop beating.

Time is of the essence now and if someone manages to get to a phone and warn the townhouse, they could get to Adryan before me even though I made sure to smash every mobile, landline and computer that I could find. But I'm taking no chances and every single soul was compelled not to contact help.

Unfortunately, this leaves me with little comfort as loopholes exist and I'm sure someone in there is crooked enough to figure something out.

There's also the fun fact that Nolan has hours at most, and for that reason, I need to be fast. If his body gives out before I get there, my abilities will be no more, and I don't think I can manage without them.

All I can do is to try and run faster, to try and get there sooner to help my friend and to kill anyone who has hurt him.

I don't have time to process how my heart has just been ripped out and shattered into pieces.

I don't have time to think about how everything I knew was a lie.

And I certainly don't have time to think about how I gave up everything, everything for a man that never even liked me.

The air rushes past my cheeks so fast that I can't even feel my tears as they fall and fly behind me, so this will be the only release that I will allow myself before I get there because I can't be distracted.

The wedges I lovingly kicked into Nolan's stomach have long since been discarded and it is just my bare feet pounding down the main road towards my destination. The cement is hot, and I don't know if it's from the heat or from the friction of my speed.

I keep chanting to myself over and over again, I have to get there in time, I can't let my foolish belief in his brother cost Adryan his life and if I don't make it, then I don't deserve to break the curse.

I don't deserve to be human, not after all I've done. Let this be the decider, the one thing I do to try to make up for it. My redemption.

Who am I kidding? It's too late for that now.

As I reach the city it is just a blur of lights. The sun is going down and the vibrant red in the sky reminds me of the scene I have left behind, so I smile. I can't be far now; I can't have long to go before I find the house.

Scenarios run through my mind as I prepare myself to attack the second I get there, but there's nothing they could have that will keep me out. No guns, no knives, no nothing.

Every single person in there is going to rot for hurting my friends and when I know they're free, I'm going to enjoy it. I may not get to see Nolan die, but I'm going to say goodbye to my powers with a bang. A last hurrah if you will.

Park Lane comes into view and in less than a minute I am at the front door of a white-stoned house. The brightest, most boring house on the block, which seems fitting given his taste.

The door barely needs a pull to be thrown from its hinges and behind it is a second one made up of steel. It's a nice effort, I must say, and I'm sure if it was anyone else it would have stopped the onslaught of violence from entering the building, but it's not anyone else. It's me.

The entrance is ripped apart with effortless vigour and I feel the weak slaps of bullets pelt against my face within seconds. I welcome it to be honest, it helps me focus and removes any other distractions from my mind.

I take in the dimensions of the hall. The stairs are to my right, the black and white chequered floor is filled with guards and there is a rather vulgar crystal chandelier hanging from the ceiling to the point where I swear, the Ambrose family are too tacky for their own good at times.

Before any of them can say a word, six bodies lie on the marble tiles, bleeding out from the throats that I ripped out with my teeth. I lick my lips to savour the taste as this is the last time I will have to do this. The last time I have to be a monster and I'm going to use it well.

Shouts come from upstairs but my gut points me to the door down the corridor. The blood stains my feet and I give out a cold laugh as I slide through it all.

I kick it open with half a thought and it reveals a set of stairs descending into a cellar. Like father, like son.

As I hear a moan my teeth grind together so hard that I'm surprised that they don't snap in two. The sound is

David and he's in pain and I hope for vengeance's sake they're both in there as it would mean that I get to take my time.

I don't know how I look, but I can only imagine. The torn pink dress and the ragged, windswept curls with blood dripping from every surface. I hope it's terrifying and I want that to be the last thing they remember.

I see them as I descend to the floor and the rush of anger rises further.

A chair is placed in the centre of the room with David tied to it, accompanied by goons crowding him. Aside from hairstyles, they may as well be identical. Black clothing covers every inch of them and only the occasional bulb lights my way.

"It appears as though David doesn't want to play." My voice is cold and dangerous. "Step away and I'll make it quick." I lie, knowing fine well that I'll do what I want either way.

Three pairs of hands rise into the air and a fourth makes the mistake of shooting at me. I catch the bullet with my teeth and spit it back so hard that I watch it shatter his kneecap.

"Tsk Tsk." I shake my head, refusing to look at David again.

His left eye is swollen shut and the right is focused on me. For once there is no fear behind them and I'm glad that he trusts me. They're done hurting him now and I think it's fair to say that we all know that.

"The first to free him can walk." I step aside to make way for them and stand roughly onto both legs of the arsehole that shot at me. He cries out and I end him there.

Spinning around, I tilt my head and watch them as they scramble over each other to release the cuffs and rope binding David to his seat but before they can even turn to face back at me, they're on the floor.

I could have dragged it out further and as much as I'd have loved to, I don't have time to waste as Adryan is still here somewhere. Will he be hurt like this?

"Can you walk?" My voice is rough, but my eyes are gentle. Nolan did this to him, he did this because I saved him and because I was foolish enough to believe him.

"Yes." He says but I watch him wince as he tries to rise, he can't but won't admit it and my respect for him grows.

He must know that Adryan is around here somewhere but there could be people all over this place waiting to take him back if I leave and I'm not going to let a thing happen to him, not after what I've just seen.

"I'm going to need you to hold on for a few minutes, is that okay?" I ask, stepping towards him and he swallows.

"Okay." His voice is dull and lifeless, and it takes a lot to hold back my thirst for vengeance.

I carry him up the stairs and out the door, leaving him a block from the house and close enough to call for help. He's to tell them that he woke up in the street and to give away nothing about the house I'm returning to as I don't want interruptions if I can help it.

When I return the whole place is quiet, eerily so and my stomach starts to do flips.

They now know I'm here and they could be hurting him. I shouldn't have left, I should have made David wait, but it was too dangerous, and I couldn't risk leaving him there unprotected.

Without a second thought for the bodies on the ground, I start to scale the house and rooms. The first and second floors are empty and have clearly been scattered as people have rushed to hide.

The third floor holds what I want but the smell of blood fills my nose as I enter. A snarl rises from my mouth as I find them all cowering in the attic with Adryan hanging by his hands underneath a skylight.

Just looking at him threatens to break me in two. He's been beaten unconscious and all of the anger I held back to help David is released with venom.

The walls are red, and my chest is on fire to the point where I half expect to breathe it as I hiss out at the relief that it's done, and they're gone.

Nobody is left to hurt them, and Nolan can now die.

I pull Adryan down and my hands shake as I check him for injury. There are so many, and I can't help but let out a frustrated scream that shakes the walls.

I let this happen, this happened because of me. Nolan tortured him for information about *my* cure. What if he dies? Fuck he can't die, he can't, I won't allow it.

Adryan's eyes don't open, and I hope that it means that wherever his mind is right now, he's not in pain. I can't imagine what all of this must have felt like and I can't even imagine what they must have done to achieve this.

Before anything else, I quickly wipe my face and body to try not to sully him further, but my dress is a lost cause at this point, so I leave it at that. I scoop him up into my filthy arms and bound over to where I left David.

He's lying against a wall, waiting for help still and when checking the phone I left with him, I can't have been gone more than ten minutes. The ambulance is on its way but it's not going to be good enough for all this bleeding.

So, I do the only thing that I can and take them both under my arms and run.

Adryan's injuries look bad, I can only imagine them internally and as each second goes by I'm praying that he doesn't get worse.

David holds in his pain, and I slow as I reach the Accident & Emergency entrance, summoning the ice for the cameras and ordering every person in sight to help the men I have with me with a voice that could crumble mountains.

Gurneys are flown over; shouts are heard all around and I'm screaming orders for them to go faster and to help better. David is still conscious but fading fast now that the adrenaline is gone. Adryan still hasn't woken up and people are rushing around him to diagnose the biggest issues.

I follow them as they take him to an operating theatre and it isn't until they tell me that what I have on could cause an infection that I allow them to seat me outside.

Hours pass and the only time I leave my post by the door is to change into a pair of scrubs brought to me by a trembling intern. Which are thin, cold and uncomfortable.

Exactly what I deserve, and I dump the dress into the nearest rubbish bin, hoping it'll end up in an incinerator somewhere.

Chapter 32

I've spent the last two days next to his bed in those same scrubs. Two days have gone by, and my powers haven't shifted, meaning that Nolan is still alive somewhere.

David was discharged last night, and his wife and children have come to collect him. Nobody knows what animal must have been roaming the streets that day or how it broke into that townhouse but it's all the news can talk of.

David, Adryan and I are the only survivors, and the Ambrose family are all assumed dead.

Nobody knows that the house was owned by the Lord of Ashes, and nobody found the stacks of weapons, tools and machinery that must have been moved. Clearly, it's not the only base in the city available to the organisation and any traces of unforgiving behaviour by the owners have magically disappeared.

I should move but I can't. I should hunt Nolan down, destroy his whole group and cover my tracks, but there's nothing that will allow me to leave this room until I know that Adryan is okay.

His broken arm has been cast, his leg wound sown and internal bleeding cauterised in surgery. The only thing left to wait for is for the swelling in his brain to go down and the doctors seem optimistic but part of me thinks that they're too afraid to consider the consequences.

Any change on his monitor and I call them in like a banshee, screaming across the floor. There's a nurse permanently sitting outside the room in case he needs anything, and I've threatened half of the staff that have walked in as for all I know they're on Nolan's payroll which has me constantly summoning the ice to my eyes.

None of them will remember this, of course, I've made sure of that but when in my presence the fear eats away at them and I'm unable to find it in myself to care. I've got too much to worry about as it is.

I keep trying to, but I can't process the betrayal Nolan revealed. My whole mind is numb, and I keep waiting for something to break through, but it doesn't.

I can't tell if it's because I'm still waiting to know if Adryan is okay or if I'm in shock or something.

David visited earlier and gave me a phone to call him should anything change but I keep staring at it every now and again, wishing I had something I could report.

By 6:00pm I realise that I need to wash myself and dress. The grime is clinging to me, and I can still breathe in the smell of the people I killed but I can no longer use the emergency as an excuse to justify it.

Pressing the assistance button by the bed, I compel a man only just finishing up his shift for the day to go to my apartment and bring me back some clothes and I also ask him to bring coffee and a meal, any meal.

I've missed eating and I need some normality. The hunger I feel isn't for food but maybe it will help with things anyway, it can't hurt to try.

I should have known something was off from the fact that Nolan didn't want me to eat, what sort of a person would do that if they cared? Adryan never let me go a day without it, just on the chance that it could make a difference and *that's* what it means to care.

After an hour the man returns, and I use the shower in the en suite to wash myself off. I scrub until my fingernails bleed and pull on the jeans and jumper I requested.

It's a grey jumper, a dark one and it comforts me. The gloom and the misery of it feels like home and I realise how stupid the past week has been as I've been trotting about like a princess, forgetting that I'm really a dragon in women's clothing.

How could I just sit there and pretend that I wasn't cursed? I feel the urge to kick myself every time I remember the weak attempt at freckles, as if that could hide the bigger picture. Who was I kidding?

The meal the man brought is just a bunch of sandwiches and some teddy bear crisps. The look I gave him when I spy them is enough to have him scamper off; it looks like something from a child's lunchbox.

After staring at the packet for a few minutes now that I'm washed and dressed, I say to hell with it and just laugh at myself as I open them up. I mean, I acted like a child before, how's this any different?

"I didn't take you as the type to laugh at the dying." A voice calls to me and my head shoots up to Adryan who's now staring over at me.

"No wait, I did. You're totally the type to do that." He laughs and winces as if in pain which makes me shoot to my feet.

"Drugs. We need drugs." I shout across the room to the nurse sitting outside and if she moves any slower, I'll rip her legs from her body. She walks in as if joining a cage with a tiger and I snarl at her to hurry up.

"Take it easy will you?" Adryan says and the nurse shoots him a worried glance, probably thinking I'll try to kill him too.

"I wouldn't need to if she drugged you faster." I say through gritted teeth and Adryan puts his hand over mine to calm me down.

But I flinch and pull it away as if stung. Never again, that can never happen again.

The drugs are distributed and then I watch the droplets fall down into his IV, reassuring myself that they will help him and ease his discomfort. The discomfort that I caused.

"Do you want to tell me what happened?" He asks the second the door closes again and my shoulders sag from the relaxed look on his face.

"No." I reply curtly before offering him half of my sandwich.

He laughs and this time I wince, expecting the pained expression to return but it doesn't.

"I don't even know why I asked." He rolls his eyes at me and accepts the food gingerly. I haven't even asked if he *can* eat food. Surely he can eat, right?

"You'd think you'd know better by now." I agree, scanning over him.

Now that he's awake I can look at all the other, less permanent bits of damage. His skin is peppered with cuts and bruises while his knuckles are almost shredded. Did he fight back?

"I'm really fucking pissed at you; do you know that?" He turns serious as if remembering something and I snap my head back up to him, breathing in.

"Are you now?" I ask casually, not wanting to give the stress in my stomach away.

He has every right to be, I almost got him killed and I am the reason James got killed if Nolan looked deep enough into my story. I should have killed him when I had the chance and none of this would have happened.

"Yes. I am." He gets out, trying to adjust himself higher into a seating position and I bawl my fits to stop from yelling at him to sit still. I can't stand to see him like this.

"That's not good." I add, taking a bite from my sandwich so I'd have at least something to throw up when he kicks me out, I could compel my way back in, but I won't.

"You made me leave." He says, his tone flat and irritated.

I try not to laugh. "That's at the bottom of my offence list."

I'm waiting for him to say it, to lay against me the real charge. To tell me that I caused all of this and to voice the fact that I'm the reason he's hurt, even though I promised that I would look out for him.

Some friend I was. Am? I don't know.

"Not to me, that's at the top." He says through his teeth, and I raise my eyebrows.

"Maybe I should get the doctor to come in here." I turn to stand, and he grabs my wrist which makes me hiss at the contact.

If I have to live through the rest of my life, I would very much prefer it to go by without another person touching me. Ever again. The last time someone touched me was Nolan and that's a fact I will never be able to forget.

"You made me leave." He repeats and I nod, unsure what he wants me to say. "You could have died." He adds and this time I do laugh, shaking off his hand and rubbing where his touch had been, as if that can remove it.

"You almost did die." I remind him, hoping it'll shake some sense into him.

"Because you sent me away." He growls and now I'm lost.

"What?"

"If you didn't go in alone, you'd have been able to see through him. I'd have been able to show you the truth." His face resembles pity and I close my eyes and count to three.

This is taking a turn I didn't expect, and I don't have the emotional capacity for it. Everything is very delicate and maybe it's a good thing that I can't process what's happened yet.

"I wouldn't have listened." I reply flatly.

"I would have made you listen; no one knows him better than me. That's why he was holding me there, to keep me from showing you." He shakes his head.

I don't want to have to think about this. To have to think of Nolan holding him, of Nolan even breathing in his direction because all that does is make me rage at the fact that he's still out there somewhere, living.

I pause for a second before speaking again. "You told him about the cure?"

I wasn't sure if I was going to mention it. Not everyone can keep things to themselves under duress, but it shocked me when I found out. What did he do to him?

"I had to leverage it for my deal." Adryan looks angry and I have no idea what he's on about.

"Come again?"

"I traded the cure for him swearing not to touch you."

My sandwich falls to the floor as I stand to my feet in frustration. Too many words want to break free from my mouth and my lips are shaking too hard with rage to do anything with them.

"Are you stupid?" I finally shout out, resisting the urge to throw things around. "You could have bartered your freedom, you idiot!"

"I couldn't risk it; he could have killed you." He yells back and I pinch the bridge of my nose for strength.

"He. Didn't. Know." I hiss back, trying to lower my voice to reduce the stares coming our way through the glass but I take a second to flip them off and they all go running.

"Are you deaf? I just said I couldn't risk it."

He clearly doesn't care about the volume which annoys me all the more.

So I sigh in irritation. "I could have killed him, but someone took away that option." I narrow my eyes in his direction so he can't miss that *that one* is on him.

Adryan's mouth drops and his eyes go wide. "You haven't killed him?"

"Please, speak louder! I think someone on the ground floor didn't quite catch that." I snap looking around. "No, I haven't killed him, I needed to get you both out alive."

"You had the opportunity?" His eyes don't slacken, and I grind my teeth.

"This is why I don't tell you things. You react too much." I start pacing around the room to burn off the energy building.

"Why didn't you kill him?" He insists.

"I couldn't risk it," I repeat his own words back to him and we both stare in silence.

I tried to kill him but what point is there in mentioning that?

I beat him black and blue and within an inch of his life and I don't know how I didn't kill him for that matter, but I didn't, and that's all that counts right now.

He's out there, hopefully on his deathbed but I have no way of knowing that and no way of finding him without leaving Adryan behind. Something I know I will not be doing until he's better.

"I forgive you." He finally says and my throat almost bobs.

"I don't care." I lie.

"I forgive you anyway." He shrugs and I finally crack.

Chapter 33

After about a week of asking how Adryan is every five minutes and getting on the case of every resident doctor in the hospital, he's finally well enough to be discharged.

I swear, it feels like being able to breathe again now that I know that he's not going to drop dead and die on me at any second as we're finally out of the woods and I can tell that I was starting to get on his nerves after checking up on him so much.

But as far as I am concerned, I'm seeing this through to the end whether he likes it or not. I got him into this mess and I will not relax until I know that he is out of it. We're close now and it feels so damn good.

I've ended up spending the week camped out on a pitiful little cot stationed at the end of his bed. I'm lucky if I get a few hours of sleep a night and I hate curling up in a ball to fit myself under the sheets, it makes me feel weak. Irritation aside, it's enough to get me through the day and while there's a hotel just across the road, I'm not thrilled about the idea of splitting up when Nolan's location and status are still unknown.

The only mention of him came a few days ago when a lawyer visited the room. Apparently, all of the Ambrose fortunes are signed over to Adryan now that Nolan is assumed dead and oddly enough, he isn't eager to be claiming otherwise.

I expected as much.

This means that Adryan now has the power to sell off all of the townhouses, the estates and everything else that comes with it. Leaving Nolan with nowhere to hide and it's only a matter of time before we find him again. At least that's what he says anyway, to soften the fact that he's still out there.

The same day he got that news saw everything go on the market, and in this economy, half of it is already being processed by now with multiple offers. It comforts me to know that I'll never have to go back to the place and if he wasn't able to sell it, I'd have been tempted to burn it to the ground.

I can't count how many forms are sitting on Adryan's desk when I return with lunch and that's just to get him out of here. He's lucky to be left-handed because his right arm is still in a cast and on every other page, he seems to have to tick something or sign a dotted line.

Watching him work through it almost makes me laugh, the concentration on his face is comical with his brows screwed together and tongue poking the inside of his cheek while he thinks.

"I don't think they want you to go," I comment when he's almost halfway through.

If it was me I'd have given up by now and just walked out. It seems like far too much, especially when considering he's basically come back from the dead not long ago.

"Trust me, they do." He mutters, half to himself and half to me.

"Why's that?"

He looks up now and scowls at me. "The dark-haired psycho sitting on the end of my bed for starters."

I think he's referring to the fact that I almost bit the head off the chief of surgery this morning when she and the interns were doing rounds. But in my defence, I'd only just gotten to sleep and the last thing I wanted was the blinds to be opened, resulting in the rising sun glaring straight onto my closed lids.

"She deserved it." I tilt my head and grin at him, offering a sandwich. We've been living on the things since he's woken up and I can't wait for an actual meal.

"Please, prove my point more." He returns and I swallow the urge to scatter the sheets of paper across the bed, just so he has to start again.

"I'm thinking of grabbing a bite later, something warm and actually cooked," I say as I finish my picnic and start to pull together the few bits and pieces that I've migrated over here.

"Is that a statement or an invitation?" He looks up from his work and raises one eyebrow.

"Undecided." I laugh.

I'd rather not leave him alone just yet, but at the same time, he probably needs some space. He's been sharing a room with me, and I bet he's gagging for it at this point. The same way that I am for a bath.

The memories of Nolan hit differently now and rather than reminiscing on what was lost, I'm dying to claw away what has been. Each time I wash, I scrub a bit harder and I'm hoping that all the skin he has ever touched is pulled away. At least with a bath, I can relax after the assault on myself.

"Why tell me then?" He lifts up the paper and stacks it neatly to imply his completion.

"Call it a conversation." I shrug, zipping up my duffle bag and moving to his things now.

He's got less than me which was surprising as I half expected him to be the type to have 5 different shampoos, as his hair always looks so soft in comparison to mine. All he has here is a change of clothes, a toothbrush and a bottle of 3-in-one body wash.

"Here's me thinking you were getting better at it." He chuckles to himself.

"Bite me." I roll my eyes and push the food over to him.

Now that the shoe is on the other foot, he's not the biggest fan of having food forced down his throat and I'd be lying if I said I don't enjoy it.

He eats with his good hand, and I place the bags on the edge of the bed before taking the paper and running them over to the main desk. I watch the staff member carefully as they process our request to finally leave this hell hole and I never want to see another hospital again.

The woman gives him the all-clear and passes me a rather clunky set of crutches. His leg wound is healing well but he still has a limp and he's going to need physio. It stresses him out less when I tease him about it, so I pull a rather mocking smile when carrying them back into the room with me.

"Now it's definitely an invitation, premium seats are guaranteed with these puppies." I hold them in the air, and he rolls his eyes at me.

"As if you couldn't have compelled them anyway." The sass is coming back to him more naturally now as for the first few days, I was worried that he would be different.

Naturally, he's going to have some sort of trauma after his ordeal in the townhouse and he was quieter at first.

Either way, it was to be expected, a brain injury isn't a minor thing and it's going to take some adjusting. He's always able to crack a few jokes but I can tell when he's not 100%.

"Chinese then?" I ask, wondering if he'll want to go somewhere else with me and knowing that I won't push it if he doesn't.

"As long as it's not a buffet." He gestures to his new accessories, and I laugh.

"Plates that are brought to the table? They might as well eat it for you too at that rate." I tease him and he throws a crutch towards me like a javelin.

We've found a Chinese place not far from his apartment and he hired a car to drop us off right outside. It had all tinted windows, leather seats and a divider from the driver that made it like a smaller version of a limo. It seemed rather excessive to me but why not? He has the wealth now and he might as well get used to it.

When getting out I can tell that he's having a hard time moving around again, even with his extra gear and I offer to carry him just to distract him from his anger within himself to which he graciously replies with a middle finger.

I've lost track of all the things we have ordered since being seated as we both have been given a little iPad that lets us do it all without having to speak to someone and I ended up clicking all of the side dishes while Adryan did the same with the starters. Leaving no room at all for our drinks on the table.

The spices dance on my tongue and for a good fifteen minutes we just sit here in silence.

I don't know why, but I'm hit with a strong emotion when I notice this and I think it's because after going through so much, we're back to doing something that is normal for us. It's a comfort to have my friend back and it helps to distract me from the grief of Nolan.

"What's the plan for tonight then?" He breaks the silence before offering me a dumpling.

"Eat lots and get fat?" I question, accepting it and swallowing it down along with a mini spring roll to follow.

"Where are you staying?" He rolls his eyes and I shrug.

"I don't know, I figured you'd want a bit of space." It doesn't bother me to say, because I understand.

Being around someone too much can be exhausting and while I don't feel that, he might. I know that before we'd always see each other on a night but he'd have his job and I'd have my hunting to break it up. We've been around each other nonstop for a week now and I'm very conscious of that fact.

It's probably why I haven't cried as much as I thought I would. I mean, that's the sort of thing you do in private and it's still a foreign concept to me.

I think I'll try and get it all out tonight while I can as my chin has a dull ache to it and I know that it's an emotional, not physical pain from holding it all in still. I cracked when he first woke up, but I've kept it all together since then as he's been healing, and this isn't about me. He doesn't need to see me fall apart over his arsehole brother.

"Is that your way of saying you're sick of me?" He questions with an eyebrow raised higher than the other.

"I think we both know that if I meant that, I'd say that." I throw back with a grin.

His plate is piled high with rice, salt and chilli chicken and Chow Mein though I don't know how he's going to eat it all, never mind the dumplings he's hoarding.

"Yours or mine?" He asks, ignoring my comment so I decide to ignore his.

"I want a bath." I gesture to my hair and clothes that are in desperate need of washing.

"That doesn't answer the question, yours or mine?" He sighs and I scowl at him.

"I assume that means we're sticking together?" I clarify because that would alter my choice.

My apartment only has one bedroom but a fantastic bathroom, while he has a spare room but only an average bathroom and it's probably something I need to look at improving for him, mostly for selfish reasons.

"Naturally." He returns, not even looking up.

"Yours, I think we both need a proper bed after this week." I know I do.

But for now, I add to my plate by scooping more fried rice onto it, along with a mountain of chips, curry sauce and some dumplings when he's not looking. This place is good and it's just what I needed after a week of nothing, and another filled with cold bread. Food might not be fuel anymore but it's a treat that I intend to make the most of.

"How long were you planning on keeping the place anyway?" He looks over at me and I have to think as I didn't really have a timeframe in mind, I suppose whenever someone noticed that Elisabeth was really dead or that I wasn't her.

"I don't know, why?" I question before shovelling more food into my mouth.

"Maybe you should think about moving into mine?" He hesitates. "You know, while he's out there."

I appreciate that the name remains unspoken between us, and I didn't realise that he was as nervous about it as I am. He's done a pretty good job of masking his fear if that's the case. It's impressive.

"Are you scared?" I tease to lighten the subject a bit but also to judge how deep it goes.

"Not for me." He stares at my face without blinking and I sigh.

Not this again. He has this irrational want to protect me from Nolan, when the second I see the man, I know that his head will be removed from his shoulders. There's no point.

"What could he possibly do to me? You'd think a week in the hospital would awaken a sense of personal security and common sense." I scold.

"If he finds out that he can hurt you he won't hold back Cam." He snaps and I roll my eyes very obviously so that he can't miss the gesture.

"Neither will I. As long as I know that you're safe he has no leverage, hell, he'd not even know I was there before it'll all be over." I promise, to try and rationalise with him.

He stares at me rather than reply straight away and I can almost see the cogs turning in his mind. But surely he can see the sense behind what I'm saying?

"Fine, keep your apartment, but I can't promise to answer my phone or stay inside when you're not there." He threatens, knowing that it will bother me, and I grind my teeth audibly.

I rack my brains for some sort of leverage but then I realise that he's threatened to do that because that's exactly what would bother him as well. Finally, his stupid protectiveness will come in useful.

"Oh don't worry I will, and news flash Ambrose, I can't promise that either." I snap.

We both just stare at each other for a second, a stubborn personality trait is something we have in common and we're trying to see which of us will break first.

Chapter 34

I broke first.

Since the standoff, we've spent most of our time at Adryan's place and he doesn't seem to mind the fact that I hover around him like a lost puppy at times. It's probably because he has a habit of treating me the same, but I don't say anything because he already won the first round and I'd rather not give him another victory.

But in all honesty, what I struggled with at first was battling the strong sense of owing him. I mean he was letting me live with him for free. Four years like this and at least I had the means to be self-sufficient, but to give up Elisabeth was like giving up my freedom.

It's not like I could go out there and get a job, I look nothing like my real ID and staying with Adryan full time meant that hunting wasn't an option.

It was hard for me to treat him normally with this in mind.

But it got to the point where he had to sit me down to demand that I stop walking on eggshells around him, as naturally he'd felt the shift in my behaviour with the lack of teasing and stupid threats, and he didn't understand what had changed.

When I explained, there was no denying how embarrassing that felt to lay it all out on the table, but Adryan blew my mind when he came back that evening as he landed a stack of papers on my lap that could probably make up a book.

"You're hired." He'd said while looking down at me and my questioning glance went back and forth between the paper and his face.

I didn't realise I applied for a job, never mind that he was hiring and at first, I wondered if it was a joke meant to make light of the tension between us, so I just laughed.

"You're the new head of security at Ambrose Industries. Here's your salary and I've deducted the monthly rent from your paycheque." He pulled a face daring me to challenge him before continuing. "Can you quit being nice now?"

At that point I was hysterical, the idea that my being nice to him is so hard to handle that he'd give me a token job and ridiculous salary just to stop it was insane, but the man was serious.

We spent the night arguing over the details which felt good after trying not to ruffle any feathers for the full week before and I actually have some responsibility now while I've talked the number down considerably.

It was a weird way of getting a job, him trying to pay me more and my trying to get more work but just looking at the contract at first made my head hurt. I could mortgage Elisabeth's whole apartment block if I wanted to and never have to lift a finger.

This gives me the freedom and options I've always wanted and I'm sure that when things die down I'll move out again, but this works for the time being as we get along as well as ever.

David is healing well and yesterday I got to meet his wife for the first time when we all went to meet up for coffee. She's absolutely beautiful and I had to do a double take when seeing them sitting there together. They were both smiling and laughing, and I realised that I'd never actually seen David happy before.

Her skin is a beautiful dark colour that beams in the sunlight and her lips are shaped in the way that most people pay to get done cosmetically. It was sweet to see them together, but I can't deny that it stung as well. Naturally, I thought of what I had with Nolan and when being reminded once again of the lie, I went quiet.

Adryan led the conversation like he usually does, and he and David bounce off each other like a game of table tennis now that he's comfortable having me around. They are the only leaders of their organisation left and there is a bond that has been made there that you can tell will last a lifetime.

At that point, it was hard not to think of Paul and James, and it still doesn't quite register that they're both dead and no longer walking the earth. A part of me wonders if it was James that planted the doubt in my mind that night as how else would I connect a vague reference of a guard to him? But maybe it's just guilt.

Adryan insists that it's not my fault but that's just something I can't believe. If I had let Nolan die in the first place, things would be different.

The news of Elisabeth came out quickly after I moved all of my things into the spare room and today, we'll be attending her funeral which is the last place I ever expected to end up. The actual woman being buried in the ground isn't something to be upset about, she was a real piece of work and I stand by what I've always thought, she had it coming.

But the funeral today almost represents a part of me coming to an end, if that isn't completely selfish to say and it marks the end of my limbo that has lasted for four years that consisted of being trapped in a place of ignorance and violence.

Now I have no reason to be Elisabeth and things will be different.

I still have an eternity threatening me with only one way out though and to be honest I find that terrifying as I won't age, I won't die, and I will just be here.

Usually, I can keep those thoughts at bay but as the coffin lowers into the ground that's all my mind can focus on. This won't be an option for me and the only way to get back to a normal life is to find Nolan and to kill him but at least I know I won't hesitate next time.

I have this underlying fear that keeps haunting me when I think of this. I keep questioning all that I know, and it feels dangerous to rely on him surviving my attempt on his life. What if he is actually dead and I'm still like this?

What if we got it wrong and he was really killed by someone else four years ago? Or what if it doesn't count if I leave him to die from injury and not a direct blow? I wasn't exactly handed a rule book when I made the deal and not hearing from him or of him gives me a constant ache of suspense.

The only options I am left with are that either he got away, or I'm trapped like this forever.

"You okay?" Adryan nudges me with his elbow, and I nod grimly. He has awoken me from my thoughts and I'm lucky that my grief blends in well here as he's the only one that could know that it isn't for Elisabeth.

"Let's go." Adryan nudges me again and gestures toward the mourners that are starting to move away. His crutches are gone now, the limp is still there ever so slightly but he's improving daily.

When he nudges me, I don't tell him that the contact hurts me because there's no point. Every touch, skim or pressure from his hand is like a knife to my core and because he doesn't do it often, I don't feel the need to say.

Since the hospital, he hasn't tried it really, not that way at least and now it's only if he needs to get my attention or take something from me. Nolan has ruined touch for me completely and I don't have time to wonder if that should bother me more.

All I want is justice for Adryan and a cure for my curse, that's it. I'm too tired for anything else.

I'm so incredibly tired and I try not to think about what it would feel like to be without so much anger and sadness building up inside of me all of the time. Without this curse maybe some of it will go away and even if it's just a drop, it would be an unimaginable relief.

"See any old friends?" I ask as we walk.

I'm remembering that he knew Elisabeth before me, and I wonder what he thinks of what I did. He didn't want me to kill Jason Easton, but he wasn't as bad in my opinion. What would he have done with her confession?

"One or two." He pulls a face when answering to indicate that it's not a welcome remembrance.

A few of the faces around us are familiar to me too and that thought distracts me as we walk. Some of these people were to be my next targets if we never found the Lord of Ashes and I know that they were working for Nolan.

I can't help wondering if they are still in contact with him now, if they know where he is or if their allegiance has changed. Maybe one of them cleaned out the townhouse and has the answers I need to actually form a lead.

Since leaving the hospital I've never really been away from Adryan, and I wonder if tonight is the night that I should try it out again. Sitting around and doing nothing drives me crazy and I don't like relying on other people for intel, even if they are my own connections.

Derek, my contact has been working around the clock and we have partnered him with Chrissy who was Paul's protege before he passed. They work together well and while we've got a better chance than we have ever had before, there's been nothing to come from it.

I wake up each morning to check my phone, willing for a message to appear from one of them with an address and a status but instead, I wake up with a full battery and a bad mood that only Adryan can dilute.

The car we took is parked on the curb and Adryan opens the door to let me in like he always does. While I made a comment the first few times, I've realised that this is just like the eating thing for him and it's not worth questioning anymore.

He has his own driver now too and it's the same sort of car that we took to the Chinese restaurant the day that he got discharged from the hospital, but rather than step inside as I should probably do, I stop and look at him.

"I'm going to hang out for a bit," I say hesitantly before biting my lip.

"What?" He asks, hovering by the door as if he must have heard me wrong.

"I need a bit of space." I use the first lie that comes to my mind. "I'm going to check out the apartment again and... You know, say goodbye."

It's a lame excuse but he nods as if trying to understand and I plaster on a smile to convince him that it's fine.

"I'll be back later." I promise, and I ignore the frown that is working its way onto his face.

"When is later?" He pushes and it's my turn to frown now.

"I don't know Mother, when's my curfew?" I tease sarcastically which makes him realise that this is as much as I'm willing to divulge, much like old times.

CURSE ME

But after a pause, he just shrugs and tells me to text him if I'll be back early enough to eat and I watch the car pull away not long after, wondering if I've just made the right decision.

The crowd is dividing in two and I follow the familiar faces from before while holding my head down towards the ground as if I'm upset.

This is the first time since Nolan that I'm going to go and hunt, and I honestly don't know if this is going to help or hurt me.

But there's only one way to find out

Printed in Great Britain
by Amazon